Everything around me seemed to slow, and I turned to make eye contact with Toad number two. All that anger I'd tucked away, all that fury I had to hold back, surged in me. "You helped slice my friends up and skin them alive?"

He grinned at me, showing broken teeth and tiny fangs in behind the teeth, retracted like a snake's. "They cried like little girls as we peeled their hides."

A scream erupted out of me, rage I'd never known coursing along each nerve ending until I saw nothing but Trolls and the edge of my sword. Blood and viscera flew around me, heads rolled, hearts pierced, and none of it was enough. None of it would bring back Dox.

The seconds blurred, and distantly I knew I'd never fought like this, never moved this fast or killed with such intensity. The movements of my body and blades blended together, a perfect killing machine that felt nothing but fury.

There may have been tears on my cheeks, but I couldn't be sure, the stimulus of the death around me overwhelming anything else.

Their screams matched mine in intensity until they began to fade. And then just me, screaming, sobbing, kneeling in a pool of blood, hands still gripping my swords as my arms hung to the side.

PRAISE FOR SHANNON MAYER AND THE RYLEE ADAMSON SERIES

"If you love the early Anita Blake novels by Laurel K. Hamilton, you will fall head over heels for The Rylee Adamson Series. Rylee is a complex character with a tough, kick-ass exterior, a sassy temperament, and morals which she never deviates from. She's the ultimate heroine. Mayer's books rank right up there with Kim Harrison's, Patricia Brigg's, and Ilona Andrew's. Get ready for a whole new take on Urban Fantasy and Paranormal Romance and be ready to be glued to the pages!"

—*Just My Opinion Book Blog*

"Rylee is the perfect combination of loyal, intelligent, compassionate, and kick-ass. Many times, the heroines in urban fantasy novels tend to be so tough or snarky that they come off as unlikable. Rylee is a smart-ass for sure, but she isn't insulting. Well, I guess the she gets a little sassy with the bad guys, but then it's just hilarious."

—*Diary of a Bibliophile*

"I could not put it down. Not only that, but I immediately started the next book in the series, *Immune*."

—*Just Talking Books*

"*Priceless* was one of those reads that just starts off running and doesn't give too much time to breathe. . . . I'll just go ahead and add the rest of the books to my TBR list now."

—*Vampire Book Club*

"This book is so great and it blindsided me. I'm always looking for something to tide me over until the next Ilona Andrews or Patricia Briggs book comes out, but no matter how many recommendations I get nothing ever measures up. This was as close as I've gotten and I'm so freakin happy!"

—*Dynamite Review*

"Highly recommended for all fans of urban fantasy and paranormal."

—*Chimera Reviews*

"I absolutely love these books; they are one of the few Paranormal/urban fantasy series that I still follow religiously.... Shannon's writing is wonderful and her characters worm their way into your heart. I cannot recommend these books enough."

—*Maryse Book Review*

"It has the perfect blend of humor, mystery, and a slow-burning forbidden-type romance. Recommended x 1000."
—Sarah Morse Adams

"These books are, ultimately, fun, exciting, romantic, and satisfying. . . .Trust me on this. You are going to love this series."

—*Read Love Share Blog*

"This was a wonderful debut in the Rylee Adamson series, and a creative twist on a genre that's packed full of hard-as-nails heroines. . . . I will definitely stay-tuned to see what Rylee and her new partner get up to."

—Red Welly Boots

"*Priceless* did not disappoint with its colourful secondary characters, unique slant on the typical P.I. spiel, and a heroine with boatloads of untapped gifts."

—*Rabid Reads*

TRACKER

Books by Shannon Mayer

TRACKER

A RYLEE ADAMSON NOVEL
BOOK 6

SHANNON MAYER

TALOS

New York

Talos Press books may be purchased in bulk at special discounts for sales promotion, corporate gifts, fund-raising, or educational purposes. Special editions can also be created to specifications. For details, contact the Special Sales Department, Talos Press, 307 West 36th Street, 11th Floor, New York, NY 10018 or info@skyhorsepublishing.com.

Talos Press® is a registered trademark of Skyhorse Publishing, Inc.®, a Delaware corporation.

Visit our website at www.talospress.com.

10 9 8 7 6 5 4 3 2 1

Library of Congress Cataloging-in-Publication Data

Names: Mayer, Shannon, 1979- author.
Title: Tracker / Shannon Mayer.
Description: First Talos Press edition. | New York : Talos Press, 2017. |
  Series: A Rylee Adamson novel ; book 6
Identifiers: LCCN 2016039143 | ISBN 9781945863004 (softcover : acid-free
  paper)
Subjects: LCSH: Missing children--Investigation--Fiction. | Paranormal
  romance stories. | BISAC: FICTION / Fantasy / Urban Life. | FICTION /
  Fantasy / Paranormal. | GSAFD: Fantasy fiction.
Classification: LCC PR9199.4.M3773 T73 2017 | DDC 813/.6--dc23 LC
record available at https://lccn.loc.gov/2016039143

Original illustrations by Damon Za www.damonza.com

Printed in Canada

ACKNOWLEDGEMENTS

As with all of my books, there are many, many people to thank. First off, my editors Melissa Breau, N. L. "Jinxie" Gervasio, and Tina Winograd You three ladies have helped me polish this story to a high gleam, and as always, have helped me be a better writer in the process. The splendid cover art by Damon Za continues to blow me away, and I am so grateful you are on my team.

To my readers. You are why I keep writing and I cannot express my thanks enough. This journey would not be the same without you.

Of course, I would be in deep trouble if I didn't mention my friend, personal cheerleader, and sounding board (these are only a few of her titles), Lysa Lessieur. Thank you for going above and beyond in all you do. And for listening to me when I feel like pulling my hair out.

Yes, this is it. The part where I get mushy. He still hasn't read any of my books (he says he's waiting for the movie), but he stands behind me and helps me keep my feet on the ground when I start to get ahead of myself. Thanks can never be enough to the man who has helped me find my path in life, the one who believed in me when no one else did. So he'll just have to settle for my thanks, and all my love.

CAST OF CHARACTERS

Rylee Adamson: Tracker and Immune who has dedicated her life to finding lost children. Based near Bismarck, North Dakota.

Liam O'Shea: Previously an FBI agent. Now he is a werewolf/Guardian as well as lover to Rylee.

Giselle: Mentored Rylee and Milly; Giselle is a Reader but cannot use her abilities on Rylee due to Rylee's Immunity. She died in *Raising Innocence*.

Millicent: AKA Milly. witch who was best friend to Rylee. Now is actively working against Rylee for reasons not yet clear.

India: A spirit seeker whom Rylee Tracked in *Priceless*.

Kyle Jacobs: Rylee's personal teenage hacker—human.

Doran: Daywalker and Shaman who helps Rylee from time to time. Located near Roswell, New Mexico.

Alex: A werewolf trapped in between human and wolf. He is Rylee's unofficial sidekick and loyal companion. Submissive.

Berget: Rylee's little sister who went missing ten years prior to *Priceless*. In *Raising Innocence*, Rylee found out that Berget is still alive. In *Shadowed Threads*, Rylee discovered Berget is the "Child Empress" and a vampire.

Dox: Large, pale blue-skinned ogre. Friend of Rylee. Owns "The Landing Pad" near Roswell, New Mexico.

William Gossard: AKA Will. Panther shape shifter and officer with SOCA in London. Friend to Rylee.

Deanna Gossard: Druid, sister to William. Friend and help to Rylee.

Louisa: Tribal Shaman located near Roswell, New Mexico.

Eve: Harpy that is now under Rylee's tutelage, as per the Harpy rule of conduct.

Faris: Vampire and general pain in the ass to Rylee. He is in contention for the vampire "throne" against Rylee's little sister, Berget.

Jack Feen: Only other Tracker in existence. He lives in London and is dying.

Agent Valley: Senior in command in the Arcane Division of the FBI.

Blaz: Dragon who bonded (reluctantly) with Rylee in *Shadowed Threads*.

Pamela: Young, powerful witch whom Rylee saved in *Raising Innocence*. She is now one of Rylee's wards.

Charlie: Brownie who acts as Rylee's go-between when working with parents on all of her salvages. Based in Bismarck, North Dakota.

Dr. Daniels: AKA "Daniels". a child services worker and a druid Rylee met up with in *Raising Innocence*. Rylee and Daniels do not like one another.

1

A wet woolen coat on a pair of frail shoulders wouldn't be as heavy or oppressive as the silence in my car. The quiet was broken only by the occasional suck of air as Milly tried to keep her tears quiet. She sat beside me, chin to her chest, moisture tracking down her cheeks. I kept my eyes on the road, but every time I changed lanes or took a corner, I saw her grief. I tried not to think about my own, forced myself to quell the tightening of my throat and the blurring of my eyes.

Easy enough to do when I let my anger burn hot, let myself obsess over how many ways I could kill Faris and Orion. How I could make them pay for all they'd done.

Though I'd spoken the words, and set myself on a path to wipe the two fuckers out of existence, it was a hell of a lot easier said than done. Both of them were powerhouses in ways I never would be. But that wouldn't stop me from trying.

Night fell as we drove into Bismarck. The darkness erased the shadows the dying sun scattered across the faces around me.

Behind me sat Pamela, her hand rested on the back of my seat. "Rylee, what will happen to Dox and the others? Why didn't we cut them down? Why didn't we bury them?"

"You don't touch the bodies of supernaturals who are killed or even those who die naturally," I said, gripping the steering wheel, fighting to keep my voice even. "I don't know the process; I just know they are taken somewhere supernaturals go."

"That seems rather vague," Pamela said.

"It's all I was ever told. I never questioned it. I killed someone and the body was gone the next morning." I hoped that would satisfy her and she'd be done with her questions for a bit.

Nope, wrong again.

"Where are we going?"

That, at least, was cut and dry. I cleared my throat. "Giselle's home. It's as good a place as any to plan our next step, and I sure as hell am not staying at the farm tonight." No, I couldn't stay that close to the skinned bodies of Dox, Sla, Dev, Tin, and Lop. Even knowing they'd be gone by morning, I couldn't handle that.

Liam and Alex would meet us at Giselle's. Blaz, on the other hand, had been quite happy to stay on the farm to meet Eve when she came back from the unicorns. Blaz had no connection to the ogres, so their deaths meant very little to him. And being a dragon, he wasn't exactly worried about dealing with any intruders. There weren't many things in the world that would tangle with Blaz and come out on top.

I flicked on my indicator light and took the next exit, slush gripping the tires and pulling us sideways for a breath. I adjusted my hands on the steering wheel and eased through the section, comfortable driving in snotty snow.

"You don't think Orion will look there for us? He knows we were raised there." Milly lifted her head, her voice thick with her tears.

I could have been gentle, but the time for pulling punches was long past. I all but spit my words at her.

"How the fuck should I know? You were his pet; you tell us what he's doing?"

She went very still beside me, her jaw tightened and tears dried with her next breath. Truth be told, I wanted her pissed off, even if I was the one to push her buttons. I needed her to overcome her grief and fear. Grief would get us killed; fear could make her hold back. None of us had either of those luxuries. I needed her angry and ready to fight, to battle for us, to keep us on this side of the grave. I needed her to train Pamela to use her magic as witches were no longer taught. I needed her to push away her fear of Orion and focus on the task at hand.

Deanna had refused to teach Pamela anything but defense. But this was war, and kill or be killed. Emotions could no longer come into play. I glanced in the mirror, caught Pamela's eyes watching me and knew she trusted me to make the best choices for our pack family. Such faith was unnerving at times, but I would carry it the best I could.

Milly straightened in her seat, snapping out of her tear fest. She folded her hands in her lap and I knew, for now at least, Milly was back to using her brain. "He won't waste any more effort tonight. Orion likes to make a point and then let people simmer in their fear before striking again."

I gave a slight nod. "Good, because we need at least a night to plan our next step."

Pamela—as always—was full of questions. "Why did you send Will and Deanna home to London? Will is as deadly as Liam, at least. If it's a fight we're facing, can't we use them close to us?"

"They are going to rally as many people as they can on their side of the ocean." Much as keeping them close would have given us higher numbers, we would need help on a larger scale before this was all done.

"You mean *Will* is rallying people. Deanna won't fight." Pamela gripped the leather seat, making it squeak. We were banking on the fact that Will *could* get us firepower. And fuck Deanna for being such a pussy at the worst possible time.

Milly shifted in her seat so she was sideways, one hand cupping her belly bump. "Druids can do other things. They can help without fighting."

Pamela snorted. "Seems cowardly." I tended to agree, but didn't say anything.

"If you stand for nothing . . ." Milly's words resonated in my head and heart, Giselle's voice echoing in my ears.

"You'll fall for anything," I said softly. Milly's eyes met mine. Giselle was with us still, tying us together even if she was gone. Even if Milly had caused her death.

Milly's lips thinned and she faced Pamela. "You don't have to agree with them, but Druids have beliefs they live up to, to the best of their abilities."

I chose not to mention the psycho Druid, Daniels. Fuck, at least she was finally gone, though it would have been nice if in the process she hadn't caused the first volcanic eruption on the west coast since Mt. Saint Helens's. Okay, maybe that had been a little bit my fault; dropping the demon stone into the lava in order to cut ties between Orion and Milly probably wasn't the best decision, but I wasn't mentioning that to anyone.

Pamela pushed back into her seat and changed the subject. "How long before we get there?"

"Less than half an hour," I said, checking the rear-view mirror as a long black sedan slid in between traffic, getting right on our ass. If this was the driver's idea of a tail, he was doing a pretty piss poor job. "Milly, you recognize that car?"

She turned in her seat, one hand on her seat belt, the other on the armrest. Pamela followed suit, staring out the back window. "No, I don't know who they are. How long have they been following us?"

"Just started." I knew the area and wasn't about to get boxed in. "Buckle up, ladies."

I put my foot down on the gas pedal and the Jeep obliged, the four-wheel drive making the difference between being in the ditch and staying on the road. A glance in the mirror showed the sedan cruising along, keeping up easily. We were closing in on the suburbs, a veritable rat's nest of streets and houses. If we were to lose the douche on our tail, now would be the time.

I spun the wheel to the right, taking the corner so hard the Jeep skidded sideways and I wasn't sure we weren't ending up in the ditch. Lucky for us, it pulled back to center before we hit the edge of the pavement. "Milly, watch them."

Navigating the slippery winter roads, I couldn't help but notice all the Christmas lights. The humans were getting festive and—a loud crack ripped through the Jeep and I ducked instinctively.

"What the fuck?" I dared a look back as we sped along a short straight stretch, bright lights zipping by.

"They're shooting at us," Milly yelped as another bullet sang through the metal of the Jeep. And then another, and another. How in hell's name were they getting that kind of accuracy? With the three of us affecting the trajectory of the bullets, there should be no way they had any actual hits. Supernaturals tended to do that to technology; screw it up that is. Which is why the accuracy of the bullets was so fucking shocking.

I took another corner, bouncing over the curb, driving along the edge of someone's decorations and taking out a string of lights. "Pamela, keep your head down. Milly, can you deal with them?"

Before Milly answered, Pamela popped up. "I can do it, she doesn't have to."

"No, lay down," I snapped, but too late. Pamela unbuckled her seatbelt and spun to face the back of the Jeep. The power of her spell gathered and she unleashed it out the broken back window. The asphalt in front of the black sedan exploded, sending the front of the car straight up, exposing its underbelly.

A second spell zigzagged through the air, and forked lightning kissed the bared gas tank. Half a breath later the car exploded in a shower of flames and twisted metal that dulled the decorations around us.

"Shit." I kept the gas pedal down and wove our way out of the suburbs and back to the main drag. I glanced at Pamela. "You need to learn to listen."

Her jaw tightened. "And you need to learn to let me do what I can do."

Milly laughed softly. "I'm glad to see your wards have spines of their own. I was worried they were so obedient, they wouldn't know their own minds."

"Shut up, Milly." I glared at her.

"Act first and think later. I wonder where she learned that?" Milly arched an eyebrow at me.

Pamela slouched in her seat, the cool air tugging at her long blond hair, her blue eyes glittering. Sullen teenager was written all over her. I forced myself to unclench the wheel. "Thanks for taking care of them. Even if you didn't listen."

She didn't perk up, but she did nod, and I noticed her fight the upward rise of her lips. Damn, was I ever that touchy? Hell, people probably thought I was still that moody.

Milly reached forward and touched a bullet hole in the dashboard. "How did they get the guns and bullets to be so accurate around us? And why were they shooting at us in the first place?"

Both questions I wanted answered, too. "I don't know." I went for the obvious. "Orion wouldn't have anything to do with this, would he?" If a demon had found some way to make guns and bullets work around the supernatural, we were royally screwed. I wouldn't get the chance to pull together any sort of army, not if we could be taken out with long-range rifles and scopes.

I put a hand to the bullet hole closest to me. The metal was hot, and I jabbed my finger in to see if I could fish out the bullet. No luck. Milly frowned, her fingers tracing another bullet hole, as if we could somehow read the bullets themselves as Giselle had once Read people.

"I don't think Orion would use this technology. Nothing he ever said would make me believe this was even a line of thought for him. But if he knew it was a possibility, there is no doubt he would make use of it. It would give him an edge we would struggle to match."

Brilliant, just what I wanted to hear. We said nothing more until we reached Giselle's place. The house still sat on a tilt, but at least the insulation was in and we wouldn't freeze to death. Pamela leaned forward. "It looks . . . bloody awful."

"Better on the inside," I muttered. I caught a flash of black fur as two wolf bodies zipped around the side of the house. Damn, those boys were fast. Then again, we did get sidetracked. Nothing like a surprise car chase and minor explosion to change how your day was going. Not that the day started out all that well, either.

I stepped out of the Jeep, paused, and slid back in. Shifting the Jeep into low gear, I plowed through the snow along the dark side of the house, putting us in the shadows. Maybe it wasn't the best hiding spot, but unless someone was looking for us we should go unnoticed. I turned off the Jeep and stepped out,

Pamela following but her eyes locked on Milly. The older witch turned back to the truck's path, lifted her hands and the crunched snow trail lifted, fluffing up and falling so it looked as if no one had been in the driveway.

I watched as Pamela frowned, lifted her hands, and then along the road, as far as we could see, the snow lifted in a veritable blanket, and then dropped to the ground erasing all tire tracks.

Milly snorted. "Yeah, that isn't going to look suspicious. No tire tracks for the block around Giselle's?"

Pamela flushed and I put a hand on her shoulder, the tension in her singing through my fingers. I bent and whispered in her ear, "I would have done the same thing. She's just pissed you're stronger than her."

The growing tension slowed and ebbed. I didn't recall Milly being this quick to anger as a teenager. Then again, if what she told me was the truth, then even at that young age, Orion would have controlled her every action.

With that thought tumbling in my head, I grabbed gear from my Jeep. Pamela had an armful too, and we left the rest in the back. We'd pretty much cleared out the cellar below the farmhouse, taking every weapon, leaving just a bare stash in case of emergency before we'd left.

Pamela propped the side door open until Milly came around and held it for us. "What's going to happen next?"

The two of them asked the question at the same time, but it was Liam who answered as he stepped from the shadows inside the house to take things from me.

"We'll talk about it inside."

Pamela didn't argue, just slipped into the house, throwing a quick glance back at me. I gave a nod. Milly hesitated, and I realized Liam had moved to block her from coming in.

"Rylee." His voice curled around me; the anger and undercurrent of fear in it obvious to me, though I doubted anyone else would hear it. "Are you sure about her?"

I couldn't lie to him. "No, I'm not. But we're at a crossroads, not a lot of options left, you know, and we can use all the help we can get."

"Not if the help is a traitor waiting to kill us in our sleep." Not once had he made eye contact with me, his entire being focused on the one person who dared to chain and force him to attack those he cared about.

I laid down what was left of my gear and moved between them. Liam was an Alpha, of that there was no doubt. But so was I, and I still ran the show.

"Let her in, Liam."

He stepped aside and swept his arm across his body. "After you, Millicent."

She tipped her chin up and arched an eyebrow at him, but said nothing. There wasn't a lot she could say; her history with us put her on the bottom rung of the pack, regardless of how strong she was.

Her footsteps disappeared into the house, but Liam and I stood there, a snake of cold air wrapping around us. He leaned over and pulled the door, closing it softly, which placed him squarely in front of me.

"My wolf is not handling her being here very well." His voice was controlled, but I felt the edginess, the wolf scrabbling to get out.

I put a hand on his bicep, his skin hot under mine. "We need her help. If we're going to war—"

"I know." He jerked from under my hand, eyes narrowing. "Logically, I get it. But my wolf only knows she proved herself an enemy once, which makes her an enemy now. It's going to take a fucking miracle to change that perception."

I tightened my jaw, irritation flaring. I pushed past him and scooped up my gear. "Deal with it. If I have to be some sort of hero, you can damn well get along with a woman you hate."

He growled something behind me, but I didn't stop to listen; I made my way into the room and up the dark stairs. They creaked and groaned under my feet, but I barely heard them. I was too busy being angry to notice anything.

I knew Liam would have a hard time dealing with Milly, and I understood why. But what was I supposed to do? Pushing her away would put all that power out there to be snatched back by Orion, or maybe some other faction. At least with Milly close, I could keep an eye on her. That's what I told myself, anyway.

My old room was lit from the moon on the snow and I dropped the sash to block the view. I didn't need anyone noticing movement in the old house. I spread out my gear, checking for damage. Swords, short blades, crossbow, spears, arrows, and a myriad of other deadly weapons. These were my back ups;

my two favorite blades were almost always with me, as was my whip now. My crossbow—I ran my fingers over it . . . Will gave me this in London. I liked it, and it was a sweet weapon to deal with asshats at a distance, but it was bulky and hard to run with. Yeah, running always had to be an option when you had no magical abilities, so to speak.

I might be immune to magic and most poisons, but that wasn't a power wielding anything other than protection, defense. And my ability to Track was the same. Super handy, but no offense either. There was one reason I'd survived everything I'd faced: the simple fact I had friends a hell of a lot stronger than me in the magic department.

I stood and took a slow turn in my old room, hearing the creak of footsteps on the stairs. As I faced the door, Liam stepped in and shut it behind him.

No words, just walked to me and pulled me into his arms, burying his nose behind my ear. I slid my arms around him, felt the horror of the day seep in around the edges of my brain. A short whimper escaped me as I bit back the grief.

Dox had been one of my closest friends and had seen me through so much, stitched me up more than once, and never questioned my choice of life. His laughter and quiet strength had been a part of my world; I'd not realized how much I leaned on just *knowing* he'd been there. Liam's arms tightened around me. "Rylee, I have to tell you something."

He tipped my head up with a finger under my chin, a smile teasing at his lips. "You need to shower. You stink like Milly."

My jaw dropped open and he ducked the reactive swing of my fist. "Jerk." But he brought me out of the grief sucking at me. Smart man—far smarter than he let on to most people.

"Come on." He was still smiling. "I'll help get you un-stunk."

2

The hot water—and Liam's hands—did the trick, soothed everything away, even if just temporarily. The dark moments we'd faced, the darkness we knew was coming, the fears and uncertainties. It had been too long since he and I had a moment like this, quiet and relaxed. Moments that felt normal and helped me, at least for a moment, re-center myself.

Clean and in fresh clothes, we headed downstairs. Liam grabbed me halfway down and kissed me, fierce and hot, a reminder of the shower. I kissed him back, knowing we would fight again. Of course we would. We weren't exactly Barbie and Ken living in the pink dream house. No, more like Morticia and Gomez running with monsters, and with moments of passion that burned us both to the core. He let me go, his hands lingering on me as we started down the stairs. Stepping into the living room, I stumbled to a stop, my brain unable to process what my eyes saw: the impossible. He was a ghost; he had to be.

Charlie sat on the beaten up old couch, grinning widely at me. "Hello, Rylee. Didn't think to see mes again, did yas?"

"Charlie, holy shit!" I ran and scooped him up, noticing some slight charring on his wooden leg, but otherwise he was in one piece. I squeezed him hard, unable to believe he wasn't dead. He patted my back with both hands.

"It's okay, lassie. It's okay." I didn't fight the tears, because this time, for the first time in a long time, they weren't grief. Charlie was right; for once in my life it was okay. I had one of my friends literally back from the dead.

I put him down and crouched beside him, wiping my face dry. "Charlie, how the fuck did you survive?"

"What are you talking about?" Liam asked.

Charlie tipped his head and arched an eyebrow at me. "Didn't tell them, did yous?"

"No time." Which was true and not.

"Yous better tell them. Only way now. Cause even if you don'ts, I wills for ya." Charlie pushed himself back onto the couch and settled in.

Alex and Pamela came in from the other room. Alex waved at the brownie, then ran over to him, putting his head into the small man's lap. "Hiya, Charlie!"

Charlie patted his head. "Hiya back, foolish wolf."

I cleared my throat, thought about the oaths I'd made to Faris. "Charlie, you tell them. I don't want to start breaking my word. Even to that asshat."

The brownie nodded and gave me a wink. "I gets it. Long story short, Faris threatened Rylee that if she don'ts help him find the Blood, which is the only way he can secure the throne, he will kill all those that's she loves."

Liam snorted. "And you believed him?"

Charlie tapped his wooden leg against the couch. "He snatched me and tossed me through the Veil into the lava to make sure she agreed to help him."

"Who did, Orion?" Milly came in from the kitchen, her right hand at her neck, fingers pressed into her skin until the tips were white.

"No, Faris," Liam growled at her.

Stillness fell on the room, and the air cooled. Giselle's spirit guides didn't like this kind of talk; that much was clear.

"Listen," I said. "I'd planned to run this by you all, but there just hasn't really been a moment to say 'Hey, the fucking vampire is trying to blackmail me so we need to find a way around his shit' with what happened at the farm."

Liam touched my lower back, giving me support. "I know. And I believe you, but Charlie, that still doesn't explain how you survived."

The brownie smiled wider yet, his eyes sparkling as if he were going to tell us a particularly dirty joke. "Well, yous see, I don't think vampires knows toos much abouts brownies. If he did, he'd be knowing that brownies use doorways and windows as a way to jump around. An opening through the Veil, it justs bees another kind of doorway."

Pamela laughed softly. "Cocky vampire—even I know how brownies move around."

Milly laughed softly, shaking her head. "He was always over confident. I knew it would bite him someday."

I didn't join in the laughter, and neither did Liam. He shared a quick glance with me, his silvery golden eyes full of questions. No doubt the same ones that rattled and tumbled in my head.

Of all the things Faris was, and there were a lot of things I'd call him, stupid was not on the list.

He *had* to have known Charlie would save himself, would show up here and tell us he was alive.

So why the fuck would he do it?

I slumped into the closest chair, understanding washing over me. He'd gotten me to speak oaths, oaths I would be bound to because of my very nature. And he'd sealed my belief by "killing" Charlie.

"It doesn't matter if he's not really threatening all of you." I ran a hand through my hair, catching on a knot but not really feeling it. "He got me to say I would help him. And he will hold me to that."

Milly put her hands on her hips. "You can't be serious? You can't help him now!"

Charlie surprised me, lifting his hand. "Besides these oaths yous spoke, that's not really the issue. You hold a choice, Rylee. Whos will lead the vampires: a child gone mad with power and a belief she should rule all the world, or a man who is fighting to lead his people and keep them safe, and keep the humans ignorant of the supernatural a little whiles longer?"

If I thought the air had gone still before, it was nothing compared to the ice that crept into the room.

"There has to be another choice," Liam said.

I slumped even deeper into the chair, feeling the truth of both Liam's and Charlie's words. What they said cut to the core of the problem. There was no third choice, no dark horse to bring up the rear and be better than both Faris and Berget.

"Fuck, Charlie, you're right. One of them has to lead, and if I have to choose, it won't be Berget. It can't be."

Milly stared hard at me. "You'd help Faris, after all he's done?"

I glared at her, anger icing my words. "I haven't killed you yet, witch, after all you've done. And unless you have someone better to lead the vampires, we don't have a fucking choice."

Her teeth snapped shut and she flushed along her cheeks. Point for me.

Liam sat on the edge of my chair, partially blocking me from Milly. Subtle—not so much. But I understood he would never fully trust her, and he was there to protect me, even from her.

Charlie jumped off the couch and strode toward me, his wooden leg only giving him a slight limp. "I've gots to bees getting back to me abode. I just wanted to sees that yous was all right, Rylee. And to tell yous I is all right."

"You aren't staying?" Pamela looked to me as if I were going to stop him. "There's a war coming, Charlie, and we need everyone. Even you."

The brownie glanced at her, then at me. "Read the prophecies, did yas?"

I frowned, irritation flowing through me. "Does everyone damn well know about those fucking prophecies *except* me?"

He shrugged and gave me a half smile. "Part of why I wanted to works with yous, Rylee. I knew what you were the minute I laid eyes on yous, not just a Tracker, but the one that would bees saving our world. When yous need me and all me brethren to fight, we'll be there." As he passed my chair, he patted my hand. "It'll work out, Rylee. I believes it." Charlie stepped through the archway between the living room and the hallway and disappeared. No puff of smoke, no twist in the air, not even a feeling of power.

Just gone.

Milly sucked in a deep breath. "He didn't bend the Veil to jump it."

Shit. "Is that how it's done?" I asked, trying to sound casual.

She looked at me, and then shook her head. "You don't want to know how to jump the Veil, Rylee. The cost is too great."

"Yet you do it," Pamela pointed out, both verbally and with a finger jabbed at Milly in condemnation.

"Yes, I do," Milly said. "But I wish I had never learned." She paused, and I saw her debating whether or not to continue before she said, "It's like an addiction. There's a rush to it, despite the cost. And like any addiction, you need more and more. The only ones who do not face that are the necromancers, as they are . . . no, that's all I'll say. I'll never teach anyone to jump the Veil; I hope the knowledge dies out."

I rolled my eyes. "Dramatics, with you it's all about the big scene." I pushed to my feet and bobbed my head to Pamela. She frowned slightly, but nodded back. I wanted to speak with Liam before we talked to the whole group.

Pamela would stay behind to watch Milly.

Pretty bad when you had to have a teen watch over an adult, but then again, it *was* Milly we were talking about.

3

Liam and I headed upstairs, Alex trailing at our heels. We said nothing, the stairs creaking under our feet. Inside my room, I walked to the window that looked onto the street at the front of the house. I pulled the sash up. No movement in all this snow, nothing at all.

I turned away from the window and walked to the bed, sitting on the end of the mattress.

Alex let out a yip and leapt up beside me, burrowing his nose into the thick covers, and rolling onto his back. From there, he juggled several pillows above his head, tongue hanging out the side of his mouth. But even his antics couldn't draw a laugh from me, not today. Too much had happened and my emotions were wrung out.

Liam shut the door behind us, the door clicking closed and giving us some semblance of privacy. "So, what is the vampire's game?"

Atta boy, right to the heart of it. "Fuck me if I know." I walked across the room to peer out the window again, as if I could find the answers in the freshly fallen snow.

Liam slid his arms around me, curling my ass tight against him as he placed his chin on my shoulder. "Already done."

I swatted his hip, but let the smile on my lips linger for a moment. "O'Shea, smarten the fuck up."

He let out a growl, most likely from me using O'Shea instead of Liam. "Fine. But Faris is playing a game, and if you don't know the rules, you are going to get killed."

Hands on the windowsill, I leaned forward. My breath fogged the old glass and I drew a circle in it, and then drew a slash through the circle. "It's always a game with the bloodsuckers. Shit, look at Doran. It's fun for him to yank your strings and he does it every chance he gets."

Again, Liam growled, but said nothing. I took a deep breath, my body held tight by his muscular arms.

"Faris doesn't really want to piss me off." The words slipped out of me, a whisper now. "He needs my help, but I wouldn't help him before, not even when he asked."

Liam's voice was as soft as mine. "Because of Berget." No point in answering, we both knew that was the truth. Liam turned me around to face him. "War is coming, Rylee. Is there any doubt in your mind?"

"No."

"And you need allies." He paused and his words sank in.

My eyes widened and I stared up at him. "You agree with Charlie. You think I should help Faris."

Fuck me sideways, was he serious? Despite what I said downstairs, I never expected Liam to agree. Yet, it made sense. Hell, what Charlie said made sense no matter how much I wanted it to be otherwise. One thing held me back.

"I don't want to kill her, Liam. I don't think I could do it."

Always, it came back to Berget. I'd sworn an oath, the strongest oath I could, that I would kill the Child Empress. Of course, that had been before I'd known who the Child Empress was.

"We'll find a way around it."

"And until then?" I put my head against his chest, his heart thumping underneath my ear. "I can't take anyone with me when Faris shows up. Just because Charlie made it doesn't mean Faris won't kill someone else. He might not have known Charlie's tricks . . ."

"Really?" The dry tone in Liam's voice was not lost on me. I slid out of his arms a few inches so I could look up at him.

"Okay, so he probably knew Charlie's abilities. But again, it's a part of the game. Like chess. You do realize I suck at chess?"

He laughed. "Yeah, you're more of a checkers girl, aren't you?"

I lifted an eyebrow. "You mean smashing my opponents as I leap over them?"

"Something like that."

He held me and my mind worked over the issues. Only one question was left.

"I know what I have to do, Liam. Are you going to let me do it?" I stepped away from him and started to pace, stopping in the center of the room to face him.

His jaw was tight, and eyes steely. "You are always leaving me behind, Rylee. Always. As much as I hate it, I—" He shook his head and then gathered himself.

I waited for him to say it. Even though I knew it was coming, I needed to hear it.

"I trust you. If the prophecies hold true, you are going to be at the center of this shit for a long time. No matter what I do, or how close and tight I hold you, the danger and darkness will always come for you. Always. If I don't trust you, I'm going to get us both killed." He reached out and slid his hands up my arms, smoothing the goose bumps that rippled along my skin with his near-prophetic words. "And I will always be here, waiting on you, fighting for you when I can, healing the wounds when I must."

"Even if it means me going with Faris, without you? Only taking Alex?" I whispered, hardly believing he wouldn't fight me on this. Even if it was what we had to do. Fuck, I so hated Faris. Even if he hadn't killed Charlie.

He tugged me against his chest, arms banding around me. "Don't fucking well remind me you'll be with that bastard. And don't let him know you know about Charlie. Whatever game he has, play along. Let him believe he's in control. As for Alex—" We both looked down to the submissive werewolf passed out on the bed, ass in the air, face jammed in the pillows. Liam snorted. "He's more loyal to you than anyone else, and even though he *is* submissive, it's changing. I sense it in him; he's coming into his own and will protect you with everything he's got.

You know that. If I can't be there, Alex is the next best thing."

On cue, the sleeping Alex let out a fart that echoed in the small room. Liam reached behind us and opened the window a crack.

I closed my eyes and pressed my face into his chest, breathing him in alongside the rush of clean snow-kissed air. "I can't even kill Faris now. I have to help him take the throne, and Berget . . ."

Liam kissed the top of my head and whispered into my hair, "You'll find a way, Rylee, that much I'm sure. If anyone can find a way, you will."

He held me and everything sank in.

Liam knew I was going to help Faris, on my own, with only Alex for backup. A way to bring the vampires on as allies in this war with Orion and his henchmen. "The enemy of my enemy is my friend," I said.

Liam hugged me tighter. "Yeah, some shit like that."

I let out a heavy breath and stepped back from him. "Come on, let's see if Pamela's scrounged up food."

Alex's eyes flew open and he scrambled off the bed, making an even bigger mess of the blankets and pillows, one pillow exploding in a shower of feathers. "Alex hungry, yuppy doody!"

He bolted toward the door, scrabbling with the handle, and then clattered down the stairs. Liam grabbed my hand. "Wait. What are you going to do to convince the others? Pamela and Milly won't want you to go, either." His face shifted and his lips twisted up. "Fuck, I to have to deal with Milly on my own."

Now I did suppress a grin. "You'll be fine. Let Pamela run interference."

He shuddered. "When is Faris coming for you?"

"Seven days."

"Shit, that isn't long enough to plan."

I smiled at him, but felt the fatigue pull at me even as I tried to work past it. Not fatigue of the body, but of the heart. Though some had lifted, after seeing Charlie. "Like you said, I'll come up with something. You'll have to trust me when I do."

He brushed the nape of my neck with the tips of his fingers as I walked in front of him. "You are the only one I do trust, Tracker."

I smiled back at him, feeling all fucking warm and fuzzy. Another time, I would have scoffed, but now, I was just damn grateful I had someone who loved me so completely.

We headed down the stairs for the second time that night, and I walked toward the kitchen, expecting everyone to be where I'd left them. In front of the living room, I froze in place. In some ways, I'd been expecting this.

Just maybe not this soon.

The blinds were all drawn, candles lit, and Giselle sat in the middle of the room looking as she had when I first met her. Young, vibrant, free of the madness that took her so quickly. Alex sprawled out at her feet on his back, grinning up at her, his tongue lolling out one side of his mouth.

"You don't seem surprised to see her," Milly said, drawing my eyes to the right side of the room. The witch sat in Giselle's chair, the paisley material clashing against her vibrant red dress.

"No, not really." I stepped into the room. "Giselle, you said you could only come through the Veil a few times, that it cost you."

Giselle nodded. "That's true. But it is easier here, with my spirit guides helping me." Her eyes flicked over each of us. "I will Read you all, because there may not be many more times to do so before I am summoned for the final time to the deep levels of the Veil." She pointed at Pamela. "Come here, little witch."

Pamela didn't look to me for reassurance. She walked forward and stopped in front of Giselle. "All right, then. Will this hurt?"

Giselle smiled up at her, reached out a hand, hovering over Pamela's heart. "No, it won't hurt."

Her hand trembled, and then she pulled back and held her hand palm upward to Pamela. "You have a great deal coming your way. The darkness has not seen you yet, but it will. And when it does, it will make a bid for you that you will struggle to refuse. Hold to what you know is truth, to what Rylee is teaching you." Giselle paused and tipped her head to one side, her eyes fluttering closed. "I see you at the end of it all; when the final battle comes, you will be pivotal. Remember, when darkness comes for you, when light seems gone from your life, you will be one of the flames that beckons to those who have lost hope, showing them hope is indeed not lost."

Pamela nodded once and then stepped back. Giselle shifted and turned to Liam and me. She pointed at Liam. "Much has changed for you, Agent. Will you let me Read you?"

I found it interesting she hadn't asked Pamela, but she asked Liam. He said nothing, only stepped forward, crouching beside her. Giselle cupped her hands around his face without touching him.

"Ah, wolf. You have fought the darkness well, *and* have fought to stay at her side. She's a tough one to stick close to, isn't she?"

He laughed and Giselle laughed with him. The mirth spread through the room, lightening the solemn mood created by Charlie's visit, until everyone was laughing except me. I shook my head. I wasn't that bad.

Giselle took a deep breath and lifted her hands back to his face, her eyes widening, filling with a sorrow I'd seen more than once on her face, and my gut twisted into a large knot.

"The rest of my words are not for anyone ears but yours, wolf."

I knew a dismissal when I heard one. Pamela and Milly stood and followed me into the kitchen. Alex stayed, but since Giselle didn't send him out, I figured it was okay. And no, I wouldn't try and pry it out of Alex. Likely, he wouldn't understand the complexity of what I was asking anyway.

But what did Giselle have to say to Liam that we couldn't hear?

Stomach tense with all the possibilities, I walked out holding my breath.

He stood quietly, uncertain why the rest couldn't hear what Giselle said to him. Her eyes were soft with a sorrow that made him think of the mermaid's words, her prophecy of his immanent death. Made him wonder if this was about to be a repeat.

She stared up at him, her eyes searching his. "You know what I'm going to say, don't you?"

"No, not for sure, and I'm hoping I'm wrong." Hell, he really hoped he was wrong.

She lowered her hands, clasping them in her lap and he crouched down beside her. "The dark times have come, and they are interspersed with flashes of light. Of love. The moment you understand why you are what you are, when you fully come to know your own soul, you will give it all up to save the ones you love, those three who are most important to you." She leaned forward, and her hands slid up to cup his face in a motherly gesture. "You will not be at the last battle with her, so you must prepare all you can now."

Chills swept down and through him as her words hit him. "You mean I'm going to die?"

She closed her eyes. "We all die, Liam. Here I am, dead, yet not. There are tasks you must accomplish. Things only you can do; they will keep Rylee safe, allow her to do what she must. Seek out the Wolf, the one who can tell you the origin of the wolves and the guardians. Power is in that knowledge. Power you will need."

He nodded, remembering the old wolf he encountered in the northern forests. "Why couldn't anyone else hear this Reading?"

She laughed softly and opened her eyes. "You tell me."

Liam let out a long, slow breath. "Because she would fight to keep me alive, no matter the consequences."

Giselle smiled up at him. "She loves you as she will never love anyone else. For the first time, she truly belongs somewhere, and she would give up the whole world to keep you at her side. I tell you these things, but you must carry them on your own."

His body stilled, feeling the weight of it, but understanding it was the only way. Rylee could never know he wouldn't be around forever. But how could he keep a secret of this magnitude from the one person who held his heart?

4

Less than five minutes passed before Liam came to get us from the kitchen, his eyes dark with shadows that had nothing to do with the poor light. I searched his face, wanting to ask him what Giselle said, maybe in large part because she couldn't Read me. I thought of Doran and his words, the first time I truly had someone Read me and the heavy message he'd given. Maybe I didn't want to know what Giselle told Liam. What if she told him he would love another? No, I didn't want to know.

Giselle hadn't moved from where she'd started. As we all stepped into the candle lit room, Giselle held her hand up. "Alex is next."

Alex rolled from his back to sitting upright in a split second. "Alex plays, too."

Giselle ran her hands over the top of his head and over the ruff of his neck. "A soul that is pure resides within you, Alex."

"Yuppy doody, spooky lady."

I bit the inside of my cheek, and Giselle laughed. "Yes, I suppose I am a spooky lady. You will see Rylee to the end; you will be at her side through it all, though not always as you are now. Loyalty is the core of your heart, and that will never change. Believe in all that you are, Alex, for you will be the lynchpin to this world's fate, as Rylee is the key to its survival. But that is a ways off yet."

Holy shit. I couldn't stop my eyes from widening. Lynchpin? I needed to get my hands on Jack's books again. If Alex was a lynchpin, I needed to know how that was going to happen.

She lowered her hands and then looked to Milly who stood on my left side. "Come here. We have much to say to one another."

I thought Giselle would dismiss us again, but to my surprise, she didn't. Nope, she dove right in.

But not with the Reading, not right away.

"You have betrayed us all to your master. And even knowing the reason why—that you were tied to him—at no point did you come to Rylee or me for help."

"I didn't think—"

Giselle lifted a hand, cutting her off. "No, you did not think. And that cost me my sanity, and could yet cost this world its entire being. I have been given a gift. A form of punishment that I may hand to you in penance for the wrongs you have committed. Are you willing to take it?"

Sheee-it. I hadn't expected this, and obviously neither had Milly if the size of her eyes and the pallor of her skin were markers.

Moment of truth . . . and Giselle brought us to it. Would Milly show her willingness to take some punishment for the wrongs she'd done?

The silence stretched and that last little hope I had nurtured flickered, as if a candle re-sparked by a cold wind.

"I will take whatever penance you have for me," Milly whispered, dropping to her knees in front of Giselle. Giselle's eyes shot to mine. "I need your help, Rylee."

Surprised, both for the request and Milly's willingness to take a punishment, I stepped forward before I thought better of it.

"Rylee," —Giselle pointed at my hand— "pull back your Immunity."

I did as she said, exposing my right hand to whatever magic she wanted to put on me. But she didn't do anything to me, not in the way I thought. Giselle slid her hand over mine and *took* a piece of my Immunity. How the fuck she did it, I don't know.

"What the hell?" I managed not to jerk my hand back, and watched as Giselle placed that Immunity on Milly.

"You will not have access to your magic until you grasp what you have done, truly understand the way you have broken our family, and truly understand where you belong in all of this. Then, and only then, will your power return." Giselle's words rippled through the room, and with them, she faded away. As if she hadn't ever been.

Pamela was first to speak. "You mean she took away your magic?"

Milly lifted her hand and whispered a spell, a doozy if I remembered correctly. One that should have taken out the entire sidewall of the house.

Nothing.

Like she was human.

"Damn it, Giselle!" I shouted. "Couldn't you have waited until *after* we were done facing a big fucking demon?"

No answer, of course. No, that wasn't entirely true. The bare echo of laughter floated through the house, Giselle's guides finding our predicament amusing. Assholes.

Milly stood and brushed off her dress. "That was . . . unexpected."

I shook my head and laced my fingers around the back of my neck. Understated much? Yup. "Can you still teach Pamela?"

"Yes, I should be able to." Milly made her way back to the paisley chair. "But is she strong enough to take on whatever comes?"

I snorted. "Even I know you're jealous because she has the potential to be stronger than you already."

Milly's eyes snapped with anger and I smiled. Oh, maybe this wasn't such a bad idea, taking away her magic. A little humility would do her good.

I lifted both hands into the air as I attempted to organize my thoughts, choosing not to discuss Faris. Let's move on from that.

"First things first. Who were those motherfuckers shooting at us? And how the hell did they get such accuracy on a Jeep full of supernaturals?"

"Someone was shooting at you, and you didn't tell me?" Liam grabbed my arm and turned me around to face him. I frowned at him.

"You distracted me."

Milly snorted. "We heard the 'distraction' all the way downstairs."

Pamela snickered and Alex let out a sneeze. I was grateful for the candlelight because the heat in my face grew at a rapid rate I couldn't control. I didn't think we'd been that noisy; then again, it had been hard to think at all . . .

Liam snapped his fingers, drawing all of our eyes to his face. "Regardless, tell me what happened."

We quickly went over the events, and the shock of the guns' accuracy struck me again.

"Rylee." Liam's eyes were distant and I saw his mind working. "Have there been other times when the vibrations of supernaturals has been blocked?"

"No."

"Think harder."

What the hell was he getting at? I racked my brain and then it hit me like a slug between the eyes.

"The FBI's private jet." I wanted to bang my head against the wall. Between the dark cars that followed us and the jet, I should have known.

Alex sat up and moved to my side, pressing himself against me. He tugged at my jeans. "Alex hungry."

"In a minute." I dropped a hand to his head and he grabbed my hand in his mouth.

"Hungry," he mouthed around my fingers. I stared down at him. This was weird, even for Alex.

"Alex, I said in—" He tugged me so I faced the side window, where the sash was closed except for an inch or so. Just high enough for me to see the ice blue eye staring in at us.

Holy fucking hell, Faris was here? Why now, why so soon?

I grabbed Alex around the ruff. "I'm taking Alex for a pee."

"I thought he was hungry?" Pamela stood.

"That too. Could you see what there is for canned food in the house?" I was all but dragging Alex, who was now trying to go with Pamela. Liam stood on the far side of the room, opposite Milly, and seemed lost in thought. Another time I would have been worried, but at that moment I was glad he wasn't noticing me.

"Pee first," I said and opened the front door, all but shoving the werewolf out. I didn't really want to see Faris, but since we all knew I was going to help him, no time like the present to start working with the prick.

Alex went tearing around the side of the house and I ran after him, our footsteps muffled in the snow. I yanked a sword from my back as I rounded the window where I'd seen Faris's eye—just in case. A pair of boot prints were set in the snow, but no vampire waited for me.

Alex sniffed the ground, lifted his leg and peed on the boot prints. "Piss on vampires," he grumbled, showing his teeth. I stepped closer and lowered my blade to rest into the snow. Etched into the window, where the sash covered, were two words:

Watching
You

Well, that was just fantastic, just the way to end an already shitty day. Like I needed that reminder when it had been less than twenty-four hours since I'd been locked in his stupid cement coffin of a room. A shiver traveled the length of my spine that had nothing to do with the cold.

"Come on, Alex. Let's go inside. And don't mention the vampire. Got it?" I slid my sword back into its sheath. No need to freak out anyone, or get Liam riled up. Fucking vampire and his games.

"Gots it." Alex shook his leg a couple of times, shaking off extra pee. We went inside, and no one had missed us. Pamela puttered in the kitchen, and Alex raced into her, yelping about his empty belly. Milly sat in her chair, curled up and brooding. Liam sat on the other side of the room seemingly watching her, but I saw he was zoned out, not really here.

Good and bad, I suppose. I didn't want anyone knowing I had to deal with Faris so soon, but to have Liam be so out of it . . . again, I wondered what Giselle said to him. The only obvious thing was, whatever she'd said, it likely hadn't been good. And I had a bad feeling it had more than a little to do with me.

Just fucking peachy.

I sat beside him. No point in beating around the bush. "Hey. What did Giselle tell you?"

He glanced up, his silvery golden eyes, a not so subtle reminder he was no longer entirely human, there was no going back for him. "Nothing that concerns you."

I blinked a couple of times, surprised. "No? Then why can't you tell me?"

His jaw ticked, and his voice grew in intensity with each word. "It was for me, and no one else. If Giselle wanted the rest of you to know, she wouldn't have told you to leave."

A pit opened, somewhere near my guts, rolling with acid. This wasn't like Liam; he didn't keep secrets. Neither of us did, not from each other.

"Seriously?" I strode away from him, hurt curling through me. The shitty part about loving someone was this kind of crap, and how easy they could stab you with mere words. I'd prefer to get run through with one of my own blades. Stupid-ass male.

He followed me out of the living room, through the kitchen and out the back door onto the rickety porch.

A whisper of voices made the hair on my neck stand up, even knowing what I heard was Giselle's spirit guides. No time for that right now.

"You don't get it, do you?" Liam growled. "You don't get to know everything."

Oh, so that was the game he wanted to play. "You're right, but I thought with you, at least, I would have someone I could damn well finally trust. I guess I was wrong." I kept my back to him, pissed off, and worse, scared. I hated being scared.

"You can trust me, you know that. You're just pissed you can't bully me into spilling."

I spun around, my jaw dropping. "Are you fucking serious? I *know* what kind of Reading would make you clam up like that. So I know it was bad, and the fact that even now you are pushing me away tells me it's even worse than I think. Which is pretty fucking bad after everything we've seen in the last twenty-four hours."

His mouth snapped shut and thinned to a hard line. That was it, I knew him; he would say no more. As if to hammer the point home, he turned his back to me and stripped out of his clothes, barely making it out of them before he shifted. The oversized black wolf glanced once over his shoulder at me before he loped off into the darkness.

I leaned against the house, the wall sagging with my weight. He decided he wasn't telling me, and there was nothing I would be able to do to change his mind. Shitty part was, my imagination was more than apt at filling in the myriad of possibilities. Maybe Giselle's words *had* echoed Doran's.

You will love another.

A shiver ran through me and I wrapped my arms tightly around my middle. He was bound and determined to carry this on his own, whatever it was. So we were not the team I'd thought we were.

So be it.

5

Sometime around two in the morning, Liam slipped into the room and lay beside me, his hand icy cold from the snow slipping over my hip. Within minutes, he conked out, twitching every now and then as he slept. Alex and Pamela slept on the floor, curled up together. Milly was in the room across the hall—her old bedroom. No one would admit they didn't want to be alone after what had happened to Dox, Sla, the triplets, and the Coven—all powerful supernaturals in their own right, and they had been wiped out like they were human and unable to defend themselves.

Sleep came to me after a long while, but not kindly.

Oh, I knew what I saw in my sleep was just a dream, but it still bit at me, tearing my heart as if a test to see how much more I had in me.

Berget sat with me on the swings in Deerborn Park where she'd been taken so many years ago. The air smelled like early spring, fresh growing things and new life, and the wind drew on her golden locks, teasing them around her face.

"Rylee, you won't give up on me, will you?" The shake in her voice and tremor in her lips tugged at me. Her blue eyes were full of her soul, not like the

Berget I'd seen below Venice. The one who'd try to kill all those I loved. These were the eyes of the little girl I knew as my sister.

"How am I supposed to help you, if this is even the real you?" I pushed myself on the swing with a bare toe in the soft sand, my loose skirt blowing around my knees.

Berget shrugged. "I don't know all the answers, I only know you will save me from this. If you don't, I will never be free. I will forever be in limbo. I know it will be hard. I know my body will fight you, because I don't have control of it anymore."

I closed my eyes and tipped my head back, breathing the air deeply into my lungs. "Can you tell me anything that might help?"

She stepped off her swing and moved behind me, pushing me higher. I let my head fall back to look at her, balancing on my seat. Without warning, her hands were around my neck, squeezing, just hard enough to stop me from breathing, her fingers digging into my skin.

"Whatever you do, don't let me bite you; it will bind you to me."

My eyes flew open, sweat soaking the pillow beneath me, my heart pounding like an oversized drum in my chest. I leaned over and checked the clock. Just after three. I'd been asleep for maybe an hour if I was lucky. Fuck, I was exhausted.

Yet, I lay in my bed unable to sleep. To have Berget beg me not to give up on her, her words dug into my brain and wouldn't let my eyes close again. How did I know it wasn't Berget the vampire, the one who was mad with the power her parents had bestowed on her? It made no sense, other than to say when Berget came to me in my sleep, I saw her as if it were her soul. And if her soul still cried out to be saved, how could I deny her that?

I slipped out of bed, stepped over Pamela and Alex, and went to my weapons. I scooped up my two blades, whip, and hesitated over the crossbow. I was just going downstairs to think, what the hell did I need any of this for? Yeah, good question. I took my weapons anyway, left the crossbow behind, and then went out the door. My jeans and t-shirt weren't warm enough without Liam's body heat beside me and I ran my hands over my arms. In the hallway, I stood silently, staring at Milly's door.

I wanted to talk to her about everything that had happened. Not as enemies, but as the friends we had been for so long. I wanted to discuss with her all the things going through my head, the worries, the concerns at one time she would have listened to. She would've been the one I'd turn to. Especially with Liam blocking me from him . . . .

She'll use you again, break your heart with her lies. In the process, you could lose those who truly love you. Shit, that was the truth. I bypassed her door and headed downstairs, avoiding the steps I knew creaked without even thinking, sliding on my weapons in a rhythm as natural as breathing.

The living room was dark, but I didn't need light to find what I was looking for. In the old Victorian desk Giselle had so loved was a stub of a pencil and a few blank sheets of paper.

"Okay, get your brain wrapped around this," I muttered. I lit two candles, placing one on both sides of the desk.

I paused, the pencil hovering over the paper for a split second before writing.

> *–Oath bound to Faris—leaving in six days. Must help him gain throne.*
> *–Guns that are accurate around supernaturals?*
> *–Orion is on the hunt for my allies and is going to try and take over the world. Fucking peachy.*
> *–Berget.*

My sister's name stilled my pencil. What the hell was I supposed to do about her? I'd sworn an oath to Faris that I would kill her, despite the fact I didn't know who she was at the time. An oath was an oath, and he was holding me to it. I looked at my list and knew, while they were all important, no way could I deal with them all. Not on my own. In helping Faris, I would try and secure the vampires as allies. That would help with Orion and was about the only damn good thing coming out of helping the bastard vampire.

I closed my eyes, tried not to think about Orion for a second, because while he was the biggest threat, I didn't know how to stop him . . . so at the moment, trying to figure him out was a waste of time. My train of thought skittered sideways. Maybe not so wasteful . . . I had the demon book of prophecies tucked away that *could* have information in it, information that would give me what I needed to wipe out Orion. Mind you, it was in New Mexico in a safe in the Landing Pad. My heart constricted as I thought about Dox, about how much he would have suffered to have his skin removed while he still lived. I clenched my hands; no time, there was no time for this grief, and that hurt.

Later, the tears could come later.

I let out a tight breath, and tapped my pencil on the desk. Doran was near Roswell too. Doran could potentially have information, or know where to go for information on Orion. Or maybe even one of the other Shamans there. A few of them still owed me favors. What the hell was I thinking? No one knew how to deal with a demon like Orion. If someone did, they would have dealt with him by now.

My mind flicked back to Doran and his connection with Berget. Again, there was a possibility he could help me. It looked like everything pointed to New Mexico. The thing was, I knew I was going to deal with Berget, probably sooner rather than later. Saving her would have to be before I went to "work" for Faris. There was no way he would go along with saving his sworn enemy.

Death or dishonor: that's what I faced.

Take what was left of my sister's life—filled with the mad rage and power of her adopted parents—or try to find a way to save her, to work around Faris's stupid fucking oath. I shook my head. Too many tasks, not enough time.

I continued to tap my pencil. Two things had to be done without any fucking dawdling, and there was no way I could manage both. One, we had to find out who the hell was putting together weapons that worked around supernaturals, because Milly was right. If Orion got his hands on them, if he found out . . . I shuddered. A demon with working guns? We were in seriously deep shit if that happened. Might as well just lie down and let him take us.

Two, I needed Doran and that black-skinned demon book. If I was lucky, Doran would have some info on Berget that would be of use too. Either way I looked at things, it meant a trip to Roswell.

Two tasks, two teams. Son of a bitch, I had to split us up again to make this happen. Apparently, my subconscious already knew this when I got out of bed. My skin tingled, chills racing. Splitting up hadn't worked well in the past. Someone always ended up hurt, or worse, skinned alive. I tried to swallow, struggled to work around the sandpaper feel of my mouth.

The creak of a foot on the stairs snapped my head up. I lifted the sheet of paper and held it over the candle on my left, and let the flames take the words.

I turned in my seat as the last of the paper burned to ash and floated to the desktop.

Pamela stepped off the bottom stair and peered around the corner at me. "Rylee, Alex is snoring and Liam is talking in his sleep."

I lifted an eyebrow. "Did he say anything interesting?" Her eyes dropped and with them, so did my stomach. "Pamela, what did he say?"

She gripped the bottom edge of her shirt and lifted her face. "He said, 'I can't tell her, she'll never let me go.'"

I gave a sharp nod, like I knew what she was talking about. "Don't worry, it's nothing." But hell, it wasn't *nothing*. Even in his sleep the bastard was close mouthed. Shit, for once I was glad I couldn't be Read. Except by Doran and that had been temporary. Seemed little good came from knowing the future, and rarely could you do anything to change it.

Pamela let out a sigh.

"Oh, good. I was worried he was going to leave us."

A twang around my heart reverberated through me. Us. Yeah, we were family, a pack, whatever the hell you wanted to call it.

And I was about to break us up in order to try and save us.

Days like this, I wished I were human and had no knowledge of the life that hovered on the edge of darkness. That I could just go to sleep at night and wake up in the morning knowing it had all been a bad dream, not reality.

There was no doubt in my mind Liam would fight me on this decision to leave, even though he'd said he was okay with me going with Faris. This was different. This wasn't Faris anymore; this was me leaving without even telling him. Yet he was the only one I trusted to go after the weapons. Despite his assertions he would be okay with me doing what I thought was best, he would be pissed. And I couldn't really blame him

But he isn't exactly trusting you right now. I did my best to ignore that little voice in my head. Still, I could soften the blow by taking along someone to watch my back. Someone Liam said he trusted only second to himself.

"Pamela, wake Alex and bring him down here. Quietly. If Liam wakes up, tell him you are taking Alex for a pee."

Her lips tightened. "You're leaving us, aren't you?"

I reached out and grasped her forearms. "I need you to stay with Liam, keep him and Milly from killing each other. Find out who is making those weapons. Liam has connections with the FBI, and they can help us on this."

Her jaw twitched. "But you're still leaving us."

I wanted to shake her, to scream she had no fucking idea what was going to happen, forgetting for a split second she had been the one to find Dox and the other ogres hung from the rafters of the barn. She knew exactly what was going on, and what was at stake. "Yes, for a day, no more. I need to get information."

"Where are you going?" Damn her persistence, yet I was proud of her too. She wasn't backing down.

I let her go, decided to tell her the truth. "To Doran. I won't be gone long. I need to speak to him and maybe the other Shamans. I'll go through the mineshaft."

"Liam will come after you." She said it with the certainty only a teenager has. That certainty where teenagers think they know it all and the adults couldn't possibly get how wrong they were. I wondered what he said in his sleep. Maybe he was done with us, maybe he'd finally seen his life was pretty much forfeit if he stayed.

No, I didn't really believe that. Of all the things Liam was, disloyal was not one of them.

"Go get Alex. I'll deal with Liam."

Pamela turned and headed up the stairs. I wasn't sure she wouldn't wake Liam; the girl had a mind of her own. But if she did, I would remind him that he said I would make the right choices. A few minutes later, Pamela and Alex came down the stairs, him creeping on his toes with exaggerated steps that I just shook my head at.

"Alex beeees quiet," he whispered, lifting a claw to his lips.

Pamela stood with her arms folded across her chest, jaw twitching periodically. I pulled out a second sheet of paper and scrawled a note on it, folded it in half, and gave it to her. "Give this to Liam when he wakes up."

"And if he tries to go after you?" She arched an eyebrow at me.

"He won't. Not when he sees the note." I was not that confident, actually, but she didn't need to know that. I was betting on him remembering our earlier conversation, and even if he didn't trust me with his Reading, he could trust me on this.

She took the folded paper and tucked it into her back pocket. "I don't want you to go."

Her blue eyes welled up with tears, and I felt my own emotions curl up toward the surface. I pulled her into my arms and held her tight. "I think there's going to be a lot of things we don't want to happen, that we will have no choice in. Not if we want to survive what's coming."

A hiccupped sob escaped her and I held her tighter. There was nothing else I could do. Alex crept forward and wrapped his gangly arms around us both. "Alex loves Pamie and Rylee."

I ran a hand over his head. "We love you too, buddy."

A minute passed and I pushed her away. "I have to go. Before Liam wakes."

"If you think he'll let you go, why don't you wait to tell him?" Pamela wiped her cheeks, her eyes questioning me.

I shook my head, unable to tell her the truth. It wasn't just Liam I worried about; I had doubts about myself, too. While being dependent on Liam wasn't totally bad, it was making me soft. I had to be strong enough to do things on my own, like before I'd started my own pack.

Good practice for when Faris showed up and I had to leave.

Again.

Fuck, this shit was getting old.

I slid on my heavy winter jacket, the leather-lined coat had as many stitch-up jobs as I did. Weapons already on, I nodded at Pamela. "This time tomorrow, I'll be back. Don't worry, okay? You just help Liam get the info he needs, however he needs to do it. I'll leave the Jeep for you three. Alex and I can make it on foot."

She gave a quick nod, but the doubt was in her eyes.

"Come on, Alex, let's go."

He and I headed out the side door. I turned back on the threshold to see Pamela standing in the candlelight, Giselle behind her.

Go, Rylee. You must. Giselle's words hummed inside my head, a reassurance I needed. I lifted my hand to them both, and stepped into the blowing snow.

6

Sleep, though it stole him away from his worries, was not restful. Giselle's words haunted his dreams, and a myriad of ways to die filled his mind. He couldn't tell Rylee, he knew that, but he hated to keep secrets from her. Hated how her eyes had filled with distrust when he couldn't tell her. Hated that he pushed her away, even if it was for a good reason.

Morning sunlight woke him as it snuck past the drawn sash and bathed his face in weak winter light. Liam groaned and rolled to his side, his hand reaching out for Rylee's body. Nothing but a cold spot beside him. Not really a surprise, she was probably downstairs working out already—the woman could rarely be pulled from her routine, even when the shit hit the fan.

And hit the fan it had. The entire local coven wiped out, Dox and his friends skinned alive, Eve dead and then brought back to life, Giselle's Reading of him. Liam ran his hands over his head, still not fully believing everything they'd seen.

Not to mention Rylee was as pissed as a cat in a rainstorm at the moment. Nothing he could do about any of that now, so he shook it off and got out of bed.

His spine cracked as he stretched and his eyes were drawn to Rylee's weapon stash.

Her two best swords were missing.

The winter ice might as well have slid down his back. He threw on his clothes and was in a flat out run in a matter of seconds, down the stairs, and into the kitchen where Milly and Pamela stood side by side, heads bowed together. The murmur of Milly's voice as she explained something about subtle magic to Pamela. No Rylee and no Alex. Maybe she'd just taken the submissive werewolf outside.

Maybe he was just trying to delay the inevitable once he finally asked the question.

"Where is she?" He drew in a deep lungful of air, trying to scent Rylee. She'd been here, but it was faint, like it had been hours since she'd last been in the house.

Pamela turned and pulled something from her back pocket, handing it to him. He noticed the red around the rim of her eyes, the smell of sadness clinging to her, and anger.

He took the note and flipped it open.

I won't be long, twenty-four hours at the most. Take Pamela and see what you can find out about those fucking guns. We can't let Orion or his lackeys get their hands on them.

That was it, nothing about where she'd gone, or what she'd left for. But he knew this was a dig at him. He hadn't opened up to her, and so now she was fucking off on her own. Having a fucking snit.

"You know where she is, don't you?" He folded up the note and tucked it into his pocket as he lifted his eyes to Pamela.

She tipped her chin up ever so slightly. "Yes, I do."

"Are you going to tell me?"

Uncertainty flickered through her eyes, her age showing. "If I do, you'll go after her and then she'll be angry with both of us."

Milly said nothing, just watched them, her green eyes thoughtful.

Liam put his hands on his hips and dropped his chin to his chest, thinking, as he tried to work his mind around the anger coursing through him. A few deep breaths and he managed to get himself under control. He'd told Rylee that she would have to make choices and he trusted her to deal with Faris on her own when the time came. There weren't a lot of options and, though he and his wolf were pissed as hell, what Rylee was asking him to do made sense. Even if her reason for leaving on her own was stupid and more than a little childish in his eyes, he did understand why she'd done it.

He hurt her, pretty much told her he didn't trust her, and she'd run away.

Fuck it all.

Through the anger, the logical side of him—his FBI training—said what she'd done was the best division of labor. Whatever task she was after wasn't danger-ous; at least, that's what he told himself. Trusting her was one of the hardest things he did, mostly because he knew how quickly she found trouble, whether she wanted it or not.

The faster he tracked down where the guns were coming from, the faster he could go after Rylee. If he had to. But no matter what, he couldn't tell her what Giselle told him. Hell, he needed to make something up. Twenty-four hours was enough time to come up with a plausible reason he'd held back. Right?

"Let's get this done and get back here." He turned and headed for the side door.

"I'm coming with you," Milly said, stopping him in his tracks.

Pamela cleared her throat softly, only loud enough that Liam heard. "I don't think that's a good idea, Milly. It's not like you can actually help now that you have no magic, and besides, Liam wants to kill you."

Ah, for the simple honesty of a teenager.

He looked over his shoulder. "Pamela's right."

Milly lifted an eyebrow, then dropped her gaze. "I can still teach her as we go, and I don't want to be left alone. I am totally vulnerable without my magic. At least if I am with you and Pamela I have a chance."

Teeth clenched, he tried to see how he could deny her. Hell, he could have Pamela tie her up and leave her in the hallway closet until they got back.

His wolf paced inside him, snarling at the very thought of sharing close quarters with Milly. Then again, she had no magic, so he could kill her if he had to. With ease, actually. She might even give him just cause to break her tiny little neck. His wolf settled with that thought.

He gave a sharp nod. "Fine, you can come. Teach the kid, stay out of the way, and don't touch me."

The two women grabbed coats and followed him out. Rylee's Jeep was parked in the same place she'd left it last night. His eyes dropped to the ground, looking for tracks, but the falling snow had covered them firmly. Her scent pulled him forward a few steps, drawing him down the path she'd gone.

"Liam." Pamela's voice drew him back. "How are we going to use the Jeep?"

His eyes flicked over the compact vehicle, and he wondered the same thing. Whatever he was, he packed far more of a 'supernatural' wallop than the others. "We'll have to try, see if it will start with all three of us."

"And if it doesn't?"

Well, that should be obvious, but he said it anyway. "Milly stays behind, regardless of how vulnerable she is."

Milly lifted her chin, and he saw the fear in her eyes. Orion wasn't just coming for Rylee and her pack; he was coming for Milly and her child too.

Shit, he was not going soft on her.

He wasn't.

Before we left Giselle's, I took a wrapped torch, lighter fluid, matches, and a long coil of rope from my Jeep. Looping the rope around Alex and tying it firmly, he was able to carry it easily. Everything else was light enough for me. At least I'd thought ahead enough to take the majority of my gear from the root cellar. Alex and I ran for two hours, until the light stained the snow around us a faint pink. With the snow falling steadily, I wasn't worried about leaving tracks, though I knew Liam would be able to scent us. I had to believe he would do as I asked and wouldn't follow me. That, and I was pretty sure he would get the subtle jab that trust had to go both ways, or it didn't work at all. The run with Alex helped with the anger and the hurt.

Going to New Mexico on my own wasn't a big deal, there was no danger waiting for me. But Doran loved to poke at Liam, loved to drive his wolf into a rage. Which was one more reason to send Liam in a different direction. I could handle Doran on my own.

It wouldn't be long before we hit the highway, and from there we would snatch a ride to the badlands exit with one of the big rigs, they were always headed along that route—

A blood red, meticulously clean pickup truck rolled to a stop beside us, the windows tinted pitch black. The passenger window rolled slowly down to reveal Faris sitting in the driver's side, a grin on his face, fangs fully showing. "Fancy meeting you here, Rylee. Get in, I'm losing heat."

The shock didn't last long, a mere split second before my rage spilled all the way to my fingertips. The only thing that kept me from launching myself at him was knowing Charlie was alive.

Seven days, he'd promised me seven days before I had to help him. I wrenched open the door. "How am I not surprised—you fucking liar—that you didn't keep your word to me?"

His grin didn't falter. "I thought you would be grateful for the ride, seeing as you mistakenly left your Jeep behind."

He still thought I thought he'd killed Charlie, threatened my family, forced me into oaths that bound me to help him, and he wanted me to be fucking grateful?

Then again, it was morning, and the sun was shining, if dimly. "Actually, I am grateful." I smiled at him and opened the door fully, yanking it backward until the hinges squealed. Oh, what a joy it would be to see him fry to a crisp in the early morning sunlight.

His eyes narrowed and the grin settled into a snarl. But that wasn't what pissed me off the most, no. That fucking asshat jumped the Veil. Just sitting there, he jumped the Veil.

My temper cooled and I realized it was probably for the best anyhow. After all, I needed him. Sure, I wasn't happy about it, but without Faris I wouldn't be able to unify the vampires—or worse yet, Berget would gain true control. Add to that I was really hoping to find a way around killing my little sister.

I slapped my hand on the door. "Get in, Alex. We have a ride now."

As I slid into the driver's seat, I wondered if somehow Faris had done this on purpose, if I was already falling into a trap he'd carefully laid out. I gripped the steering wheel reflexively. No, I couldn't worry about it now; I had a way to get to the mineshaft and that was all that mattered.

Still, knowing he'd suckered me into my oaths while not actually hurting anyone only compounded my belief he was far smarter, and far more devious, than any of us gave him credit for.

The truck spun out as I gave it gas, the back end fishtailing before the tires found traction in the wet snow. Probably had four-wheel drive, but it wasn't that nasty out. I'd save that for going through the badlands, which would be rutted and snotty at best.

Alex all but vibrated beside me, claws tapping on the dashboard. "Alex hungry."

"You can eat when we get to Dox's."

He slumped in his seat, bottom lip sticking out. "Bugger."

I ignored him and peered through the darkened windows, the tinting making it look like midnight than morning. The passenger door had closed better than I thought after I wrenched the shit out of it and the interior heated up nicely. In the center console, a cell phone beeped. I grabbed it and held it up. The color still stayed on, the cell phone still worked. A tingle of apprehension slipped along the surface of my body. I flicked the phone open and it continued to give me the high definition color screen. The connection was simple; Faris had something to do with the guns being used. Yes, I had an old cell phone, but it was ancient and as simple as they came, and even it chose not to work sometimes. This phone was shiny and new and hurt my eyes the screen was so damn bright.

I flicked the "answer call" button.

"Who is this?"

Faris laughed softly. "Be careful, Rylee. I need you in one piece, and there are new enemies coming your way. Not that you should be surprised, Tracker."

"Why the fuck would I believe you?"

I could almost hear the smile in his voice. "Because I believe they were following me, and now they are following you. Since you stole my truck, that is."

"Fucking idiot!"

I hit the end button and quickly dialed in a number, holding the phone gingerly to my ear. It rang three times before picked up.

"This better be good," he grumbled, sleep heavy in his words, the sound of static belying the fact he was a supernatural using a phone.

I snorted. "Doran, I need a ride."

The phone was so damn sensitive I heard the slide of sheets over his body as he moved around. Unreal.

"Do you know how long I've waited to hear you say that?" Doran all but purred into the phone, all trace of sleepiness gone.

"From the cave, to Dox's. Then maybe to Louisa's. I'm not sure yet." Always best to ignore his less than subtle innuendos. His punk-rocker boy style wasn't really to my taste, even if I hadn't been with Liam. Not to mention, being a Daywalker did nothing for his stock with me.

"When?" Good, he was back to business.

I checked the clock. "Half hour to the mine shaft, half hour to the doorway. Hour at most."

"Shit, it'll be close. Wait for me, I'll be there." He hung up and so did I.

Everything was coming together better than I could have hoped when I'd left Giselle's in the dead of night.

Which should have made me feel good, but the rolling in my gut made me question whether I was wrong about this whole trip. No, I needed that book, needed help. And if there was nothing else I'd learned in the last few months, it was I couldn't do it alone. I needed those around me to help with the nastiness in the world.

Then again, the tingle of fear and subtle twist of premonition in my heart could be due to the fact I was driving a truck that had belonged to Faris and he'd been followed—oh yeah, he had a phone in it that worked around supernaturals.

I stared at the phone and then picked it up, flipping it open. The call log was easy to access and I re-dialed Faris.

He answered right away. "Technology is a beautiful thing when it works, isn't it?"

"Where the fuck did you get this phone?"

"It was a gift. From a lovely lady with mocha skin and *delicious* lips, amongst her other delicious bits . . . would you like the details of how we met, and how she showed me her gun, so I showed her mine?"

I hung up on him with a snarl and threw the phone onto the dash. Pig. The phone may have been a gift, but no doubt strings were attached. Could Faris be working with those who had the deadly accurate guns? A shiver rippled down my spine at the thought. For now, there was nothing I could do, nothing to change this.

Half an hour later we were on the highway, cruising toward the mineshaft with no issues. Red and blue lights flickered behind us, and I checked the speed-ometer. Nope, all good there.

No doubt Faris had reported the missing truck and set them on me. Fuck a duck, Faris was an asshat. For a brief moment, I thought about making a run for it, knowing I could outrun the cop once we hit the badlands. No, I had time to deal with a cop. I took my foot off the gas pedal and let the truck slow, steering it to the side.

"Fucking hell," I muttered and Alex nodded.

"Bad guys."

I shook my head. "No, not bad guys. Just pain in the ass cops doing their job."

When the first shot ricocheted off the back of the truck, I thought I was hearing things. The second and third shot, I knew we were in shit. Again.

"Motherfuckers!" I yelped when a bullet slammed through the back window and out the front. "Faris, I hate you, you bastard!"

I put the pedal to the floor, taking us back onto the highway. Horns blared around us as I did a half-assed merge into traffic. At that moment, I didn't care if Faris was using me, I was grateful he had the foresight to steal a truck and not some pansy-assed girly car.

The shots kept coming and again, I wondered how the fuck they were doing this, and with what technol-ogy—how they were able to overcome the vibrations supernaturals gave off. Our exit came up fast and I waited until the last second to yank the truck to the right and skidded sideways to the off-ramp. Teeth gritted, I fought the wheel to stay in control, the slush and ice pulling at the tires.

"Weeeee!" Alex bounced in his seat, not understanding the severity of the situation. If it had been magic or monsters chasing us, he might have got it. But he didn't understand guns; they had never been a factor in our lives.

"Alex, sit still."

He slammed his butt onto the seat and gripped the dash, claws digging into the plastic. "Fun, Alex likes rides with Ryleeeeeee!"

He bounced into me, and the wheel slipped through my hands, spinning the truck in a 180-degree circle so a brief second we were staring back at our pursuers. A black sedan was alongside the police car, like the last one. Just like all the cars the FBI drove. What the fuck was going on, had Agent Valley decided we were a liability—and if so, was Liam in trouble? But that didn't make sense. The thoughts ran through my head faster than ever, slipping through before I could do anything about them.

The truck continued to spin until we faced the right way, though looking at the wrong side of traffic. Cars peeled off around us, fishtailing and sliding in fresh snow. A mess of metal and rubber collided around us.

"Son of a bitch." I slammed the truck into four wheel drive, the extra grip giving me the power I needed to get our asses back on the right side of the road and avoid the collision of cars that sprung up around us.

I glanced in the rearview mirror to see the sedan stuck behind the pile up of cars, unable to cut through the snow and grass median as we had. A figure stepped out, tall and slender, feminine with a distinct *mocha* hue to her skin highlighting her jet black hair. At this distance, I couldn't tell anything else. She lifted a hand and saluted us as we sped away.

I rolled down the window, stuck my hand out, and saluted her back. Though not with the respect she'd shown us. How the fuck had they found me? Had Faris actually called in the stolen truck? No, that wasn't his style.

But how else . . . my eyes landed on the phone. If it was null to the supernatural, they could easily put a tracking device in it.

"FUCK!" I grabbed the phone from the dash and tossed it out the window.

Whoever had the guns, also had a desire to deal with vampires. Not good, not good at all. I hoped Liam would be able to handle this shit for a few hours until I was back.

The road twisted to the right, the wreck disappearing behind us, and then it curved to the left. With the speed we were going, and the kickback from the last curve, I was pretty sure we were going to eat it. "Hang on, Alex!"

Sweat slid down the back of my neck as I did my best to keep the truck on the road. As the tires slid off the pavement and onto the gravel, the truck finally gained traction and I was able to give it some actual direction.

One more fishtail as the truck settled onto the road, and we were good. I glanced in the rearview mirror, expecting the black sedan to be on our asses. But the road was blessedly empty.

Less than a half hour later, we were bouncing and sliding across the badlands, and I was doing my best not to get us stuck. Even with the four-wheel drive, I knew there were holes and slush that would suck us down with ease. Ahead, I could see the edge of the mineshaft peeking out of the fresh blanket of snow. Almost a foot in fewer than twenty-four hours. It didn't seem that long since we'd crawled out the mineshaft with the ogres in tow.

I put the truck in park, and Alex and I jumped out. I sank to my knees in the snow and had to slog my way through to the top of the mineshaft. I had a sudden vision of coming back through the mineshaft, the tall FBI woman with mocha skin at the top with a gun waiting for us.

Shit, that would not be good. There was a chance the phone wasn't a tracking device, and it was not a chance I was willing to take. Not with my life, or Alex's.

I swallowed hard and sent out a silent call to Blaz, knowing even though he was at the barn, he could hear me being this close.

Tracker, where are you?

I licked my lips and concentrated on forming the words clearly in my mind, finally gave up and just looked at the mineshaft.

There was a pause before he answered. *Yes, I see it. But what is that in your mind about Faris?*

Oh, fuck a duck, that was the last thing I needed—Blaz on a rampage after the vampire for being, well, Faris. I blocked everything to do with Faris and concentrated on the mineshaft and a desire for Blaz to keep an eye on the place while I was on the other side.

I waited, hoping he didn't pursue the Faris thread. The downside of Blaz was he could be inside my brain and there wasn't much I could do about it. All part of the bonding between him and me.

Yes, I will check. But I'd rather not leave the farm unless I'm needed.

"What the hell?" I grumbled and apparently that went through loud and clear.

We can discuss it later; it is not urgent. But I am . . . somewhat in hiding.

My eyebrows shot up and I leaned my hands on the mineshaft edge. Hiding? What the hell could a dragon be hiding from?

An image of a large, red dragon flashed inside my head, then was gone before I could be certain of what I saw.

"Fine. Hide. We can 'discuss' this when I get back."

Eve is not back yet; that is another reason to stay where I am. There was a slight overlay of worry in his thoughts, amusing since he ate Harpies on a regular basis.

I Tracked her and felt her not too far from us actually, out with the Tamoskin Crush. The unicorn group wouldn't hurt her, of that I was certain. Not after their future leader Calypso had brought the Harpy back to life. Eve's emotions were smooth, and while not necessarily happy, she was at least calm and not afraid.

I let him see her, feel her emotions and that she was not far. Through me, he could in a sense "Track" as well. This was so damn frustrating, not being able to speak like he did. Seemed some things didn't go both ways. As it was, I did my best to soothe him.

"Don't worry about her, she'll be fine," I said out loud.

I almost felt him snort. *I wasn't worried about the Harpy. I knew you would worry about her.*

"Whatever," I muttered, then called Alex to my side. There were still ropes leading down into the shaft from the last time. Probably not the safest practice, but hell, not many people wandered the badlands this time of year.

I tested the ropes. "Alex, can you . . ." I trailed off as he expertly wrapped the rope into a harness, holding it out for me to finish off the knots.

"Alex watches Boss."

Well, I'll be damned. After I tied the knots, Alex climbed carefully over the edge and lowered himself down. Like he'd done it a hundred times. Shit, that was a hell of a lot easier than I had planned. The werewolf could still surprise me. Then again, he was growing up in a way, losing his submissiveness, and as it went, he became more mature. Day by day, he seemed to be gaining back his humanity, and with it I was losing the goofy werewolf who'd shown up on my doorstep two years ago.

Again, I set my thoughts aside to pay attention to what was in front of us.

The cave was no different than any day before, but it *felt* different. More than likely it was the backwards footprints we followed. Every now and then I saw the outline of an ogre's foot, and I found myself wondering which of the boys it was; my heart aching for their loss, and had to push it away. One day I would honor all those who had fallen, all those I'd loved and lost.

One day. Just not today.

Alex and I crossed the Veil with no difficulty, sliding through without anything pushing us to cross. Of course, that didn't mean what was waiting for us on the other side wasn't difficult.

Worse, it wasn't Doran.

7

The castle was quiet—eerily so—and the stiff hair on the back of my neck told me it wasn't a good thing. For the moment, I ignored my gut. On our side, the doorway from North Dakota opened onto the first floor of the castle. Nothing fancy. But we needed New Mexico and that meant descending the stairs into the dungeon. A walk I'd taken more than a few times lately. Again, I was surprised at the quiet. Not that the castle tended to be noisy.

"Alex, you smell anything?" I paused at the juncture of three hallways, the torch in my hand burning the pitch with a spitting hiss releasing the scent of pine into the air.

Alex sat back on his haunches and sniffed the air several times, tipping his face toward one hallway after the other. "Funny air."

"Yeah. I got that much." We were in a hurry, but I had a feeling something was off. Which meant I had to look into it, I couldn't just leave it alone. I set the torch into a wall sconce and pulled a sword free. With one finger to my lips, I signaled Alex to follow me with a head jerk. He tiptoed, taking in long breaths as we went. I didn't think about where I was headed, just followed my instincts.

We stood at another intersection, this time with a flight of ascending stairs. My gut tightened as I stared the steps.

"Here we go." I crept up, feeling the tension rise as I went, the tingling sensation of imminent danger I knew all too well working its way along the edge of my nerve endings.

At the top of the stairs, Alex bumped gently against my legs, stopping me.

"What?"

"Bad smells. Rotten smells." He shook his head as if to clear the scent. We could have turned around, pretended whatever was going on had nothing to do with us, but past experience told me that was stupid. Lately, everything seemed to happen to me, or was about the stupid fucking prophecies. I gritted my teeth and started down the dimmed hallway. Ahead, a glimmer of steel caught my eye. I yanked my second sword clear of its sheath and pressed my back against the wall.

Alex mimicked me, his claws scraping against the cold stone. We waited, two heartbeats, three, ten, twenty. Nothing happened.

I inched along the wall while I searched the shadows for a figure, or something.

Nope. False alarm, apparently.

But then why was my heart still pounding with adrenaline? Good fucking question.

At the end of the hallway was a window, sealed shut, but light peering from the moon through the cracks. I strode to it, sure we were alone and flung the window open.

"Wowsers. Big door," Alex breathed out behind me.

I turned and stared at a door recessed deep into the wall. In front of it was a black Veil, like something you'd put over the pictures of someone deceased. Not really thinking, I pulled the Veil down. It fluttered to my feet with a soft hush.

The doorway itself had my attention. It stole my thoughts as I stared at it. Thick, I could tell without even touching it, the whole thing was solid steel, shining as if polished. That must have been the glint I'd seen. Three solid, shining steel bands lay across the door, each with a lock the size of a melon hanging off it. Etched into the door were symbols I was unfamiliar with, swirls and designs that drew my eye and made me think I almost understood what they said.

What they meant.

"Big door, no kidding." I reached up and was unable to touch the top of the frame, not that I really expected to be able to. It had to be at least ten feet high and almost the same width. More of a square than a rectangle. Set deep into the stone as it was, I wondered if the purpose was an attempt to hide the doorway. Where did it lead? I put my hand on the metal, lightly, tracing one of the designs with my finger.

From the other side, something rammed into the steel door, making the doorframe shudder and flex, the solid bands groaning under the impact. But they held.

Barely.

I stepped back, swallowing hard. Alex let out a whimper.

"Not good."

No, this wasn't good. But there really wasn't anything I could do about this, nor was there time. I needed to get to Doran, get what I needed, and get my ass back to Liam.

The thing on the other side of the door rammed it again, harder this time. I took a few steps back, and the ramming eased. More steps back and it stopped altogether.

Whatever it was knew when we were close. Which left us with only one option.

"Time to go."

The thing on the other side of the steel door could stay there. Even I knew when it was time to leave well enough alone.

Liam would be proud. I couldn't stop the smile that slipped across my lips as I headed back down the stairwell.

We had learned there was a door we would never open, and what lay on the other side of it was awake and less than pleasant. No doubt that was the tension I'd picked up on.

I was glad we could walk away from the door. Because I had a bad feeling one day we would have to find out what was waiting for us on the other side of it.

Yippy fucking skippy.

Once more, we were back in the dungeons, facing the doorway that would take us into New Mexico. Or more accurately, a cave on the outskirts of Roswell.

Doran would be waiting for us there. He'd better be. I wasn't walking all the way into Roswell to find his fanged ass. We stepped through the doorway.

My torch flickered as a gust of wind ripped through cave, blowing it out. A single figure waited at the mouth of the cave. A woman I recognized from the tunnels below Venice. She was one of Berget's slaves, a human who had taken blood from a vampire but hadn't been turned. Might not ever be, according to what I understood.

"Hello, Rylee." Her voice carried well in the cave. I dropped the torch at my feet so I could pull my two blades free.

"Hey, bitch. On a suicide mission?" I stepped toward her and she smartly stepped back.

"No, I am here to give a simple message. The Empress hopes the death of your Harpy was enough to convince you to help her now. She would hate to take the life of any more of your 'wards.'"

I couldn't help the laughter that poured out of me. So similar to Faris's tactics it was unbelievable, yet with Faris it had been a ruse. With Berget, she'd been serious about killing Eve, though Berget couldn't know Eve had survived. It took me a good ten seconds to pull myself back together. "Oh my, you see that's how I know it isn't my little sister in charge of things, but her two psychotic parents. My sister would know better than to try and *kill* a member of my pack to gain my loyalty."

She gave a startled twist to her head. "We did not *try* and kill her. We *did* kill her."

I grinned at her as I walked the slight incline that would lead us out. "And my friend brought her back to life. Lucky for you, because now your death will be quick."

I lunged forward and she stumbled back, surprise flitting across her features before she was snatched out of reach of my blade.

"What the fuck?" I yelled. Doran came out of nowhere. He spared me a glance as he wrestled the woman into submission.

"Rylee, don't you know it isn't polite to just kill someone when you haven't wrung all the information you can out of them?" He stared down at the woman and smiled as he ran a finger along her cheek.

She screamed and tried to pull back from him, her cheek blistering where he'd touched her.

Shit, he was stronger than I thought, in ways I hadn't imagined. Doran had been holding back on me.

Since we'd used the existing ropes to rappel into the tunnel, Doran used the rope Alex and I brought to tie up the woman. He tossed her over his shoulder like a sack of screaming potatoes for the walk to Doran's classic '67 Mustang. He dumped her into the trunk, her head hitting something with a thud and she finally shut up.

Sleek, silver, and chromed to the gills, the Mustang glittered in the weak winter sunlight. Though it was cold as a witch's third tit, very little snow was on the ground. Which was a good thing with the girly car. Alex piled into the backseat and lay down, his eyes taking in everything, yet remaining remarkably quiet—but that didn't last long.

He let out a long trumpeting fart as if to deliberately contradict my thoughts. He even had the audacity to throw me a big wink. As if he knew what I was thinking. I rolled the window down and said nothing.

Doran glanced at me, his green eyes curious. "Why did you come back so quickly?"

"I left the black-skinned demon book in Dox's safe."

"And where the hell is the big ox? I'd planned on heading to his place for a drink tonight."

"Dead. Him and a bunch of his friends." I closed my eyes, swallowed hard, the words like chunks of glass in my throat. Doran's hand slid over mine.

"I'm sorry. I know he was your friend."

"And he wasn't yours?" I jerked my hand away.

Doran's lips tightened. "No. I drank his liquor, and we lived in the same territory, but we were not 'friends.' Daywalkers do not have friends any more than Shamans do." His eyes wouldn't meet mine, he stared straight ahead, the teasing Doran I knew gone as his voice hardened. "Shamans bargain for their services. Daywalkers bargain for the pleasure they can bring. I get hit up on both counts. But not as a friend."

I stared hard at him wondering if he liked not having friends. For years, I'd thought I could do it on my own, thought I was strong enough to face the world one on one. It had taken friends and love to show me I was stronger with them than without.

I couldn't help challenging him. "You think pretty highly of yourself to think everyone wants you."

His eyes darted to mine, then back to the road. "That's why I like you, Rylee. No games with you. You say what you mean, no filters involved. I don't get that with anyone else."

Something in his tone told me it was time to change the subject. "Aside from that shit, we have a rather large problem."

I quickly went over the guns and the phone I'd found, though I didn't say who it belonged to.

"You think the humans are manufacturing technology that works around us?" Doran didn't look at me, kept his eyes on the road.

"Yes. They know about us, or at least a portion of the FBI does, and it would make sense they are trying to find a way to protect themselves from us. It's the same old shit with them—whatever they don't understand, whatever frightens them, they want to annihilate."

Doran blew out a soft whistle and shook his head. "All right, I assume there is more to this visit than all that."

I took a deep breath and a chance, voicing the thoughts that had been spinning through my head since I had the dream about Berget. "I think we can still save my sister."

He hit the brakes, the car skidding sideways to a stop in the middle of the road. My seatbelt jerked tightly and the thump from the trunk told me our passenger got the short end of the stick.

"What did you say?" Doran's cool demeanor was gone; instead he sounded almost panicked. "I thought you were going to kill her. In fact, I would agree with Faris that killing her would be the smartest choice.

She's been inside my head, Rylee. She's controlled me. I know her better than anyone else."

I undid my seatbelt and faced him. I had been thinking long and hard on this, and there was a chance I had found a loophole in Faris's stupid oath. Or at least, part of it.

"You know her when she is controlled by her dead parents, who happen to be fucking loony tunes. We were able to stop Giselle's madness for a little while and the same stone worked on the necromancer I fought in London. You said it yourself, Berget is *mad* with the power that comes from her parents. Berget is not the one who has been doing these fucking awful things. I know I swore to kill her, but I swore to kill the *Child Empress*. If I can bring Berget back from the brink, she isn't the Empress anymore, is she? She won't want to be the Empress." I could only hope I was right.

The words hovered between us and he opened his mouth, blinked a couple of times, and then snapped it shut. "Shit, you might be right."

Hope, bright and pure, flared in me. He thought I might be right.

And that meant that maybe, just maybe, we had a chance at saving Berget.

The Jeep, much to his surprise and dismay, started with barely a cough. Worse, it had started when Milly sat in the driver's seat and him in the back.

"Head to the old library on 10th Street." He leaned back, tried not to breathe too deeply. To him, Milly stank. Her rose perfume and use of magic created a heavy fog that irritated his nose, even with the holes in the windows from the bullets bringing in fresh air. Yet Pamela didn't smell like that, and it made him wonder if the smell had more to do with the nature of the person, or the kind of magic they used, rather than what perfume they wore.

"What's at the library?" Of course, the question came from Pam; when did she not have a question?

"That's the Arcane Arts division of the FBI for the central region. Best place to start asking questions."

"And you think they can really help us?" The young witch twisted in her seat, one hand gripping her seatbelt so she could look at him.

He thought for a moment before answering. "They should have some idea of what's going on, and if they don't then they need to know. This is the sort of problem they are trained to deal with."

Telling Agent Valley he would periodically give the AA division information had been a hard choice. Now, though, that co-operation should serve them well. Didn't matter he hadn't brought any information to Valley yet; he was now.

Milly slowed the Jeep for a stop sign. "And if they want more from you, from us, in exchange for their help?"

Liam narrowed his eyes. "What do you mean, more?"

"They already have you on their list of informants, do they not?"

If she knew that, what else did she know? "Witch, you are already so far down the shit list you may never see the light of day again. So make sure you consider that when I ask you this—how do you know?"

She took the corner, checking several times for traffic. "Agent Valley has reached out to anyone who has a connection with the supernatural. That includes me. He doesn't understand I am your least favorite person."

That didn't make sense. "What about the fiasco in London?"

She smiled, but it didn't reach her eyes. "A misunderstanding. He is desperate for help, which makes him very dangerous. He will take help from anyone, even those he should be avoiding. There are rumors that he was reaching out to a certain vampire."

Liam thought back to when he'd seen Valley in London, before they'd left. There had been a distinct smell of rot about him, but at the time he brushed it off.

"He's working with a necromancer." The words slipped out of his mouth as his brain put it all together.

Milly started in her seat. "I don't know about that. Why do you think he's working with a necromancer?"

"He smells like death."

Pamela's heart rate kicked up several notches and the smell of fear rolled off her. The last time she dealt with a necromancer had been ugly, at best. She peered back at him, obviously trying to control her fear.

"Are we going to be dealing with zombies again, do you think?"

Before he answered, they were pulling into the parking lot of the "library."

"We're going to find out," he muttered, stepping out of the Jeep, the two witches following closely.

He looked down at his clothes: loose t-shirt, ripped jeans, scuffed sneakers. Not exactly the Gucci suits he'd been used to for so long. The other Feds might be more bothered by his clothes than he was. To be fair, it was likely his old coworkers would be more bothered by the fact he was no longer human. He couldn't help the grin that slipped over his lips.

This could be fun. He paused for a split second.

Good lord, Rylee was turning him into a delinquent in no time flat.

"What are you smiling about?" Pamela moved up beside him.

"Just thinking that Rylee has changed us all."

Milly snorted. "She is the catalyst. She's going to change the world whether she wants to or not, and with that, she with that will of course alter all those around her. I have seen it in myself, seen her change me even when I wasn't sure I could. She *has* changed us all. You included, Agent."

He ignored her and took the lead, pushing his way through the heavy, bulletproof glass doors. The secretary, Diana, if he remembered correctly, looked up from her desk as they stepped in. She'd been working here when he'd been in the department.

She adjusted her glasses. "I'm sorry, the library is closed for renovations."

Liam saw her hand slide under her desk, no doubt for a gun. He said nothing, waited for her to recognize him. It took another few seconds.

"Agent O'Shea? Oh my god, we'd heard that . . ." her words stumbled to a stop and her face flushed a bright red.

"That I'm not human anymore?" He arched an eyebrow at her.

Diana nodded. "Obviously, that isn't true if you are here. Are you bringing in new . . . recruits?" Her eyes slid from Milly, obviously pregnant, to Pamela far too young for any sort of recruiting.

"Not exactly. I need to speak with Agent Valley. Is he in?"

Diana shook her head. "No, I'm sorry, he's not. He's on medical leave. You can speak with Agent Ingers; she's taking over things while Agent Valley is out of commission."

Liam's mind raced. Agent Valley had been fine just a few days ago, so what could have happened so quickly that he was now on medical leave?

"Agent Ingers would be fine."

Diana pointed to the waiting room chairs, which he chose to ignore. An itch started between his shoulder blades and his wolf was suddenly on high alert.

He'd never heard of an Agent Ingers, which meant she'd been brought in from somewhere else. That might not work in their favor at all, depending on her views of the supernatural. Though if Valley had approved the new supervisor, she was likely going to be someone they could work with.

They waited for almost half an hour before Agent Ingers strolled into the room. She was a stunning woman, as tall as he was but far slimmer, her body fit and toned. Mocha-colored skin, blue-black hair, and dark brown eyes that would give Milly's a run for their money when it came to drawing men. She took him in with a single, cool glance that seemed to skip over him, dismissing him.

She smiled at them and held out a hand that was perfectly manicured, her skin soft and without any calluses. She smelled of sweat and gun oil, with a hint of witchcraft hovering around her. Almost like she had tried to scrub the scent off her. Shit.

"So, you are the infamous Agent O'Shea."

He didn't bother to correct that he was no longer an agent; every part of him ready to walk away from this.

"Yes. These are my friends." He didn't name the two girls and when Pamela opened her mouth to introduce herself he shook his head ever so slightly. The same smell of rot that had hovered on Valley lingered here too, stronger with Ingers's entrance. He didn't know the woman well enough to trust her yet—even if she was with his old FBI team—with Pamela's name, or even Milly's. He took another deep breath, his nose crinkling with the sour scent. Maybe a sickness was running through the department, maybe that was what he picked up on.

"If your 'friends' don't mind waiting here, we can speak in my office." Agent Ingers gestured to the back of the department. As they walked through the nearly empty building, it hit him what was off. When he'd worked here, they'd had twenty-five agents. In the short walk, he'd seen two: Ingers and Diana.

"Has the department been downsizing?"

"A flu has run rampant through the department." She shook her head. "It has not left us with much staff."

The itch between his shoulders intensified. She was lying; he smelled it on her, a sour bite in his nose that competed with the growing scent of witchcraft.

"Really? I haven't heard anything of the sort going through the city." He let her get further ahead of him, wanting space between them. Now it was more of a "how much information could he get and still get them all out" situation. Thin ice, this woman was thin ice in a heat wave.

"Well, you haven't been around much, have you?" The words were spoken with a soft intensity he really didn't like. Ingers didn't like him, and he was betting it had nothing to do with him leaving the department, and a hell of a lot to do with not being human.

They were in her office, but he didn't shut the door. She sat at her desk and leaned back, her hands hidden from him. He heard the nearly silent click of her releasing the safety on a gun.

"If you're going to shoot me, you better fucking well make it count."

Her mouth dropped open and he lunged forward, tackling her to the ground. The gun went off with a pop, and the bullet ripped through his guts, the wound healing as fast as it opened. She opened her mouth to scream and he slammed his hand over it. Her teeth started to close over the flesh of his palm.

"I wouldn't bite, or you might end up needing to shave a hell of a lot more." He grinned down at her. Yes, Rylee's bad behavior was definitely rubbing off on him.

From the front of the department a scream erupted at the same time a shot rang out. He dragged Ingers up with him, and took the gun from her with ease. He tucked it into the waistband of his jeans then spun her around, cranking her arms behind her back hard and fast, feeling her wrists creak under his fingers. She gasped—whether with the speed of his actions or the pain, he didn't know or care.

"You better hope my friends are okay, Ingers." Pushing her ahead of him, he worked his way through the department until they were at the front desk. Diana was strung upside down by her heels and Pamela clutched her own arm, Milly holding Pamela tight against her chest.

"What happened?" He barked, twisting Ingers's arms a fraction more, just because she had shot him.

Milly pointed at Diana, but kept one arm around Pamela. "She shot Pamela, for no reason; we were just sitting here."

Diana screamed again and from deeper in the office he heard the start of running feet. Shit.

"Stick her to the wall, Pam."

"Gladly." She flicked her hand on her uninjured arm and Diana slammed against the far wall, upside and squawking. "You want that one stuck too?"

He nodded and she took Ingers off his hands, tossing her against the wall.

Ingers glared at him, but she didn't panic. Her eyes glittered with a hate he'd rarely seen, not even on Berget, which was saying something. "O'Shea, you are going to die. You and all your fucking freak friends. You have no idea who you are dealing with."

Milly and Pamela stepped out the door, but he paused on the threshold, the truth burning though him like a hot branding iron.

"I know exactly who I'm dealing with." He stared hard at her. "And for the record, we all die, Ingers. It's just a matter of where and when."

8

Doran's home was the same as always, hidden behind a fold in the Veil, his fountain spewed water that steamed the surface of the catch pond below. I couldn't resist letting my fingers trace the surface of the water as I walked by. Bathtub warm, the water housed fancy koi that swam lazily around the circular pond, one even coming up to nibble at my fingers.

"Don't tease my fish, Rylee," Doran said without looking back at me. He pushed our prisoner ahead of him, controlling her with ease.

"You teased my Harpy. I think I can play with your fish if I want to."

He grunted but said nothing more. I tapped the top of the water for good measure and watched as all the fish raced to the surface for food. Alex, watching me carefully, stuck both paws into the water, pinioning a fish between his paws.

With a strangled squawk, I smacked his paws. "Let it go." It was one thing to tease the fish, another to kill them.

Alex stuck out his bottom lip and let go with an exaggerated flip of his feet. "Fine."

Damn, he'd picked up the sullen teenager act from Pamela.

"Don't touch anything, got it?"

He rolled his eyes before answering. "Fiiiiiiiiiiine."

I didn't know whether to laugh or smack him. I went with neither, snapping my fingers to the side of my leg. That, at least, he listened to. We followed Doran inside.

Doran took us into his house, to be clear, into a room I'd never been in. The kitchen's thick adobe walls held the heat from an open fireplace snugged into the far wall. Knives hung from a rack above a monstrous butcher's block that was big enough for Liam to lay on with room to spare.

I pointed at the well-used block. "Carving up bison sides?"

"Nah, just prisoners." He gave me a wink, but Berget's servant stiffened and a low moan slipped out of her. If she was that easily scared, this was going to be as simple as—

She lashed out with her foot, catching Doran in the shin, knocking him off balance long enough to get out of his hands. She grabbed one of the hanging knives and bolted out of the room while he hopped and cursed in what sounded like Russian.

"Damn it, Doran!" I ran after her deeper into the house.

A part of me wondered how Doran could let her get away; the other part wondered if he'd done it on purpose, if he was somehow still working for Berget. I slid around a corner and pure instinct saved me from losing my head. A flash of metal and I dropped to my knees as a cleaver buried itself into the wall where my neck had been.

"Sneaky bitch," I snarled, pulling my sword free and driving it upwards, catching her in the hip. The tip of the blade drove between the ball and socket, the feel of it in my hands telling me exactly the damage I was doing. A scream erupted out of her mouth as she jerked away from me, fighting for every step she took. I had to give her credit, she was a tough one.

That didn't mean I wouldn't take her head.

She ended up backing into a bedroom that had no exit, no windows. A dead end.

"Well, you about done with the fucking theatrics?" I leaned on my sword as she hobbled around the room, feeling for a way out. "Listen, I know a coffin when I see one." Hell, I'd been in one similar enough to this recently; I knew what I was talking about.

A sob hitched in her throat and she put one hand to her mouth, the other clinging to the bloodstain on her hip. "You have no idea what you're about, what's happening. You aren't vampires, you don't have any right to interfere." She took a deep, gulping breath. "The Empress will kill you for this."

I didn't try to suppress the laugh that rippled out of me. Alex crept up to my side and mimicked me, laughing with his head thrown back. "Ah, no. You see, the Empress, as you call her, is a callous bitch with no love for anyone or anything except her own power. Your death will mean nothing to her. You aren't even a vampire, you dumb fuck."

Not nice, not nice at all. But I spoke the truth and the woman stood, her lip trembling, her eyes hard with a hatred I wasn't sure was entirely directed at me.

"I don't want to die."

I shrugged. "Who does?"

Doran limped up to my left side, a glower on his face. "And you haven't killed her yet, why?"

"Oh, we're just having a girl chat. By the way, hate the bedroom. You need at least one window. The whole vibe is off for you, Daywalker." I glanced at him with a single arched eyebrow.

"Really? I was going for mysterious and sexy." He faced me, and suddenly the game was on.

"Shit no. Creepy and gloomy is what this is." I waved my sword in a circle in front of us, keeping an eye on our hostage without staring at her.

Doran frowned. "Damn. That designer cost me a gods-be-damned fortune, too. I have to see if I can get my—"

"Excuse me, are you going to let me go now?" The confusion on her face was exactly what I'd been hoping for. Not a technique I often used. Hell, I knew I was quick to kill. But this one time, maybe a little technique was the better part of valor.

"Only if you answer our questions. Answer them all, and Doran here can wipe your mind of all your memories and you'll be free to go." Slumped onto the edge of the bed, she bowed her head. Doran blinked several times and from the corner of his mouth whispered, "That's demon magic."

"Fake it," I whispered back.

She didn't notice our exchange as she stared at her lap. "Berget is hunting for the same thing Faris is. I don't know what it is—"

"Old news. Move along," I said.

She lifted her head and licked her lips several times. "There are rumors the madness is getting worse. That if she can't find this thing they are looking for, she will lose what is left of her sanity, and kill anything and everything around her."

Chills swept through me and I felt, more than saw, Doran shiver beside me. Bad news when the shaman gets the willies.

I leaned forward. "Anything else?"

"The other vampires have stepped back. They will not side with either of the two contestants for the throne until one of them has been declared properly." She shook her head. "I don't know anything else."

"Doran, you hungry?" Faris had shown me memories when he'd taken my blood, I was hoping . . .

"Excellent idea, Tracker." He grinned at me and strode to her, grabbing a hunk of her hair, and bending her head to one side at an extreme angle. Gentle is definitely not the word I'd use.

A single strike and his teeth buried into her neck, but he lifted his eyes to mine, a grin sparkling there. The woman let out a moan, this one not of pain. Her hand drifted upwards to cup his crotch and I turned my back. "Alex, let's get you something to eat."

I wasn't worried about Doran and the woman; he would either drain her until she was dead or drain her to the point of unconsciousness. Either way was fine by me.

You can be a cold bitch, you know that, right?

Yup, I did, and I knew it to the core of me. At times, there was no other choice but to be that hardass bitch in order to survive. I was used to it.

Alex galloped ahead of me repeating over and over, "yummy in my tummy."

The kitchen was well stocked and Alex wanted pasta. Though I'd been on my own for years, cooking was not what I'd call my forte. Spaghetti noodles with a can of sauce poured over it was the best I could do for him. He didn't care.

As Alex dug into his oversized mixing bowl of noodles, slurping them into his mouth, Doran swayed into the room.

"Drunk?" I leaned a hip against the butcher's block.

Doran held his finger and thumb an inch apart, paused and then held his hands two feet apart. "Maybe just a little."

I went with the obvious. "Coffee help?"

"Nope. Just give me a few minutes, the buzz won't last long—unlike with you, where I had a hard-on three days later." His grin was unrepentant and I ignored him. That was Doran. Serious and full of wisdom in one breath, a raging horny man in the next.

Alex slurped up the last of his noodles and red sauce and pushed the bowl away. "Goody good." He lay flat out on the floor, front and back legs pointing in the four directions, a long low sigh slipping out of him.

Doran cleared his throat and took a step, then another. His green eyes were clear, and while he shook his head once, there was no sign of the drunken Daywalker he'd been moments before.

"Better?"

"Much. And, may I say, that was an excellent idea. Though there wasn't much information she had, there were things she's seen that we can use."

Damn, I'd been hoping as much, but wasn't sure it would pan out. "Like what?"

He smiled and gave me a wink. "All in due time."

I slapped my hand on the butcher's block, the sting of my flesh only sending my anger further into orbit. With difficulty, I managed to keep my voice level. "No fucking games, Doran. Not today. You are either on my side or you aren't. Too many people have died already to play this shit. And I am running out of time."

A flare sparked in his eyes, defiance pure and simple. "And if I refuse to play by your rules, Tracker? What then? Are you going to take my head?"

There were days I felt much older than my twenty-six-and-a-half years. This was one of them. I tried another route. "Doran, I can't make you help me, but you said you would. I broke the bond between you and Berget; I freed your ass from her. But if you play these games now, we are done. No more friendship, nothing. I can't afford to guess anymore."

He closed his eyes and stepped closer to me, close enough that he was well within my guard. Everything in me told me to back up, to put space between us.

"Rylee," he breathed my name and my pulse hammered in my throat. Doran had become a friend. I didn't want to kill him.

"Doran, are you my friend, or are you my enemy?"

His eyes snapped open. "You would call me friend?"

I frowned. "What the fuck do you think, that I let just any Daywalker get this close to me?"

He let out a laugh and wiped his face with his hand. "No, I suppose not. She saw fear in Berget, though she didn't know it was fear. I did. Berget is afraid of you, and like the humans, what she fears she wants to kill, even though she needs you. A very human trait, which is surprising. From what I could see, Berget is going after Jack again, but she seems to have some means of hiding him from you."

I swallowed hard, forcing the words "we'll save him" to the bottom of my gut where they belonged. "Jack is on his own. He's made that clear."

Doran's eyebrows shot up and he took a step back. "Well, then this last bit should be of utmost importance." He took a breath, started to speak and then stopped. "Shit, Berget plans to bespell Jack, possibly even make him a vampire. He would be an immortal Tracker then. That is, if she hasn't done it already."

Holy mother of the gods. I sagged against the edge of the butcher's block, my legs suddenly weak. Jack had been terrified of dying, of dying alone. But that didn't mean he'd buckle, did it? Fuck, was that why Berget had taken him the first time, not to use him against me, but to use him for herself? "I thought you said the process was long and tedious?"

He nodded. "It is. Which makes me wonder if it had already been under way when you met Jack. If his miraculous recovery was because he was already taking . . . the steps to become a vampire. He said it himself, he doesn't want to die."

"Who the hell does?" I muttered.

Doran lifted his hands, palms facing me. "Here is what I am wondering, that I couldn't divulge from the woman's mind. If Berget has Jack, why is she continuing to pursue you?"

That, I was pretty sure I knew the answer to, but to be sure . . . "How much stock do vampires put in prophecy?"

Doran snorted. "It is their whole lives. They are guided by it. Ah, I see. You are the one Berget believes will fulfill the prophecy, hence, she still wants you to work for her."

I rubbed a hand over my eyes. "Jack is just a back up. If she can't have me, then she can at least have the only other Tracker in the world."

"Devious little thing, isn't she?" Doran muttered as he walked past me.

"Where are you going?"

"I thought you needed to go to Dox's place, to get the book?" He half-turned and arched a pierced eyebrow at me.

Not that I'd forgotten exactly, more that I'd just been sidetracked. "Alex, let's go."

The werewolf groaned and rolled onto his side. "Too much pasghets."

With much prodding, I got Alex back into the Mustang and we were off, headed toward Dox's place.

We drove in silence for the first few minutes until I couldn't stand it. "You killed her?"

Doran glanced at me. "You didn't expect me to?"

I turned my face from his and shrugged. "If you hadn't, I would have."

And that was that. In some small ways, ways I would admit to no one, Doran and I had similarities. Survival was always at the top of our lists, and we would do anything to make sure we stayed on this side of the Veil, unless our friends were in harm's way. I vividly recalled Doran begging me to kill him before he hurt me or Pamela when Berget set him on the young witch. Yeah, for a Daywalker, he wasn't half bad.

Even if he liked to tease Liam far more than what was good for his health.

We pulled into an empty parking lot, Dox's "Temporarily Closed" sign hanging crookedly on the door of the bar. Days, it had been only days since we'd left his place and headed out to the west coast, yet it felt like a lifetime had passed.

"Still deserted," Doran said as he opened his door. Alex pushed past him, bounded toward the Landing Pad.

"Brownies, brownies, brownies!"

I clenched my teeth to keep the emotions snugged down tight. With each new tragedy, it was getting harder for me to hold it in.

Anger, just focus on that. Good idea. "Dox didn't have anyone else he trusted to run the place while he was gone."

"You have a key to get in?"

I pulled a sword from my back. "Yup."

Doran shook his head, a smile ghosting across his lips. "A girl and her weapons—such a pretty sight."

"Shut up." I was at the front door and pressed my hand to it first. A slight tingle and whatever protective spell Dox had laid on it dissipated. I checked out the lock. Light burn marks around the edge of it looked fresh, but nothing else was out of place. There wasn't enough room to slide my blade between the door and the door jam. I stepped back and raised my blade to my ear, then ran it forward, straight through the locking mechanism.

Twisting my blade, the feel of metal on metal ran up the length of the sword into my arm, but the lock gave.

I gave a silent thank you to Milly for spelled blades that cut through pretty much any shit I threw at them. I pulled my sword back, but didn't sheath it. I hadn't known Dox to have any ability whatsoever with magic, which made me wonder whether it was Dox who'd spelled the place or someone else.

I slipped into the darkened pub; the only light came through the door window behind me. I flicked the light switch, nothing happened. Shit, there was no reason his power would be cut off, and I was pretty sure he hadn't turned it off before we left. "Doran, you didn't lay a protective spell here for Dox, did you?"

"Nope. But someone did, and it isn't a Shaman I recognize." He moved beside me. Alex crept forward on his tippy toes and whispered, "Alex smells Troll shit."

Oh, shit. There was a scuffle from the back room, where Dox's office was and where the safe was that held the black-skinned demon book. I moved to the bar and crouched, pressing my back against it. Alex followed me, and Doran moved across the room to the wall and disappeared in a shadow.

Trolls, I hated the fuckers with all I had in me. Trolls helped skin and kill Dox and the other ogres, and they had been dodging me and causing problems for longer than I cared to remember. If I could kill them, I would. Just on principle alone.

Three of them sauntered out of the back room, laughing and joking. In the poor light it was hard to tell, but I thought two of them were similar in color and size, their bodies giving off an almost neon yellow glow. Tall, but thick in the body, they were buck fucking naked, their double pronged dicks hanging limply to their knees. The third Troll looked to be of a darker color, maybe green, and his body was squat and lumpy, reminiscent of a toad. When his tongue flicked out and grabbed a fly, I realized he wasn't just reminiscent of a toad. I wracked my brain as they got closer. Toad Trolls had a poison they secreted out of their mouths that they could spit quite far. Wouldn't bother me any, but it would burn through pretty much anything else. Like locks and safes. In his hands, he held the black-skinned book.

I drew in a quiet breath, getting ready to start slicing into them when Toady boy decided to get clever.

"Here, hang onto this, stupid. I want to leave the Tracker a message of me own." He threw the book at the other two Trolls, both of which scrambled to grab it out of mid-air. They ended up landing on the floor, pounding the shit out of each other.

Toady boy wasn't watching though. If I thought Trolls were disgusting before, it was nothing to this shit. A dick in both hands, he started to whack off on the bar, just to the left of me. Yeah, that's what I said.

Nope, I was not getting *that* in my hair, thank you very much. While he moaned and panted, oblivious to the world around him, I snapped my sword forward and up, taking not only his two dicks, but both hands too.

The other Trolls were still wrestling on the ground when Toady began to shriek, acid spraying out of his mouth and onto the bar in a steady mucous stream.

"Alex, behind me," I shouted as I jerked my second sword out and, with the two, sliced Toady boy's head from his shoulders.

Now, most creatures notice when their leader goes down. Not Trolls. Not smart, but mean as hell, they were too busy bashing the shit out of each other to notice their buddy was headless, dickless and, more importantly, dead.

As the two Trolls rolled across the room, I scooped up the black-skinned book and waved at Doran. "Got what I came for."

I walked to the door, Alex snickering at my side. "Dumb Trolls."

Yeah, when a submissive werewolf who was stuck permanently at the mentality of a two year old thought *you* were dumb, that was bad.

Doran held the door. "After you."

And just like that, we were outside, in the fresh air.

Surrounded by Trolls.

Ah, fuck, it was never that easy, was it?

9

"**W**here are we going now, Liam?"

He did his best not to sigh. Pamela meant well, but there were times her constant questions grated on him.

Like now.

"Agent Valley should have answers to the questions we have, so we go there. And quickly."

Milly made eye contact with him briefly in the rearview mirror. "You think they'll try to silence him?"

"If he's not with Ingers, and she's willing to kill us on sight, with no provocation, yes. I think they would try to shut him up." Which would be bad on a lot of levels. If Valley was gone, and Ingers was in charge, they would no longer be able to say they had allies with the humans. And with a war coming, they needed all the allies they could get.

At the moment, Liam realized he was going to tell Agent Valley everything they knew about Orion, about Rylee, and the coming war. The agent and the FBI would need to know everything if they were going to help. And Liam was damn well making sure they would help one way or another.

He gave directions to the area he knew Agent Valley lived in. When Milly pulled over on the street intersection he'd given her, she said, "You don't actually know what house he's in, do you?"

"No, but I can figure out quick enough." He shimmied out of his clothes, his nudity not something that bothered him. There were far bigger things to be worried about than a witch ogling his ass.

He folded the clothes and handed them up to Pamela.

"Here, hang onto these for me, would you?"

She kept her eyes forward, a pink blush staining her pale cheeks. "Okay."

He opened the door and stepped into the snow. Pamela and Milly slid out of the Jeep to wait for him. This time of day the road was quiet, and most people were at work, so there was no one to peer out a window and see them. Without another thought, he let the shift take him, trusting if a human did see him, they would see something else. He didn't know, didn't care. Bones turned to liquid for a brief moment as they bent and twisted to that of a wolf's, and then he was on all fours. Nose to the ground, it didn't take long to pick up a scent, though it wasn't Agent Valley's.

The smell of death and rot lay heavy all along the road. Rotting meat, molding clothes . . . he wrinkled his nose and let out a snort. He twitched his ears as Pamela moved up beside him and put a hand on the ruff of his neck.

"Any luck?"

Of course, he couldn't answer her. He just put his nose to he ground and kept scenting. Somewhere in here he should find Agent Valley. He checked cars and walkways, and when the occasional curtain twitched Milly, and Pamela waved and smiled.

Again, he understood that humans saw what they wanted to: a large dog being walked by two nice young ladies. Probably sisters.

He worked his way up and down the road twice before he finally understood what was bothering him. The smell of rot . . . as he'd told Milly, Agent Valley had smelled of rot when they'd spoken London. Maybe there was more to it than just working with a necromancer. Excitement flared through him and he picked up the scent with ease, tracing it to the peach-colored house at the head of the street, right at the intersection.

When he approached the door, the curtain beside it twitched ever so slightly.

Bingo.

He glanced over his shoulder and the two witches walked swiftly to the left side of him.

"It's about time, wolf," Milly muttered under her breath as she rubbed her hands up and down her arms.

Pamela snorted at her. "You could have stayed home. We told you that you didn't have to come."

Liam couldn't stop the grin that crossed his muzzle. That was Pamela. Milly stepped to the side, out of the way so Pam could knock on the door, his clothes gripped tightly in her hands. Inside, there was a sound of feet shuffling. And the light click of a gun being loaded.

Without thinking, he body-slammed Pamela against the wall as silenced shots popped softly, driving through the door where they'd been standing. Snarling, he leapt forward, taking the door out with his body in an explosion of wooden shards. Being part-Guardian had its perks. Two more shots went off before he could see clearly, the bullets tearing through his chest.

Liam looked up as the wounds healed closed, the shooter a young man with pimples on his cheeks. Loose clothes, baggy jeans, and underneath the smell of death was a three-week-old case of body odor.

"Oh, shit," he squeaked, half-lowering the gun before seeming to realize he was going to need it again. Liam bared his teeth and took a step closer, the fur along his spine stiff with his anger.

The kid took a few steps back; the scent of magic filled the air and then the gun was jerked out of his hand, seemingly plucked away by an invisible person. The kid's jaw twitched and he looked past Liam to Pamela.

"You stupid witch. Stay out of this." Of course, that was when the kid lifted his hand and a black thread of *something* coiled from his palms. A supernatural using a gun against other supernaturals? Wasn't there a rule about that kind of stuff?

Liam didn't wait to see what the kid could do. Leaping forward, he covered the distance between them with ease, and took the kid to the floor. Pimple face's head smashed against the fake tile floor with a resounding thud and his eyes rolled back in his head.

The black smoke, or whatever the hell it was, faded and drew back into the kid's hands.

Pamela sucked in a sharp breath. "I think he's a necromancer, like Anne." She pushed him with her toe. "At least he's not going to be raising anything nasty with his noggin conked."

Liam took in a slow breath, couldn't get past the stench of rot and knew this form wasn't going to help him anymore. Breathing out, he let the change take him and within seconds stood on two feet. Pamela handed him his clothes as she turned her back.

Without hesitation, Liam scooped up the fallen gun. If it worked in the hands of a supernatural, he wanted it. He tucked it into the back of his pants, a feeling of familiarity rolling over him. Sure, he could use a sword, but a gun was his weapon of choice, and always would be.

Milly, though, had no such qualms. She watched him dress, her eye calm and assessing, but she said nothing. He forced himself not to hurry, knowing this was a power pull with her. She wanted to make him nervous, to put him off balance.

"Not going to work, Milly," he grumbled as he pulled his shirt over his head and slipped on his shoes.

"What's that, Liam?" Her eyebrows arched high, giving her a falsely innocent look.

He turned his back on her and crouched beside the kid. Even in this form, the scent of rot was strong. "Pamela, can you lace this kid up, stick him so he can't do anything?"

"I can stick him on the wall, but I can't stop him from raising dead things." She swallowed hard, the gulp audible. Rylee said Anne freaked out Pamela worse than the zombies she'd raised. Weird.

Putting a hand to her shoulder, he gave her a squeeze. "That'll be fine. You and Milly stay here, keep an eye on him. I'm going to search the house for Agent Valley."

Pamela pinned the kid to the wall in seconds, her lips tight. Leaving them, he started through the house. Kitchen and living room were empty, as was the bathroom and two bedrooms. A full circuit left only one more door. He opened it and stared into the dark stairwell.

"Son of a bitch, it's always the basement." Above his head dangled a string and he pulled it, but the light didn't flick on. A low moan echoed up to him, the hairs on the back of his neck rising with the noise.

He shook his head. "Like a damn horror movie. Wait for it, O'Shea, next you'll see an image of your dead parents."

A shallow breath and he started down the stairs. While a flashlight would have been great, he didn't really need it; a light source came into the basement from somewhere, maybe a ground level window. His eyes adjusted to the low level with ease.

One more step and he was on the concrete floor, which happened to be covered with a think layer of water.

"Shit on a stick. Valley, what have you gotten yourself into?" He did a slow turn. To his right was an open area and a few chunks of wood, to his left another door with a faint glow coming under the gap at the bottom. The basement seemed to be circular, similar to the house above. If he wanted to, he could run tiny laps down here. A moan and a thump against the door to his left drew his attention. His feet splashed in the water, but with each step the smell of death intensified. Forcing himself to crouch, he touched the water and brought the smell to his nose.

Gagging, he stood up fast and fought not to puke into what wasn't just water, but a slurry of old blood and viscera.

"Fuck, that is nasty." Doing his best not to think about what he stood in, he made his way to the door. Hand on the knob, he twisted it. In the backlit room stood Agent Valley, swaying on his feet.

"Sir?"

His old boss seemed to stare right through him, teeth clicking together twice before he really seemed to see Liam.

"O'Sheaaaaaaa." He raised his hands and lurched forward. Liam caught him, felt the lack of resistance in Valley's flesh, fingers inadvertently driving through to the bone.

"Sir, what's happened to you?" What the fuck was going on here?

Agent Valley was interrupted with anything he might say by screaming upstairs.

Liam spun, taking Agent Valley with him. "Sir, we have to get out of here, because if I know Pamela at all—"

An explosion rocked the foundation of the house when they were halfway up the stairs, the timbers around them shivering and then collapsing completely.

Lunging and dragging his old boss, cringing as chunks of flesh heaved from the agent's arms, Liam managed to get them both to the top of the stairs.

Pamela was there, pulling at his arms. "We have to go, Liam. That lady from the police station is here." Shit, things just got better and better.

Behind Pamela stood the pimple-faced kid, who appeared to have regained consciousness. He stared at Liam and Valley.

"Don't hurt him," was all the kid managed to say. Liam chose not to point out there was no hurting someone who was already dead and rotting.

"Come on, let's go." With a single heave, Liam tossed Agent Valley over his shoulder, the older man's gut squishing and squirming in a most viscous way.

Nothing to do now but run.

And hope to hell there was enough of Agent Valley left when they stopped running, he could tell them what the hell was going on.

Trolls, while not particularly clever, fast, or empathetic, were truly not fun to deal with on a large scale. And a large scale was exactly what we were looking at with at least thirty surrounding us.

Doran glanced sideways at me. "Let me try to calm this before you start lopping off more heads. I'm not sure even you can manage this many."

While I didn't put my swords away, I did give him the benefit of the doubt. He was right, there were too many for me to be thinking I could manhandle the situation. A bit of finesse every now and then didn't hurt. Usually.

He cleared his throat and raised his hands into the air, effectively silencing the crowd. "Boys, you have a slight problem inside the bar. One of your leaders has been ambushed by those who were supposed to be helping him."

A squarely built, pebbly-skinned Toad Troll stepped forward, his black beady eyes narrowing until they looked as if he'd closed them. His double genitalia swung from side to side, hitting his knees. Didn't look comfortable to me, not in the least.

"We don't fight amongst ourselves anymore, fucking stupid fang face." He spat at Doran who sidestepped the arc of poison easily. With his sidestep, he was now right next to the door, which he pushed open. The two Trolls alive inside were *still* beating the shit out of each other. It looked like I wasn't the only one who'd gone about causing grief by chopping off a cock or two.

The leader of the pack let out a long, gurgling hiss and about half the crowd rushed into the building. Doran lifted an eyebrow at me. "Can you handle fifteen?"

I shrugged, my heart picking up speed. "Better odds than before."

Without another glance at me, Doran spun and pulled two grenades from under his jacket. Grenades that looked suspiciously like the kind I'd gotten from Deanna. He threw them at Dox's bar and yelled out the ignition word, "*Ignitio!*"

The two grenades hit around the same time, or I was assuming that was the case, because I was already rushing the remaining Trolls. "Alex, go for the pink one." The werewolf let out a howl and launched himself full speed at the tiniest of the Trolls, taking it to the ground and snapping its neck in two seconds flat. I headed straight for the Toad Troll. That one could damage anyone but me. He spit at me, and I took it on the arm, the acid poison burning through my coat, but my skin only got a little bit warm. Booyah for being an Immune.

"Gotcha, fat boy." I lifted my sword to run him through, but had to spin and deal with an orange-ish Troll on my right coming in fast. A big brute, he reached for me with hands the size of turkeys and enough fingers that he could probably make a mean shadow-puppet professional. I slid toward him, using a back swing to take all those grasping fingers off. Bloody stumps fell to the ground at my feet, still twitching and writhing.

"No touching the Tracker," I said calmly, as if lecturing him on how to cross the road.

"Stupid Tracker, I'll skin you like I did the ogre bitches," he yelled, before falling to the ground, using his teeth to try and gather up his lopped off fingers. The words echoed in my head; they were the same ones on the note I'd found at the farmhouse. These were the guys who helped take out Dox, Sla, and the triplets.

Everything around me seemed to slow, and I turned to make eye contact with Toad number two. All that anger I'd tucked away, all that fury I had to hold back, surged in me. "You helped slice my friends up and skin them alive?"

He grinned at me, showing broken teeth and tiny fangs in behind the teeth, retracted like a snake's. "They cried like little girls as we peeled their hides."

A scream erupted out of me, rage I'd never known coursing along each nerve ending until I saw nothing but Trolls and the edge of my sword. Blood and viscera flew around me, heads rolled, hearts pierced, and none of it was enough. None of it would bring back Dox.

The seconds blurred, and distantly I knew I'd never fought like this, never moved this fast or killed with such intensity. The movements of my body and blades blended together, a perfect killing machine that felt nothing but fury.

There may have been tears on my cheeks, but I couldn't be sure, the stimulus of the death around me overwhelming anything else.

Their screams matched mine in intensity until they began to fade. And then just me, screaming, sobbing, kneeling in a pool of blood, hands still gripping my swords as my arms hung to the side.

"Ryleeeeeeeeeeee!" Alex's howl broke through to me and I took in a ragged, choked breath. He sat across from me, blood staining the silver tips of his fur. "Ryleeeeee," he said softer, his lower lip jutting way out. "No more, Alex's heart hurts."

Shit. I took in another, shaky breath and stood. Behind us, the Landing Pad exploded, a shit storm of glass and wood falling to the ground. I covered my head and ducked. Doran's grenades apparently had some real bite to them. Good to keep in mind he hadn't shown me all his tricks yet.

The crackle of a raging fire turned me around. The Landing Pad was engulfed in bright red flames that twisted and danced in the winter wind.

"Come on," Doran said, his eyes soft as they met mine. "We've got to get the hell out of here."

I nodded and all three of us climbed into his Mustang. The drive back to his house was quiet, beyond quiet, which was weird because I heard my heart thumping with each beat.

There was no doubt in my mind those were some of the Trolls that had taken out Dox and the others, but if I could kill them like that, then the Trolls had had help taking out my friends. The ogres were skilled warriors; no way Trolls did it on their own.

"Feel better?" Doran asked, as we pulled into his yard. I looked down at myself, and really saw what I looked like. My clothes were thickly crusted with Troll blood. Little bits of matter that could have been flesh or brain were flecked all over, like an abstract painting. A sudden longing to have Liam with me made me close my eyes.

"I think I will shower before we go. Have you got extra clothes?"

Doran rolled his shoulders. "I should have something that will fit you, but you might not like it."

"Temporary clothes don't have to be anything fancy," I said, sliding out of the car. Shit, I was going to burn these. The leather jacket I would be able to salvage, but it had a new hole to add to the mix, and

I'd have to throw out the wool lining. At least that could be replaced.

Alex padded quietly beside me, pressing himself against my leg. I realized he was doing it for me, giving me someone to lean on. I put a hand on his back. "Thanks, buddy."

He said nothing, just looked up at me with those liquid gold eyes, then away. Doran once more led the way, this time deeper yet into the house, past the bedroom where the woman's body still lay as if asleep.

With a sweeping gesture, Doran opened a simple white wood, slatted door into a bathroom of the kind I'd never seen. Floor-to-ceiling pale pink marble coated the entire room, which looked to be about thirty feet deep and twenty feet wide. An in-floor tub that took up the far wall filled with water and suds, waiting for someone to dive in; behind it a fireplace crackled, the flames dancing.

"Take your time." Doran stepped back and shut the door behind him with a soft click.

A soft spurt of air and then steam coiled out from six spigots along the edge of the wall. "Talk about being pampered." I stepped into the room and slid out of my jacket, which was already feeling too warm. "Alex, hop in the tub there and get clean."

"Yuppy doody!" He scrambled across the floor and, from ten feet out, leapt into the tub. Water sprayed up and out as he disappeared under the surface before coming up just far enough that his eyes peered at me.

Laughing softly, I peeled out of my clothes, feeling for the first time the blows and cuts I'd gained in the fight with the Trolls. The whole thing was a blur; I'd never fought like that, with a total loss of control. Angry fighting? Yes, for sure. But nothing like that. I started to count as I stripped. Both arms were bruised from elbow to shoulder, large finger marks where I'd been grabbed, two slashes from claws ran between my breasts, my left hip had what looked like road rash, and when I inspected my jeans they were missing material. How the fuck had I not felt any of this?

Each moment that passed, the aches increased until I was in a full out hobble. Both sides of the room had clusters of showerheads and I headed for the one closest to me on the left. I flicked the handle and all the showerheads came on at once. Three above me and three at different angles on the wall.

"Doran, how many fucking parties do you have?" I griped as the water hit my open wounds. Better than crying.

"Oh, I have a few a month. The ladies like the bathroom best though. I can't imagine why," Doran said from way too close. I spun around, barely able to see through the stream of water, but I shouldn't have worried. A split second later a scrawny, soaking wet werewolf stood between me and the Daywalker.

"No touch Rylee," Alex growled, hunching his back like a pissed off, soaking wet kitty cat trying to make himself look bigger.

Doran lifted up his hands, but I saw the smile on his lips. "I'm not going to touch her, Alex. Just bringing her clothes and thought we could chat a minute."

Alex deflated. "Okee dokee." He trotted back to the tub, which he slid into like a giant salamander, just his eyes and nose floating at the top, watching us.

"He is loyal to you above everyone else; not often that happens, even with wolves." Doran didn't look at me as he handed me a bar of soap. "Here, Louisa left this last time she was here."

I took the bar of soap and sniffed it. Strong scents of sage and lavender filled my nose. "You aren't going to let me have any time to myself, are you?"

"I think you were right about Berget. We might be able to stall the madness for a little while, maybe a year. No more than that, but it would buy us time." He snapped his fingers and a stool slid to him from behind the door. He sat, crossed his legs and gave me innocent eyes. "You going to shower or just stand there and get wet?"

"Fucker."

"Only if you beg." He winked and I turned my back on him.

"Oh, that's a good view too."

"Enough with the games, Doran, or get the fuck out."

"Fine." The stool scraped as if he slid it across the floor, sliding closer yet to me. "I have a fire opal that is very large, about the size of a peach pit. The thing is, if it is going to work long term, I don't want to put it on a chain—too easy to knock off and let the madness loose before we are ready."

I scrubbed the soap over my upper body, the sting of the antiseptic properties making me hiss. "So what, we make her eat it?"

He barked a laugh. "No, not exactly. I think we can implant it in her, though, let her body heal over it so it's too hard to remove."

Limping, I turned to face him. "And you think it'll work?"

His lips tightened and even through the streaming water I saw the concern etched on his face. "I have no idea. I have never dealt with a madness like this and while the theory is strong, the power and personalities embedded in Berget are beyond strong. They ruled the vampire world for generations. They will fight this."

"I think Berget will fight too, though." I finished soaping up and began to rinse off as my brain tried to tell me what a fucking fool I was.

"And if you do save her, what then? You think Faris will let her live? You think he won't try and find some way to fuck you over? He's a vicious set of fangs that cannot be trusted. Not ever."

I threw my hands into the air, sending a spray of water out. "What the hell do you want me to do, there isn't exactly a third applicant for leader of the vampire nation, unless you know something I don't?"

Doran shook his head. I turned off the water and he tossed me a towel. "No, there are no other applicants, no one is strong enough to carry the nation; it has to be Berget or Faris. My vote is for him, much as it pains me to say it."

The thing was, my brain was kicking into overdrive, pieces of my past colliding with this moment, and I wondered if it had somehow all been set up. If there were reasons beyond the obvious for the demons, monsters, and wretched souls I'd battled in the past, reasons I was only now seeing.

"But if there were a third applicant, and if that vamp finished the task ahead of Faris and Berget? Would that do it?"

Doran blinked several times. "What are you thinking, Tracker? I don't like the look in your eye. It is far too calculating for you."

I didn't want to tell him yet; I had to get the idea straight inside my own head. But, fuck, if I was right on this, I could make sure neither Berget nor Faris took the throne. I would still fulfill that stupid prophecy about being the one to bring the new vampire leader's reign into being. And I would have the leader of the vampire nation already on my side and ready to fight Orion. In one fell swoop, I would save Berget, thwart Faris, and gain allies we so desperately needed.

"Rylee, why are you staring at me like that?" A flash of fear whipped across Doran's face.

I wrapped my body in the towel and walked toward him. The Daywalker scooted backward, his green eyes wide.

"Doran, you might not like it, but I have an idea."

10

Doran, indeed, did not like my idea.

"Are you fucking out of your mind?" he yelled at me, his eyes all but bugging out of his head.

I was wearing the most ridiculous of get-ups, a tight black dress that stopped mid-thigh and had a sheer cut-out running in a deep 'V' between my breasts. With my black boots and weapons, I looked like a hooker about to go on a rampage and finally take out her pimp. Whatever, it was temporary. I carefully crossed my legs. "Doran, it makes sense. The simple fact you don't want to do this tells me you are perfect for it."

He slammed his fist on the desk between us. I'd insisted we go somewhere dry and warm after the showers. Alex lounged in front of the roaring fireplace snickering. "Doran is scaredy scared."

I smiled at Doran, calm and collected. "Tell me one good reason why this won't work."

Doran leaned toward me, hands flat on his desk. "Faris will never take me along with you two."

Yeah, I'd broken my oath to Faris not to tell anyone. But I'd made Doran swear he would do nothing to stop me, or tell anyone else. At this point, I figured it was worth the risk. I had to find a way to stop both

Berget and Faris. Had to find a way to stop Orion's gang of murderers. I had few illusions the Trolls we wiped out at Dox's were the only ones present at the death and skinning of the ogres. Much as it had been a release to kill them all.

"He will if he knows you are there to help us, if I make it clear you are going to help me kill the Child Empress."

Doran slumped, and I waited. I knew this was the best answer; he just didn't like it. Nope, didn't like it at all. It would mean going back to the farm to collect a few items, it would mean keeping a secret from Faris long enough to accomplish all the tasks. And right under his nose.

Dangerous? Fucking right it was, but the choices were narrowing and my gut said "go for it." I was inclined to listen to my instincts; so far they hadn't proved me wrong.

"So Liam doesn't know about this little idea of yours?" Doran shifted the conversation, and I knew what he was doing.

"No, he doesn't, and I still think you would make a far better leader of the vampire nation than either of those two. I have the recipe under my mattress at the farmhouse that tells how to turn you into a full vampire, Doran. It makes so much sense I can't begin to understand why you wouldn't do this. All the pieces fit, and you know it. I have to believe it." Besides, I knew Doran. As a leader of the vampires, he'd work with me. I'd have all the bloodsuckers working as a team—and more importantly, they'd be fighting on my side and against Orion.

He turned his back and leaned his ass against the desk, his voice soft with defeat. "I have an approximation of being human as a Daywalker. I will lose even that if I step fully into the night."

My shoulders slumped. Maybe it was too much to ask of him. But who else did I trust with that much power and my life? I had read the recipe a few times, and I was pretty sure I knew it by rote, but to be sure, I wanted to grab it. The end result of the process would be me offering my blood into a crucible holding all the other ingredients, with only one small addition. After that a vein had to be opened, and then I had to let the new vampire, who had very little control, feed on me. From a main artery. Yup, good times ahead.

"Rylee, I have never wanted to lead. I don't have it in me." Doran finally turned to face me, the edges of his eyes tight, his jaw twitching. I took a deep breath and stood.

"If you have another way we can stop them both, and go through with trying to save Berget, tell me."

Alex sneezed, breaking the silence between us, then mumbled. "Nope. Rylee's right."

Doran let out a bitter laugh. "Your Alex is right, you are right. This is probably the best shot we have."

The soft tread of a footstep turned us both around.

Faris stepped into the office; dressed in black from head to foot. His blue eyes glittered. "Best shot at what?"

Oh, fuck. Doran moved beside me. "I took some of her blood, and saw the oaths you put on her."

I stiffened, as did Faris. The vampire didn't move, but I felt him gathering himself. Doran didn't rush, though, and in that moment I knew I'd chosen right. He would be the best leader for the vampires, better than either Faris or Berget. That was, if my plan worked.

"I'm going to help her kill Berget. The little bitch thinks I'm still in her thrall, so I can get closer than either you or Rylee."

Faris lifted his head ever so slightly, and I could almost see the wheels turning in his fanged head. "You won't try and stop me? Or Rylee?"

Doran lifted his hand and placed it over his heart. "I swore an oath to her that I would not interfere, other than to help kill the Child Empress."

Faris turned his gaze on me. He blinked several times and a slow smile slipped across his lips. "While not exactly what I imagined you wearing, the dress is much preferable to your usual jeans and a t-shirt. You will stay in it while we work together."

Son of a bitch, he had to show up when I was in a dress Milly would balk at wearing. Nothing to be done about it now, or at least, not right at that moment.

I eyed the window; the shades were drawn and zero sunlight coming through.

Faris snapped his fingers at me, drawing my attention back to him. "If the shadows are deep enough—and the Daywalker here has made sure of it so he can entertain his previous masters—I can move around, Tracker. I see you eyeing the window as if to take the blinds off. I assure you, if I burn, I will take you with me."

I frowned and had to force myself not to cross my arms, which would have accentuated the bare skin underneath the sheer cut out.

"What are you doing here, Faris?"

He smiled. "Things have sped up, in a way I cannot control. Our seer has claimed the new leader must be crowned on the night of the equinox. I need to take you with me now."

I shook my head and sat back down. "Oh, no. I made an oath and it involved seven days, not right now."

Alex slunk to my side and stuffed himself under the desk away from Faris, muttering under his breath, and chattering his teeth in between curse words. Their last encounter had not left the werewolf exactly trusting of the vampire. Being strangled tends to do that to a relationship.

Faris let out a low laugh, and I heard the pleasure in it. He was enjoying this. "Rylee, you can bring Doran, I'll allow that, but only if you come with me now. Right this second."

I closed my eyes and tried to breathe around the anger. Liam would think I'd run off and left them high and dry. Shit, shit, shit.

My mind worked frantically to find a way around this, but there was nothing. Doran cleared his throat. "I have to put a few things together. Rylee, you can give me a hand."

I snapped my fingers at Alex, who all but leapt up, and the three of us filed out of the room past Faris, each step I took reminding me it hadn't been long since I'd tackled more Trolls than I could count.

"Five minutes. If I have to come find you, one of you will die," Faris said, as causally as if telling us a rainstorm was headed our way.

Doran broke into a jog and I followed him, a growing ache rolling up my legs and through my body. If pain really was just weakness leaving the body, then I should have been a fucking superwoman by now. I bit back the groan that attempted to escape my lips and focused on something else. How about clothes? At least I had my boots, even if I was in this stupid ass dress. "Are you sure you don't have anything better for me to wear?"

"That is the piece that covers the most. Hurry up—do you remember what we need?"

Son of a bitch, he was right. The recipe, there was no way we were going to be able to go back for it. This was all going to be on my memory and nothing else. Doran's shamanic room smelled of herbs and sharp spices. The black-skinned demon book sat on a pedestal in the middle.

"Doran, I can't leave that unprotected."

He grabbed it from me and shoved it into a bag he snatched from the wall. "I'll bind it to the house, anyone tries to take it out will be killed, and I'll make the bag look empty."

With two flicks of his wrist, the bag stiffened and then he hung it back on the wall with a wink at me. "No one looks for the obvious spot, anyway." Shit, the thing did look empty. It would have to be enough for now. Had to be.

I stood in the middle of the room thinking. Wracking my brain, I recalled the ingredients. "Sage, blood-wort, jasmine root, Troll tooth . . ." I covered my face with my hands, tried to envision the sheet of paper. "Fuck, there were three other things."

Doran scrambled around the room, stuffing things into small drawstring bag. "Crucible?"

"Yes, mortar and pestle. A diamond, that was one of the items, moon dust—"

"Wait, what?" He froze mid-step.

"Moon dust?" Oh fucking holy hell, let me not be wrong.

"Shit, I don't have any, maybe Louisa might."

"There's no way Faris will let us go," I whispered. Shit, the vampire could probably hear us as it was, why the fuck was I bothering to whisper?

As if reading my mind, the vampire called out from the other side of the house. "Three minutes, children."

"Shake it off." Doran started to move again and I saw him grab an opal and it was indeed the size of a peach pit. "We will have to see if we can get it along the way."

"How are we going to do that?" I snapped.

"Trust the gods watching over us to set things in motion. It's about all we've got. Now, what the hell was that last ingredient?"

Alex let out a woof and I stared at him, a chill sweeping through me. How could I have forgotten? "Hair from a submissive wolf."

Doran chuckled. "The gods, they do have a sense of humor. Take it from him now, I'm not sure how much longer he'll be submissive."

I ran my hands over Alex's coat, easily plucking out some long silky fibers.

"Shit, so we're only missing one thing, moon dust."

Doran pushed me ahead of him out of the room. "We'll be missing more than that if we don't get back to Faris. Grab your weapons, they're on the bed."

We ran down the hallway, parting at the juncture. I bolted into the bedroom and scooped up my two blades, back sheath, whip, and leather jacket, which looked to be cleaned, or at least wiped off. I didn't want to think why Doran had put all my weapons in his bedroom. Horny bastard. Faris began to count down in a booming voice.

"Five, four, three . . ."

Arms loaded down, I ran as fast as I could, skidding to a stop in front of Faris as he tapped his watch.

"Seconds to spare. Rylee, I do hope you aren't going to push me the entire time." He reached out and grabbed my arm, squeezing the flesh, his fingers rebruising where the Trolls had taken their toll.

I ground my teeth but said nothing. Silence was its own power sometimes. I didn't use it often enough. It didn't hurt that I knew his little secret, that he hadn't killed Charlie. Perhaps he wasn't as tough as he seemed.

"Well, well, the Tracker has learned control? I don't believe it. Now, give me your weapons."

Fuck, I'd been hoping he'd forget about that. I handed him my swords, sheath, and whip. "What happens when we run into uglies? You going to do all the dirty work?"

Faris shook his head. "There will be no uglies, as you call them. You are here just for your ability to Track. And perhaps in that dress, act as a tart piece of arm candy."

Alex blew a raspberry at him. "Uglies are always at Rylee."

My lips twitched and the vampire only frowned more. "What's in the bag?"

What small smile had been creeping across my lips dropped off my face. That he'd noticed the small back of items Doran carried was not good. We did not need him knowing what we were up to.

Doran saved us. "I have a plan to knock Berget out, but it is a powerful spell that can't be put together until right before we tackle her."

Faris looked from me to Doran and back again. Shit, he could kill us both and we would be unable to stop him. Though Doran was a Daywalker, it was the same difference of strength between them as that between a human and Doran. There would be no stopping Faris if he decided he'd had enough of us. Which I knew would happen. Right around the moment he figured he'd gotten everything he could out of me.

Control was not something I practiced a lot of, but it looked like I was about to get a crash course in keeping my tongue in my mouth. At least until that final moment when I would take Faris's fat head and remove it from his treacherous body. Which was a distinct possibility if I could set Doran on the throne instead of Faris or Berget.

"Why are you smiling, Tracker?" Faris stared at me, his icy blue eyes hard.

I stared back. "None of your fucking business, vampire."

And with that, our little ragtag bunch was off to a screaming start.

Fan-fucking-tastic.

"Roll the window down, Pamela." Liam did his best not to gag on the words. Agent Valley was in the very back of the Jeep, letting out a moan every now and then, but otherwise his old boss was being pleasant. Not including the smell. And considering he was a rotting zombie . . .

Pamela wretched as she rolled the window down. "Ugh, that is fiercely awful."

Milly's face was green as she drove, her eyes darting all around as if expecting another ambush. "How did Ingers find us? And why would she throw grenades at the house?"

Liam snorted and took a deep breath, immediately regretting it. "She was trying to kill us, Milly. That's why the grenades. And we asked after Agent Valley, that's how she found us. Logic. She is an FBI Agent."

"I . . . am . . . Valley." Agent Valley wheezed from the back, his fingers gripping the back of the seat, juices flowing down around him. They had barely escaped the collapsing house, only to find Agent Ingers waiting for them outside. Pamela blew up the black sedans in the driveway. The necromancer called up dead insects to swarm Ingers and the two Agents with her. The combined efforts between the young necromancer and witch had caused enough ruckus to give them time to get moving.

Liam looked to the necro kid next to him. Only minutes had passed since they'd all escaped being trapped in a house at the mercy of Ingers and her deadly accurate bullets. "How do you know Agent Valley?"

The kid shifted in his seat and pushed his glasses up the bridge of his nose. "He's my uncle."

Well, that explained a great deal. Agent Valley's desire to help the supernatural world stemmed from the fact he had one in his family. It made perfect sense now, but still . . .

"Then why did you turn him into a zombie?"

The kids jaw trembled and then tightened. "Because Ingers had him killed. She doesn't want him to help me. Us." His light brown eyes flicked to Liam. "I thought you were on her side. She threatened to send people to finish the job."

Damn, the woman was colder than he'd thought when first meeting her. But that didn't matter, not right now. There were more pressing matters than a bitch having a hormonal day. "What do you know about the guns? Did your uncle tell you anything?"

Pamela turned in her seat. "Do you have a name, necromancer?"

He blinked several times. "Frank."

"Aren't you going to apologize for trying to shoot us? That is rather rude since we saved your scrawny ass back there." She arched a delicate eyebrow at him and he flushed from his neck up to the roots of his light brown hair.

"Yeah, sorry about that. I didn't know who you were, but I'd seen you going up and down the street with what I thought was a sniffer dog." He paused and cleared his throat. "Did you get my gun?"

Liam snorted. "Not been around many other supernaturals, have you? And don't worry about your gun, you don't need it." It pressed into the small of his back, the steady presence of an old friend.

Frank shook his head and swallowed hard. "No, my mom and Uncle Roger didn't encourage me trying to find other supernaturals. They were trying too hard to keep me under wraps to let me meet anyone like me."

Agent Valley shifted in the back. "O'Shea. Guns, manufactured . . . with . . . witchcraft." The last words breathed out with a spray of spittle that splattered the seat.

Liam stared at Frank. "Do you have anything to add to that?"

The kid sat, unmoving before finally answering. "I followed my uncle once, to where they were making the guns. I could take you there."

Pamela twisted in her seat again. "It will be dangerous. Are you sure you can handle that?"

Frank stiffened in his seat and Liam glanced up to see Milly flash a quick grin in the rearview mirror. Yeah, Pamela learned quickly. Part of it was truth it would be dangerous if other witches were involved, but if Frank knew where they were, then they needed him. And the best way to make sure he came of his own volition was to stick his pride.

"I'm not afraid of danger. But the place, it was way out of town, at least a four-hour drive." Frank glanced back at his uncle. "And even I don't want to be this close to him for four hours."

Liam did a quick calculation. "Which direction?"

"Southwest."

"Perfect, we'll drop him off at the barn."

Pamela blanched and Milly's knuckles whitened on the steering wheel. Liam didn't apologize or back down. While no one wanted to be there—the barn—hell, the farm was safe with Blaz there.

The drive was quiet, and the smell worsened each mile. By the time they pulled into the farmyard, they'd all had more than enough. Milly hit the brakes and slammed the Jeep into park, stumbling out with a wretch, her body heaving uncontrollably. Pamela wasn't far behind.

But as bad as the smell was, Liam still remembered the man in the back of the Jeep had been his friend.

"Come on, Agent. Let's get you settled in the barn." He opened the back of the Jeep and helped Agent Valley shuffle out of the vehicle and toward the barn. The cold air was bracing and Liam took in a big drag of the clean scent.

A low rumble reached his ears a split second before Blaz slowly revealed himself coiled around the barn, his scales sparkling in the sharp winter sun. He blinked sleepy eyes at them, his jaw cracking in a huge yawn that showed off every one of his massive pearly whites.

Hello, Wolf.

"Blaz. Rylee's gone off on her own again."

Pissed her off, did you? The dragon had the nerve to give him a wink. Liam didn't think it was funny, nor did he feel like explaining himself to the dragon.

"No, I did not piss her off. She's off on one errand, we are on another." He waved at Agent Valley. "This one is going to stay here awhile in the barn. At least until we get back."

He got his former boss settled into the barn and then stepped back into the cold, grateful for the fresh air.

Blaz reached out with one claw and drew a line in the snow in front of himself. *You will have to let her go at some point. You know that, don't you? She is for the world, not just you.*

"I don't need to be schooled by an oversized gecko," he snapped, not caring that said gecko could tear him apart limb by limb, the only surefire way to kill a Guardian.

Blaz let out a low, rumbling laugh. *The others cannot hear me, Wolf. Let me guess, you know the time of your death is coming, and Rylee does not? Yet she knows you carry a secret? It will drive her mad not to know. Give her something, a false secret.*

Liam went very still, his heartbeat skipping into overdrive. How the hell could Blaz know what he himself had only just learned?

The dragon stretched his wings, the scales catching the light. *Bonded to the Tracker as I am, I know her heart even better than you, Wolf. Better because while I have some affection for her, I do not love her as you and the others do. So I see her more clearly. And if I must, I will drive her to do what the prophecies call on her for.*

"And if that means her death, you don't care, do you?" Anger surged through him. The dragon might be their ally, but he was apparently not their friend.

Blaz shrugged, his shoulder bumping into the barn and shaking the timbers. *I do care, for we are tied together, she and I. If she dies, as will I.*

"Then why aren't you with her right now, making sure she's okay?" Damn it, this dragon was the most infuriating creature—

Because unlike you, I know she will come to me when she is damn good and ready. Trust her, Wolf. Her instincts run true, even if at times they seem to be contrary to what you believe.

Liam threw his hands into the air and turned his back on the dragon. "Whatever, Blaz. We'll be back later to pick up Valley."

Ahead of him, Frank was sprawled out on his back, the two witches hovering over him.

"What the hell is this?"

Pamela covered her mouth with one hand, giggling. "He passed out when Blaz showed up."

What the hell was he going to do with a fainting necromancer, a green witch, and a witch he hated, who had no abilities at all at the moment? Yeah, not much. Not much at all.

11

Faris had a plan, or at least, he said he did. He took us via the Veil to the castle, which acted as a central jumping point to many parts of the world. For those who couldn't jump the Veil, the castle was a place that allowed one to pick and choose where they went. Of course, you had to know where each door opened, and hope they didn't get destroyed while you were on the other side. Already, we'd managed to close one permanently.

Yeah, my bad.

We were on the first floor of the castle where walls were covered with sconces, their light flickering in the air. It was not an area I'd been in before. Faris strode ahead of us, my weapons strapped to him. They looked small on his big frame, and out of place against his designer cut clothes. He stopped in front of a plain wooden door, the slats barely held together with bent and twisted nails, rusted with age. Hanging by a thread? Not even. This was not a door I would have picked to try, but since I wasn't running the show . . .

"Hurry up, Tracker." Faris snapped his fingers, and pointed to the ground beside him, as if I were his pet, a dog eager to obey its master. I tightened my hands into fists.

Doran gave me a push on the small of my back. No words, we couldn't discuss anything without Faris hearing.

I moved to Faris's side, my blood pounding in my ears, and I reminded myself of Charlie, this was a game Faris was playing. One where he didn't know I'd uncovered his secrets. But I also reminded myself he had two of my friends at his disposal now. Faris's left eye twitched. Something had been off with him since he'd jumped the Veil, which meant that no matter what I thought I knew, it could all go out the window in one big ass vampire tantrum.

Fuck, talk about being stuck between a set of fangs and a sword.

Faris pointed at the wooden-slatted door. "This is what we're going to do. We will open doors, you will step through and Track the Blood. If you find them, that is the doorway we will use."

"And if I can't?"

He glanced down at me, the glint in his eyes unforgiving. "We keep trying until we do."

With his left hand he pushed the door open. On the other side it was night and a deep jungle, the rustle of bush and wind blowing through the myriad of plants floated through the doorway. I had a sudden urge to run away, the presence of something dark, so heavy it clogged the breath in my throat.

"Step through, Tracker."

"You have to tell me their traits, idiot. I can't just guess at what I'm Tracking." I put a hand on my hip and cocked one leg, though I was not feeling all that damn confident.

The vampire's eyes narrowed. "The first vampires, vicious and wild, uncontrollable, power mad, blood hungry. Now get on the other side of the doorway and Track them."

I didn't move, sensing something through the doorway. "There is something on the other side, we should try another door."

His hands twitched now along with his eye. "I don't fucking well care, Tracker."

For all that Faris was the ultimate in asshattery, something was wrong. Like really, really wrong with him.

"If Rylee gets hurt, you will have lost your only way to find the Blood," Doran said, breaking our standoff.

"Good thing you are here then, Shaman. You can keep her alive when the injuries happen." Faris didn't turn as he spoke, just stared into the night darkened vines and trees, hands trembling with what I assumed was rage.

"Alex, come with me," I said softly, refusing to snap my fingers for him. Never again would I do that, not after Faris doing it to me.

He stepped beside me, lifting his nose to the doorway. "Uglies."

"Yeah, that's what I was afraid of. Come on, we'll make it quick."

My feet barely crossed the threshold of the doorway when the ground around us shook and a roar broke the air. Alex cried out and pressed hard against me. My first thought was we were going to face another giant, but no, there were no giants in jungle areas I was aware of. I stood weaponless, and for the first time truly, truly understood the situation Faris had me in, a position I had gone into willingly, thinking I could handle him and it.

I was completely at his mercy and completely without any way to protect myself.

Shit.

Shaking, I Tracked the Blood, or at least what I knew of it.

I didn't pick up anything, couldn't sense a thing out of the ordinary. I tried Tracking vampires in general and got a distant ping, way far to the south.

"Nothing, there is nothing here."

The creature, whatever the hell it was let out another roar, far closer this time. I spun, and froze.

Faris blocked the doorway, one of my own swords pointed at me. "Be very sure, Tracker."

"Fuck, I'm sure! Now move, that thing out there is getting closer and I'd like to be on that"—I pointed into the castle—"side of the door before the big fucker shows up!"

The crash of bush and trees behind me spun me around. Like a cross between an ogre and a giant, the creature stood easily fifteen feet tall, but it had only one eye. Correction, she had only one eye, her pendulous breasts swinging as she skidded to a stop. She blinked several times, sniffing the air, then launched toward us.

I had no choice.

I sprinted to the left, away from the door, away from Doran and Faris. If the asshole wouldn't let us through, he'd have to find me. I wasn't about to stand there and let the Cyclops scoop me up for dinner, thank you very much.

In the darkened jungle, I couldn't see where the hell I was going. "Alex, lead the way."

He brushed past me, the silver tips of his coat seeming to gather the little bit of light coming through and giving me a glowing lead. At a full tilt run, we wove through the jungle, the crash of the female Cyclops not far enough behind.

I had no way to stop her, not even a deterrent—

A tree flew through the air crashing into the ground right in front of us, dirt and bush spewing up in a wave of earth. "Over it!"

Alex leapt over the downed tree with ease and I vaulted it, felt the brush of fingertips along my shoulders. We either had to go faster, or find a way around this big bitch.

Sprinting full out in a tiny black cocktail dress in the middle of a jungle in the dead of night was, surprise surprise, not going well.

The only thing I knew about Cyclops was their hide was thicker than a giant's and their only real weakness was their single eye. But getting to that eye would prove to be the problem. I needed a weapon, something that could be used at a distance like my crossbow.

Jungle, what the hell was there in a jungle to help?

Tribes.

"Alex, find humans."

A tribe would have weapons. Spears, bow, and arrows. Anything sharp and pointy would work at this juncture.

Alex veered to the right, his tail streaming out behind him. "Close," he yelped as the ground dropped out below us and we skidded down an embankment. The Cyclops, unfortunately, was right behind us. I didn't dare look back, that was the kiss of death in chase scenes and it was a rule I lived by.

Never look back.

"Faster, Alex!" I screamed as we hit the bottom, a shallow creek gurgling along softly. On the other side, the chatter of voices erupted and torches were lit.

He'd done it; he'd gotten us to a village.

Now I had to get a weapon and pray it was strong enough to do the job.

When we were midstream, the men of the village poured out of their huts, their nut brown faces lit up with horror alongside the fire. I didn't know the word for weapons, or spears, but I didn't need to.

The man closest to me threw me a spear. I grabbed it midair and spun, facing the Cyclops. With weapon in hand, fear skidded away from me. This I knew, this I could deal with.

The big bitch swung a hand toward me and I caught it on the tip of the spear, driving the point deep, praying it would at least stall her.

Nope; the spear's haft broke in the middle, blasting apart under the pressure. I caught the broken spear, knowing I had no choice but to wait for the opening I needed to take her out.

To pop that bulbous eye like a grape.

A hail of arrows arced over my head and hit the Cyclops. None of them stuck, but it got her attention. She let out a roar and I got a good look at her mouth.

Blunt, flat teeth meant for grinding bones snapped at the tribesmen. There was no fucking way they could take her on, yet they were buying me the time I needed.

"Alex, we have to hamstring her." He ducked a swing from her, and got around to her back side, driving for the flesh and tendons above her thick cankles.

Teeth and claw, he attacked her. Clinging to her leg as she spun to dislodge him. A single thick belt hung from her waist, bones dangling as if mementos of kills. A blocky thighbone swung by me. I grabbed it with one hand and let her momentum pull me from the ground.

Clamping the spear haft in my teeth, I clawed my way to her belt, felt her stiffen as my hands touched her bare skin. I glanced down, saw Alex had gained nothing, hadn't even drawn blood.

"Alex, get away. Leave her!" His obedience saved his life. The Cyclops swung down hard, her fist sending up a spew of water and rock where he'd stood only a moment before. With her bent over, I scrambled up her back and straddled her shoulders in a second.

This was a death I would lay at Faris's feet. Letting gravity take me as she stood, I let the weight of my body pull me around her neck. As I slid in front of her I clamped my thighs tight and faced a very surprised Cyclops. I dropped the spearhead from my mouth into my hands and drove it deep into the wide-open eye.

There was no sound, no final roar of pain. Her eye frosted in a matter of half a breath, from the exterior in toward the point of the spearhead, as if dipped in ice. She slumped to her knees and I jumped off as she fell face-first into the creek bed, the water sluicing around her, her body melting into nothing as if it had never been.

"Goodnight, big girl," I said softly, for the first time in a long time feeling a sorrow at the death of a creature trying to kill me.

Breathing hard, my brain tried to tell me why I was feeling bad. The pieces put together slowly in my head. The large breasts, the sagging belly, driving me away from her territory . . .

"Ah, shit." I hung my head, shame burning through me. A mother protecting her babies. Dying to protect her children. A big ass nasty mother, but that wasn't the point. She never would have come after us if she hadn't felt threatened.

A hand touched my shoulder and I spun, settling into a half crouch. The tribesman held up his hand, palm outward.

"I speak little English. You Tracker. Yes?" His dark eyes were wide with something akin to awe. I didn't like it.

I slowly came out of the crouch. "Yes, how did you know?"

"Magic man tells us. You kill one eye. You make us safe." He gave me a tentative smile.

I swallowed hard. "Did she have babies?"

He bobbed his head. "Yes, yes. Babies are excellent."

My guts lurched and I backed away, feeling as though I'd been duped. Excellent, as in . . . "You ate them?"

He bobbed his head again. "Yes, take strength. Be better warriors."

Horror, absolute and pure, rippled along my spine, through my heart and soul. They'd eaten her babies, and then she'd come after us thinking we were the ones? Fuck, fuck, fuck. Tears pricked at my eyes, and I knew I had penance to pay for this one.

"Alex." My voice was thick with tears I couldn't seem to stem. "We're leaving."

I slogged through the stream, standing for a moment where the Cyclops had fallen. "I'm sorry."

Something drew my eyes upward, to the top of the embankment. Faris stood watching me, his eyes hooded.

I could lay this at his feet, but it wasn't all on him. I'd made the choice to run, even if he'd forced it on me. I'd chosen to fight the Cyclops instead of circling back. A part of my brain—the logical part Liam would agree with—argued with me.

You had no choice. You can be sorrowful, you can regret, but you have to live. She would have killed you, and then Alex.

My jaw clenched and unclenched. "I will make this right. I don't know how, but I will make it right."

I bent and scooped a rock from the stream, the edge just sharp enough. I dragged it across the palm of my hand, opening a shallow cut, my blood dripping into the stream. A blood oath, one I gave freely. At some point, I would make this right.

"Are you coming, Tracker?" In the dim light, I couldn't see his condescension, but I damn well felt it.

"I want my weapons back. This clusterfuck wouldn't have happened if I hadn't had to run through the damn fucking jungle, you fanged ass." I didn't step toward him. He needed me, and while I wouldn't trade my friends for obedience, I also knew at some point I had to draw the line in the sand.

"Rylee, do I need to make another point?"

I kept my eyes on him, not ready to call what I hoped was a bluff. "If you aren't going to protect me, then I need to take care of myself. I won't kill you, Faris. Unlike you and Milly, when I make an oath, I fucking well keep it."

Shit, except for telling Doran. Charlie told the rest of my family about Faris's game so I didn't break my oaths about keeping silent. About not telling anyone that Faris was blackmailing me into helping him. But since Faris knew about Doran, I wasn't going to count that one.

The tension between us grew and shifted, pulled taut like an overheated piece of taffy. He broke first. With a snort, he threw my weapons on the ground at his feet. "Come and get them, then."

I didn't hurry. Fuck, that was the last thing on my mind. Alex waited for me on the far bank. I walked over to him.

"Hate that vampire," he growled, his teeth showing in a flash of moonlight through the trees.

I ran my hand over his soft ears, taking comfort in the fact at least I wasn't alone. "Yeah, I hate him too."

Faris made me and Alex lead the way back to the door. On this side, it was situated in between two trees weaving themselves together with vines and flowers. The moonlight stretched down through the canopy and lit the doorway clearly showing the edges. I pushed the door open and stepped across. Doran was there, waiting. He scooped me into his arms and hugged me unnecessarily tight.

"You do realize if I had to go to Liam and tell him you were dead, I'd be joining you on the other side of the Veil?" He squeezed me tightly against his body, a cheeky ass grin slipping over his lips.

"Enough," Faris growled and I turned, Doran still holding me, and saw something I never would have expected.

Faris was jealous of Doran.

I let my body soften against the Daywalker, felt his surprise, saw Faris's eyes darken dangerously. Yeah, poking at the vampire probably wasn't my best idea, I just couldn't help myself. Truly.

"Doran is my . . . *friend*, and he was worried about me. Perfectly natural." I leaned in and kissed Doran on the cheek for good measure before letting go. Doran swatted my ass. "Play nice with the vampire, Rylee. He can kill us all, you know."

"Yes, perhaps it's best you remember that." Faris glowered at me, and I felt the power between us shift. Suddenly, I'd found a weakness. While he hadn't liked Liam in my bed, there hadn't been this jealousy. Seemed it took another fanged boy to really set him off. Good to know.

I shrugged again, though inside I was cheering. Fuck yeah—score one for the Tracker.

Sauntering down the hallway, I aimed toward the next door. A slight adjustment on my sheath, and this time I wouldn't be taken off guard.

12

The next three doorways were total busts, one of them actually taking us back to the jungle. This was the problem with crossing the Veil; even with actual doorways you never knew where it would take you, until you'd used the crossing, and there was no way to know them all.

"You're running this show, Faris. Did it occur to you to look for a fucking map of the castle doorways?" I snarled at him, soaked through to the bone from the last doorway, which happened to open at the base of a waterfall. "Or better yet, why the fuck don't you jump the Veil with me to each of the continents?"

His hand snapped out, faster than I could track with my eyes, fingers around my throat, squeezing hard enough that spots danced in front of my eyes. This was another power game, and I'd be damned to hell and back if I broke. I'd let him choke me before I pulled a weapon on him. "You do not understand the rules, Tracker, to this ascension to the throne, and I do not feel like explaining them to you."

He let go and I dropped. Doran caught me against his chest and I sagged against him, this time for real.

I drew in breath and it was the sweetest air I'd tasted in a long time.

Faris strode down the hallway searching for the next door.

Doran tipped my head up. "You okay?"

I ran a hand over my throat, winced as I touched where Faris's fingers dug in. "Yeah, he's just pissy because I won't back down."

The Daywalker's green eyes filled with something akin to worry. "Don't push him, Rylee. He's on edge, more than I've ever seen him."

"I noticed."

"Doorway," Faris called from around the corner, and I jogged to catch up. Doran was right, Faris was not himself, even for the vampire of many faces that he was.

This was the fourth doorway in two hours. Each one I stepped through, Faris made me stand there for at least fifteen minutes. It took me less than thirty seconds to figure out the Blood was or in this case, wasn't there.

Faris didn't trust it could be that quick. He jerked the handle and the doorway swung open.

Daylight streamed through, catching Faris along his lower leg. He threw himself backward, scrambling away from the sunlight, his eyes wide with horror.

I stood and watched, but didn't shut the door. "So eager to die, vampire? I can help you with that."

"Shut the door, Tracker."

With the tip of my sword I reached out and shut the door. "See how nice I can be, vampire?" If he wasn't going to use my name, I wasn't going to use his. "Perhaps you can tell me what the fuck is really going on."

Faris sat on the ground, looking totally and utterly defeated. "I need to sleep; you three, keep checking doorways."

My eyebrows shot up, and my jaw dropped open as he pushed himself to his feet and limped away.

Unable to process what just happened, I turned slowly to Doran. "Any ideas?"

But the Daywalker had gone pale, pasty white. "I don't think I can do it, Rylee."

Shit, I was pretty sure he didn't mean continue looking into doorways.

Time to get tough on his ass. I strode to him, stuck my face right in his, like Liam had done so many times to me, only I lowered my voice to a whisper. "Yeah, you think I want to face Orion? You think I want to fulfill this particular prophecy? You think I want any of the shit that has come my way? Fuck, Doran, you of all people should know sometimes you don't get to choose."

He let out a slow breath. "Rylee, it is not just the daylight I will give up, but my very soul. Daywalker's retain their souls; it is why we cannot carry the power a vampire can. Where their souls were, their strength fills."

My throat tightened. Shit, if that was true, then he was right; I couldn't ask that of him, not even for this. Faris would have to lead the vampires; he was the only option now. Fuck me, I hated this. "You can still help me with Berget?"

He nodded. "Yes, of course."

I turned from him and loosened my second sword. "You open the doors, I'll step through. We'll move faster with Faris asleep."

Doran opened the door that had seared Faris, and I stepped through. "Do you know why he has to sleep now? That is way too weird."

He cleared his throat. "It is a part of the ritual. They must fast for some time before they go on their individual quests, and they may not feed until the quest is complete, or their opponent claims the throne. To do so would show weakness and the inability to conquer their own flesh. This is also to prove themselves as they pass the final tests before the ceremony."

I did a slow circle as I Tracked, reaching out as far as I could with my senses. "That's why he isn't jumping the Veil, isn't it?"

"I believe so. It would take too much power, would require him to feed every day and he can't do that."

I stepped back through the doorway. "Nothing here."

Alex trotted ahead of us, much perkier now that Faris was not with us. He flung open the next door with a flare I didn't know he had, one paw flicking out, a la Vanna White. "Ta-da!"

Oh, fuck me. The other side was not a 'ta-da,' more of shit on toast we're in trouble.

"Shut the door!" I screamed as I ran toward him.

He wasn't fast enough, and the doorframe cracked as the giant spider pushed its way through. Its body brushed the top of the doorway, and its legs folded nearly in half in order to make it. A tawny golden fur covered its body, and in another time I would have said the thing was magnificent, maybe even beautiful. There was one real small glitch.

Its eyes glinted silver.

A Guardian.

And I wasn't betting on being able to talk us out of this one. But there was no choice, I had to hope this Guardian had some sense, as did Eagle and Bear.

I lowered my blades and did my best imitation of meek. "Guardian, we did not mean to disturb you. We were on the hunt for another." The arachnid scuttled forward, its furry legs flashing. Doran and I dove in opposite directions and the spider spun, going after Doran.

"Alex, keep the door open!" I swung hard with my blades, crisscrossing them in front of me and taking the leg closest to me off partway up. A high-pitched squeal more porcine than anything else erupted out of the Guardian. It spun and faced me, and I held up my blades.

The time for meek and mild was gone. "I will fucking well take you apart limb by limb or you can go back into that hole you came from."

It clacked its fangs together twice. "Child of the Lost Ones, you take my leg and expect me to go obediently where you tell me to?"

I slid my blades along each other and adjusted my stance. "No. But you need to have an option before I chop you into tiny little pieces. You can leave now, with seven of eight, or you can stick around and see how many appetizers I take before you've had enough."

The Guardian went still, only the fur on its long legs waving in some unseen breeze. "The Lost Ones were always foolishly brave. It is why they are no more. It seems their blood runs true yet."

I dropped my weight, bracing my body, thinking this was it, the Guardian was going to attack. It let out a long breath. "I do not wish you well, Lost One, for I do not think well wishes will help you with where you're headed."

It took a step back, and then another. With nothing more said, it slid through the doorway. Alex slammed the door shut and pressed his back against it, his golden eyes as wide as I'd ever seen them.

"Big ass spider."

I slumped where I stood, the adrenaline rushing out of me. "Holy fucking hell that was lucky."

Alex slid down the doorway and I pointed at him. "No more opening doors unless I'm right there, got it?"

He crossed his heart with a claw. "Gots it."

I slid my swords into their sheaths as I turned to Doran . . . "Doran?"

There was no answer from the Daywalker. He must have made a run for it down the hall. I strode around the corner and stumbled to a halt. He was flat on the floor, two huge puncture marks in his middle, foam frothing out of his mouth.

"Fuck, Doran!" I dropped to the ground, grabbed him and rolled him to his side. His body convulsed, shaking with the venom pumping through it. No wonder the freak ass Guardian didn't mind leaving. It had done damage to us already.

An eye for an eye and all that shit.

I wiped the foam away, tried to clear his throat. "Alex!"

There was a scrabble of claws on the rock floor and then he was with me, but like me, there was nothing he could do.

I lifted Doran a little, slid my hand down his arm to feel for a pulse. It was erratic and weak, but there. Only one person might, maybe could help us.

I tipped my head back and screamed his name.

"FARIS!"

Just once, I called for him. He would hear me and come, or he would ignore me and Doran would die in my arms. I quickly slid out of my jacket. Losing another friend, wasn't an option. I wiped his face again and slid out one of my blades. I pressed it gently against my arm. The blade was so sharp, I didn't feel the sting, even when the blood flowed down my arm to pool in my elbow.

I lowered my wrist over Doran's mouth, my blood dripping in, turning the white foam pink. I scooped the foam out with my fingers so my blood dripped deep into his mouth.

He let out a moan, the first real noise I'd heard from him.

"You would give the Daywalker your blood?" Faris said behind me.

I pressed my wrist against Doran's mouth, felt him latch on, his lips suctioning around my open wound. "You got a better idea?"

"You woke me to watch you two have your little love fest?"

The snarl in his voice turned me toward him. "I wasn't sure this would work, vampire."

Faris spun on his heel and limped away from me. In the back of my mind, I took note that Faris was really not healing well.

Doran sat up, his arms wound around mine, holding me to him. I didn't know how long to let him draw from me, but since he was sitting up, I figured we were about done. "That's enough for you." I slid my finger between his mouth and my arm and popped the suction.

He moaned and sagged forward. "Rylee, that was bad."

"I hope you didn't see a bright light and head toward it when I brought you back." I sat beside him, my hip against his calf.

Coughing, he shook his head. "No, not so picturesque." He shuddered. "Your blood is different, Rylee, stronger. It shouldn't have brought me back from that venom, not from a Guardian. I should have died no matter what you did."

I shrugged. "Can I do anything about it, my blood that is?"

He slowly shook his head. "No, but be aware of it. Your blood was a draw before, but it is stronger yet. Do not let Faris bite you, or Berget. Or anyone else for that matter."

His words were an eerie echo of Berget's. "Just add it to the pile of shit on my plate. For the record, I hadn't planned on letting anyone bite me."

Alex snuggled up beside me. "Sorry, don't be mad at Alex."

I curled forward to hug him. "Hey, I'm not mad at you. You didn't know it was on the other side."

"Alex sorry, to Doran." He reached out and slid a claw over Doran's hand.

Doran waved him off. "No big deal. What's life without a little poison now and then?"

We said nothing more, just shifted and shimmied until the three of us leaned against the wall and waited for Faris to show up. Wrapped around each other like children scared of the dark night, praying for their parents to rescue them. Only there were no parents coming for us, we weren't praying, and would have no rescue but the one we came up with ourselves.

The place Frank led them to was not what he'd been expecting. He'd expected an old, run down building with barbed wire twisted around the fence and gate, sluggish Trolls patrolling the perimeter, the obvious suspect.

Not a mirrored building that glistened even under the weak starlight, looking as pristine as only a brand new building could. No guards, no fence, a nice parking lot and trees planted every ten feet along the front of the property. Young trees that hadn't had a chance to be anything but saplings.

Night had fallen as they drove, and now it was closing in on midnight. Snow still fell in an icy mist, felt but not seen. Not much time was left before Rylee would be back and waiting on them. That would be a first.

Liam eyed the place, looking for a way in. "Did you get inside, Frank?"

Frank sat on the other side of the backseat and shook his head. "No, I got this close, and then slipped around to the back. They were doing some sort of demo outside to prove the guns worked."

"How did you know they were doing a demo? How did you know these guns worked against supernaturals?"

Frank swallowed hard enough that the two witches in the front seats turned to look at him.

"They had a firing squad."

Chills swept through Liam, and though he suspected he knew the answer, he still had to ask. "What exactly were they shooting, kid?"

Frank swallowed hard again before answering. "I didn't know what the creatures were, but they were tied up together and they weren't human. Not even close. I've never seen anything like them before."

It didn't matter what kind of supernatural had been rounded up for the firing squad, the point was it had been done.

"What a clusterfuck," he said softly, wondering in that moment how Rylee was faring. Hell, she was probably back at Giselle's, pissed off they were taking so long.

He made the decision quickly. "Milly, can you show Pamela a way to hide us, so we can slip in?"

Milly snorted. "Like a cloaking device? This isn't *Star Trek*, O'Shea."

The wolf in him had him leaning forward and physically crowding her across the seats before he could stop himself. A low growl slipped though, making it very difficult to think of anything but her neck snapping between his teeth.

"Liam." Pamela put a hand on his shoulder. "I can cause a distraction, I don't need her to help us get in."

He turned slowly to look at the young witch. Not a drop of fear trickled out of her; she trusted him with her life. With a slow easing of his muscles he slid back on the seat.

"What are you thinking?"

"I did it for Rylee once, I started a fire. Everyone rushes to that, and we sneak around back and in." She tucked a strand of blond hair behind one ear. "We can leave Milly in the car and take Frank with us."

Milly stiffened in her seat, and he heard the beat of her heart shift. She was afraid to be left alone, afraid Orion would come for her when she had no one to save her ass.

"Good idea, Pam. Let's get this done."

The three of them piled out of the Jeep, and Milly didn't move from her seat, didn't wish them luck, didn't ask them if they were sure.

He almost thought he saw a tremble of tears shine across her eyes, but he ignored it.

The bite of the North Dakota wind snapped at his bare face, but the fresh air was welcome after sitting in the Jeep with three other people and the residual odor from Agent Valley.

Taking the lead, he motioned with his hand for the two kids to follow him. Shit, this must have been how Rylee felt, towing Pamela, Alex, and Eve around on her salvages and such. While they were powerful in their own rights, they were children, untrained and so very young.

With nothing but the soft crunch of their feet on the packed snow, they slipped around the side of the building, staying well back from the lights.

Halfway there, Liam saw a major flaw in the plan and touched Pamela on the arm. "They will see where the shots come from. Go back to the Jeep, get Milly to drive and let off two or three fireballs. Be sure not to hit the doors, we want to drive them out front, not push them out the back."

Her jaw tightened. "And then just you and Frank go in?"

Liam drew her close. "They can't hurt me. And Frank can raise the dead. We'll be okay, but not if they are on top of us before we even reach the door. We don't want a fire fight, not with people who have guns that work against us. Double back and meet us along the road there." He pointed to a dark line passing through dense canopied trees that ran parallel to the building. He didn't point out he had a gun—Frank's—tucked into the back of his pants under his shirt.

She let out the building steam of teenage indignation in a big gush of air. "You're right." No more words, she turned and ran back the way they'd come, her long hair streaming behind her.

Liam didn't waste any time. "Frank, let's go."

They jogged around the perimeter and were at the back of the mirrored building within a few minutes, crouched low against the snow. Between the building and them was a line of dark, dirty snow, posts driven at twelve-foot intervals, chains dangling from them. Liam lifted his nose and took a deep breath.

Trolls, they'd used Trolls. Not that the killing of the slimy bastards was any loss, but if the Trolls decided they had a vendetta against the humans, and the Trolls were aligned with Orion . . . shit, clusterfuck didn't begin to cover what they could be looking at.

"How are we going to know the witch does anything?" Frank whispered, his eyes round and dilated behind his glasses.

"You'll know. And don't call her 'the witch.' She has a name. Use it," Liam said softly. There was very little finesse behind Pamela's abilities, just sheer power. With her, it was all or nothing.

"Sorry."

Without warning, an explosion erupted, lighting the night on fire as a column of flame shot high into the sky straight up the front side of the building.

"Holy shit," Frank breathed. The kid had missed Pamela's previous light show, exploding Ingers's cars, since he'd been unconscious.

"Remember that next time you try to take her on or call her 'the witch,'" Liam grunted as he started forward. A second column joined the first and then a streak of flame the size of a truck soared in an arc toward the top of the building.

Liam paced himself so the kid could keep up; even at that slow speed, they made it to the back of the building without anyone seeing them.

They skidded to a stop, and Liam pressed his hands against the door, which opened easily. Not even locked? That was cocky beyond any FBI agent or operation he'd ever known.

They stepped inside and Liam froze, his nostrils flaring, every nerve in his body dancing with recognition.

Witches, and lots of them, had been here. His thoughts connected. "Frank, we have to get some of these weapons out of here, and then we have to burn this place down."

"Isn't that what the witch—I mean, Pamela—is doing?"

Liam forced himself to move forward, deeper into the building, deeper into the thick smell of witch and dark magic. "No. And we have to hurry because we aren't dealing with humans."

Frank swallowed, his Adams apple bobbing several times. "Other supernaturals are helping them kill their own kind, that's what you're saying?"

Liam followed his nose, sniffing for gun oil, and picking it up pretty quick. He didn't bother to answer the kid. "This way." He wove through the lower levels of the building. The weapons were always stored down low in the FBI buildings, easier to grab on the way out. They didn't run into anyone as they traversed the hallways, though Liam heard footsteps now and again.

He brought them to a door labeled "Armory." With a glance at the kid, he pushed the door open and peered inside. Armory indeed. Guns of every size and type. Without questioning himself, he grabbed two handguns to replace those he could no longer use. While he didn't mind Rylee's blades, guns would always be his first choice.

"Grab two guns and the ammo for them."

Frank did as he was told and Liam gathered up ammo for himself, stuffing it into a large backpack on the floor. Footsteps coming down the hallway made him pause. He snapped his fingers and got Frank's attention. "Hide."

Frank stared around them, settling on tucking himself between two desks.

Liam loaded the weapon, almost casually, though his heart thumped hard. The last time he'd used a gun, he inadvertently killed his partner. Being as close to supernaturals as they'd been, the bullet veered sideways instead of staying on its intended course.

The door swung inward and a man in his forties strode into the room, his head down. "Gods be damned, I thought we'd taken out that meddling coven."

Liam didn't wait for the witch to bring his head up, didn't give him time to use a spell. He just pulled the trigger. Even in his hands, the gun worked and the bullet stayed true, driving through the man's head.

The witch was dead before he hit the floor.

"That was loud, Liam," Frank whispered, standing.

Liam nodded. "Yeah, guns tend to be that way. Time to leave, I think."

Frank nodded, then lifted his hand, and the body at Liam's feet twitched. Frank gave him a half grin. "I'll leave him to guard the weapons. That should scare the shit out of the rest of them."

The dead witch rose slowly, pushing itself to its feet, but only had eyes for the kid who intoned in a more than creepy voice. "Protect this room, kill all who enter."

The zombie nodded, its head lolling forward and back with far more looseness than it should have.

Liam scanned the room, saw two files on the far side. He grabbed them and stuffed them into the bag alongside the ammo.

All of this seemed too easy, too well laid out. Then again, it wasn't the FBI running the show; it seemed to be a coven of witches who thought no one could touch them. Who thought no one was left to slip through the back door and steal their things.

"Pride goeth before the fall," he whispered as they stepped out the room, quickly retracing their footsteps. The back door was in sight and he pushed the kid ahead. "Go."

The crackle of air, the scent of ozone. He didn't think, just leapt for Frank, tackling him to the floor as the lightning zigzagged through the hallway, bouncing off the walls.

Liam rolled, and brought up the gun, sighting down the barrel. The gun barely bucked in his hand as he squeezed off two shots. The witch at the end of the hallway dropped, her eyes going wide as she clutched at her chest.

"Not so much fun when your shit is turned on you, is it?" He pushed to his feet and grabbed the kid, the sound of many feet and voices coming their way. "Come on, Frank. They've taken away the welcome mat."

They shoved through the door and out of the building, bolting across the open space, across the firing squad line, and into the dark winter night.

Running hard, they met up with Pamela and Milly on the side road.

Liam jerked the door open. "Pamela, let it burn, we have to destroy it."

Her eyes lit up and she jumped out of the Jeep. Fire flew from her fingers, tagging them exactly where they were. But it didn't matter. The building was burning hard and fast and for all the witches who were left, it was too much. They scattered as multiple explosions in the lower floors burst windows.

Milly got out of the Jeep and went and touched Pamela on the shoulder. "That's enough. They won't be able to stop it, but they will come for us. I know them well enough."

Pamela dropped her arms and sagged. Liam caught her and stepped into the Jeep, her slight weight nothing in his arms.

"Okay, let's go."

Milly didn't hesitate, put the Jeep in gear and hit the gas pedal. Frank said nothing as they drove down the dark road, the raging fire behind them lighting the night sky.

13

Faris found us, asleep, waiting on him. To say he was not happy was an understatement.

"What in all the seven bloody fucking hells are you doing?" he roared, his foot swinging toward Alex with a kick I knew from past experience would break ribs. Alex scrambled out of the way, barely missing the blow.

"Resting after we almost got eaten by a spider Guardian." I yawned and stretched as though we had all the time in the world, my skirt sliding even further up my thighs. Hell, if he could have a nap there was no reason we couldn't too.

Faris spun twice where he stood, one eye bloodshot and twitching like crazy, his words making no sense. "Piece of what—do you think—there is no reason Tracker—sunrise is coming—prophecies fade . . ."

Doran grabbed me and jerked me out of the way as Faris continued to flail and speak like a maniac. "This is bad. He doesn't have the control to go without blood, Rylee. Power, yes, in spades. But not control. He'll never make it to the end."

I stared at the vampire in front of us, who twitched and jerked like an epileptic having a grand mal, his bones creaking with each jump of his body, teeth snapping and a low pacing growl trickling out of his mouth. And he seemed to not see us at all.

"Then we have to kill him, we can't be dealing with a vampire gone mental," I said, carefully removing my sword, doing my best not to draw Faris's attention. Fast, this had to be fast and without warning if I was taking his head.

Doran put a hand over mine, stopping me. "There is another choice. If we feed him, it will bring him back."

I couldn't believe what I was hearing. "Why the fuck would we do that?"

"Because he is powerful, even if he doesn't have control right now. And if we kill him, Berget wins. There is no guarantee we can stop her on our own. You do understand what we must do if the spell and opal don't work?"

I jerked my hand out from under his, and before I could say anything, Alex let out a howl.

Faris had him pinned to the ground, his face buried in Alex's fur along his neck, feeding deeply.

"Fucking vampire!" I leapt toward them, driving the point of my sword through Faris's middle. He reared back, his lips smeared with blood, his eyes no longer twitching or bloodshot.

"Enough. Enough." Faris raised his hands in submission, his movements slow.

Alex scampered away, whimpering, putting his paw to his neck. "Owie, fucking vampire."

"Stay over there, Alex." I pointed to the far wall as I pulled my second sword. There was no need for me to say what I was going to do, we all knew.

Faris, his skin dull and his eyes dim even after taking blood from Alex, continued to hold up his hands. "I am out of the running now. I free you from your oath to help me find the Blood."

Holy shit. I lowered the tip of my blade lightly. "And the other oaths."

"Even after you kill me, you will hold to your oath to kill the Child Empress."

I shook my head. "No. I won't. You killed my friend, Faris, and you threatened everyone I love. Big mistake." I raised my sword, and his eyes widened. The swing of the sword was halfway through when he spoke.

"Charlie isn't dead."

I froze, the blade mere inches from his neck, shocked that he would admit it. But I played along. "Bullshit."

He leaned back on the stone floor, bracing himself on his elbows. "Charlie is fine; he's a brownie, Rylee. He can move through time and space using doorways and windows. An opening through the Veil is a doorway."

I lowered my sword tip. "Then why?"

Faris snorted and lay down on the stone, flat on his back. "Rylee, you are the most stubborn, difficult woman I have ever dealt with. I tried seducing you, I tried to help you, I tried asking, but none of it worked when it came to getting you to help me. You forced me to resort to methods even I am loathe to use. And yet even blackmail isn't enough, is it? Berget tried the same methods, attempting to kill your Eve, yet none of it worked." He lifted his head slightly just to arch his eyebrow at me and then lay back down. "You are too fucking stubborn to do anything you don't want to. Did you tell the others that I was blackmailing you?"

I flushed. "Yes and no. Charlie told them, but I would have anyway. They're my family; we don't keep secrets."

"Do you see, Doran, what I was trying to work with? Wait, you knew Charlie was alive?" Faris lifted his head and stared at me, his eyes wide.

I lowered my blade. "Yes."

"Then why did you come with me if you knew it was a bluff?"

"Faris, you are the biggest asshole in all the world, but at least you are not going to turn the world over to the vampires. You aren't going mad with power. As much as I hate to say it, you *were* the best choice."

Besides, we needed the vampires unified—and not under someone certifiable—if I was going to convince them to help me in the upcoming shit show with Orion. Not that I was ready to spill those beans to Faris just yet.

He thumped his head back into the stone. "And now, there is only one."

I cleared my throat and slid my blades back into their sheaths. "That isn't true, exactly."

Doran let out a strangled squawk. "No. Rylee. Just. No."

Faris wobbled to his feet. "Wait, what are you talking about?"

And if Faris knows you plan to turn Doran into a vampire, and take the throne, you think he won't just kill him?

Time to think fast and lie through my teeth, something I wasn't all that good at. "I have an idea."

Faris's eyes focused on me. "And the idea is . . ."

"Not sure if it will work yet." I shrugged. "When the time comes to tell you, I will."

Doran hadn't moved, his green eyes distant, and I could almost feel him closing off from us.

"Faris." I lifted my hand, stopping him, feeling my world tighten further. "Let it go. Apparently, I am the only one who has to make a sacrifice to save this fucking world. Let's find the Blood. We'll wait for Berget there and deal with her."

I wanted Liam so badly I ached all over. I didn't trust either of these men I was with. I'd thought I could trust Doran, but apparently I was wrong.

Faris surprised me by doing as I asked. "So, it is proven now that I do not have the control to lead, but we know the Child Empress is no better. It will be difficult at best to kill her, let alone implement whatever plan it is you two have hatched." He limped forward.

I put a finger to his chest, my next words measured and slow. "What the fuck is going on? I cannot deal with this mercurial shit you're pulling, Faris. Either you are trying to hurt me, or you are on our side. I will tell you this straight right fucking now." I took a step closer, pulling my blades and pressing them into the hollow of his throat. "Turn on me one more time, play one more fucking game with me and nothing you say or do will keep me from striking your twisted head from your shoulders."

His eyes never wavered from mine, but he didn't try to bespell me.

"You have my word, Rylee. I will not turn on you again, or even seemingly turn on you. Now, what is your plan for our little Empress?"

I dropped my blades. That would be the best I could get out of him. A glance at Doran showed him still off in la-la land. Some help there.

"If we can pin her down, we can end her."

Faris threw back his head, his laughter echoing off the stone walls. "Just how do you plan to 'pin' her down?"

I frowned at him. "Hadn't got that far."

The vampire put a hand to his chin. "We can figure that out as we go, but perhaps it would be best to find the Blood first. There is a time limit on this."

I lifted an eyebrow. "Spit it out."

"Three days until the winter equinox rolls around. And depending on where the Blood resides, that could mean we have less than three days."

Why was there always a fucking time limit? Even if we found the right door, the Blood wouldn't be waiting for us on the other side, they could be thousands of miles away. "If you feed, can you jump me across continents?"

He nodded. "Yes, that would be the fastest way to Track them."

My brain kicked into overdrive. "You go feed. I'll keep checking doorways, see if we can't find what we're looking for before you get back."

"So we are a team now, are we? And you are Red Leader? Interesting turn of events." Faris turned his back and jumped the Veil, leaving me with my mouth hanging open.

"Did he just refer to *Star Wars*?"

"Yes," Doran said. "I believe he did."

"Done sulking?" I wouldn't look at him, couldn't. He'd let me down, and that disappointment was like a fire in my gut.

"Rylee—"

"Don't fucking bother, Doran. You don't want to take responsibility. I get it." I strode toward the next door. Doran might not want to lead the vampires, but what other choice was there? Berget? Fuck no.

Forcing my thoughts back to the task at hand I stared at the next crossing. Classic castle doorway, heavy bands of iron across it with round loops of iron for a handle. Sword in one hand, I grabbed the ring of iron and pulled. The door slid open on what felt like oiled hinges, revealing just another part of the castle. Also lined with doors.

That wasn't what made my jaw drop, though.

Nope, my jaw dropped because I found myself staring at Jack. Not the sickly, almost dead Jack I had met, a cranky old Tracker who couldn't stand without help or a cane.

The Jack I found myself staring at was young, vibrant with life, and had a brand spanking new set of fangs.

By the time they got to the farmhouse, the twenty-four hours Rylee had said it would take her had come and gone. And Liam was close to pulling his hair out.

"She'll wait for us, or she'll come looking for us," Milly said as they slowed to a stop in the driveway.

"She does have this nifty little trick that allows her to find people."

Liam let out slow breath. Much as he hated to admit the witch was right, she was. They might be behind, but Rylee could find them a hell of a lot easier than they could find her.

"Let's check on your uncle, Frank. See if we can't get something out of him." The four of them stepped out of the Jeep and headed toward the barn. A loud squawk drew his eyes upward. On top of the barn perched a perturbed Harpy.

"Eve." He lifted a hand, and the Harpy let out a second squawk and flew down to greet them.

"Liam, Pamela! The big lizard has buried himself in the fields, under the dirt as if he is hiding."

I'm not hiding; I'm being inconspicuous.

"Whatever, lizard."

Blaz didn't answer and so, that was that. Though what he had to be inconspicuous about was beyond him.

Eve flapped her wings, drawing his eyes to her.

"There is something," she said in a lowered voice and her words were hitched. "Dead in the barn. Please tell me it is not Dox and the others."

"No, it isn't Dox." One of these days, he would have to ask Rylee about that, about where the bodies of the supernaturals went. Because as far as he'd been able to tell, they just vanished.

"You're right, though, there is something dead in there," Liam said, reaching up to put a hand on her ruffled feathers. The Harpy shook her head, a flash of silver and gold flickering off her. That was different.

"New jewelry?" He'd never thought to see anything like that on the Harpy, yet the dangling earrings suited her.

"Gifts from the unicorns, to show they mean to honor the old ways." She fluffed her wings. "I will leave soon. I have to convince the other Harpies to stand with us."

A chill swept through Liam. "You've said they'd kill you."

She lifted her head. "I will take the chance, as we all do each day. I must try."

His wolf puffed up with pride. His pack was strong and loyal to the core, even if they were from all walks of the supernatural world. "Be safe, Eve, and come back to us."

Her luminous eyes flicked over them, then strode to where Frank stood, shaking. "Who is this?"

"Frank, meet Eve. Eve, Frank is a necromancer. He's going to help us with the dead guy." Without any more introductions, he headed toward the barn.

Eve reeled back as if she'd been struck. "Frank must come with me."

Liam's feet froze. "What?"

"He must come with me."

Frank stammered out, "I . . . can't, I have to help Liam."

Eve shook her head. "No. You will fly with me to the Harpies and help me convince them. That is all there is to that, Death Walker."

Liam's wolf nodded his approval.

The prophecies come true in strange ways. For the moment, he ignored the voice inside his head, even if he did agree with it. Though he knew no prophecy that dealt with a Harpy and a necromancer, that didn't mean it wasn't important.

"First, we need Frank's help with Agent Valley. Then he can go with you."

While Frank stammered and stuttered his way to the barn, the others didn't question Liam's decision. About fucking time they saw it was his job to run the show.

The barn door pulled open easily, but the scent of rot was not so easy to take. One of the few times Liam actually cursed his sensitive sense of smell. "Fuck, that is nasty." Though the light was dim, he saw clearly. But he wasn't so sure the others could. Reaching to the right, he flicked on the switch for the overhead lights.

The view was, unfortunately, no better than the smell.

Behind him, the two witches gagged and wretched, and a glance back showed him they were not coming any further into the barn.

Milly pointed at the house. "We'll wait inside."

Frank followed Liam into the barn. "It's not that bad, you know. I've smelled worse."

Liam couldn't help the way his eyebrows shot up. "Worse?"

Frank shrugged. "Probably just part of being a necromancer."

Agent Valley shuffled toward them, one eye sagging out of its socket. Liam planted his feet firmly, determined not to back down.

"O'Sheaaaaaaa . . . Ingers is tied . . . Black Cov-eeeeeeeeeen." Agent Valley gasped for breath, feet stalling as he wobbled from side to side.

"Frank, can you find out more information? Details, places and names?"

"It will drain what is left of him. I don't want to do that," Frank whispered, backing away. Liam lunged toward him and grabbed the kid by the arms.

"He's already dead, Frank. But he can still help us if you can pull your shit together. Do you understand? This isn't a game. It's life or death, and your uncle died to protect you, trying to protect all of us."

Frank's eyes filled with tears. "He was the closest thing to a father I had."

This was not the moment for Liam to soften, and he knew it. "Then make him proud, Frank. Do what you have to do."

Frank sniffled loudly, and then slowly nodded. "You have the questions, so you ask him. You need to touch him."

This was not what he was expecting. "How?"

The kid walked forward and put his hands on Valley's head, thumbs above the eye sockets, fingers wrapped around his head. "Press in hard, hard enough to feel . . . past the bone. I'll open the connection between you two."

Oh shit, this was not what he'd been thinking at all. But there was no way he'd back down now that he'd shamed the kid into it.

Two steps and he was face-to-face with his old boss. He lifted his hands and placed them where Frank had, the feel of dead flesh under his fingers making his own skin crawl. He couldn't stop the low growl that built in his chest. Bearing down, his fingers pushed through the dying tissue that had once been Agent Valley. Breathing shallowly, he thought for a moment that he was going to lose it, his gorge rose and he had to fight not to jerk away.

Then his fingers touched the soft resistance of Agent Valley's brain, and everything shifted.

"O'Shea. This was not how I expected to speak to you after our last visit."

Liam closed his eyes and concentrated on the voice in his head. Kind of like Blaz's, only this felt more distant. Almost like he heard the words outside his head at the same time they echoed inside his head.

"Yeah, me neither, boss."

"Did you find where the guns are being made?"

"Yes. Grabbed a few for myself."

Good man. But that is only the start. Ingers had connections within the Army, and if she can prove the supernatural world exists . . ." Agent Valley didn't have to say anything more, Liam knew.

If the Army felt threatened, then it really would be an all out war with the humans.

"Fuck, we can't let that happen."

"I agree. You have to kill Ingers, wipe her files, get rid of everything that is even mildly connected to the supernatural."

The body of Agent Valley let out a heavy groaning sigh. *"All those years I tried to tie the humans and the supernaturals together, to bring about change. To help Frank. All to see it be wiped out now."*

Liam felt the Agent's emotions as if they were his own, and he shared in the disappointment that was so much more than just a simple task going unfinished.

"Humans aren't ready, not yet, Agent. You know that."

"I'd hoped perhaps we'd finally come far enough." Another deep groaning sigh rumbled out and Liam had to hold his breath to not take in the putrid scent from the belly of the rotting Agent.

"Sir, is there anything else you can tell us?"

"The meeting is on the night of the winter equinox. I don't know how Ingers plans on showing her hand to the Army, but I know that is the night. She has ties to the Black Coven. I was coming to warn you about them when she killed me."

Liam squeezed his eyes tight and lowered his chin to his chest. "A little less than three days."

"Yes. And Liam, I would ask one thing of you. The boy is like my son. . ."

Liam knew what his request would be. "I'll do my best to watch out for Frank. There is a war coming. I can't guarantee his safety, but I will look out for him as one of our own."

Seemed Rylee wasn't the only one collecting wards.

"Thank you, O'Shea."

With that, Agent Valley jerked away and fell to the ground, his body twitching twice and then stilling.

Liam looked at his hands, goo hanging off the tips of his fingers, grey matter under his nails. Teeth clenched he turned to see Frank crying.

Nothing he said would ease the kid's pain. He knew from experience when you lost a parent, there was very little anyone could say to even begin to help. So he kept it simple.

"Come on, kid. Let's get cleaned up."

14

Doran, Alex, and I bolted through the castle, not really looking where we were going. Just running blindly.

We spun around a corner and there were Jack and Berget, waiting for us.

Fuck a duck, we were so screwed.

"Rylee, lovely to see you again, sister," Berget all but purred. As with Faris, I saw the sign something was wrong, off with her. Her whole body quivered, like a horse covered in flies, its skin twitching uncontrollably.

"Jack, be a dear and grab her, would you? I'm feeling rather faint."

Jack's blue eyes swirled three tones, so he was still a Tracker, could still Read people, and now to add to that, he was a vampire. A baby vampire, but that didn't matter.

He rushed forward, his eyes full of sorrow. "I'm sorry," he mouthed, and I saw in that moment he was holding back. Still, he was too fast for me.

Doran, though, was another matter.

The Daywalker slid between us, catching Jack off balance, and off guard, apparently. They crashed into the stone wall, shaking the place. Dust fell from the ceiling and Berget clapped her hands together. "Oh, I love a good fight. Shall we make a bet, Rylee?"

I yanked my swords out, and didn't bother to answer her crazy fucking idea. "Alex, start opening doors." We had to get out of here. I was banking on at least one doorway leading into the daylight.

Alex yanked doors open left and right. Night time, night time, and then, bingo.

Sunlight filtered in, early morning or late evening, I couldn't tell. Didn't matter. I jumped toward Doran and Jack, driving my blade through Jack's chest. He reared off Doran long enough for the Daywalker to scramble from under him.

A mad dash was all we had, and the three of us tumbled through the doorway and into the sunlight, the door slamming behind us. Sand and surf, we lay on a barren stretch of beach. Alex, the previous danger immediately forgotten, ran toward the waves, diving in and under like a seal.

Doran sat up and I got a good look at him. "Not bad for tangling with a vampire, I hardly see any marks."

"He was holding back. I think he is tied to her, like I was, and is fighting her."

I snorted. "So? He chose this life, Doran. Did you choose to become a Daywalker, or did someone just take you?"

His eyes clouded over. "I see your point."

I noticed he didn't answer the question. Jack, in choosing to become a vampire under Berget's power, made his choice. He was not on our side anymore.

Maybe he never had been. I stood and brushed the sand off my dress, checked my weapons, and looked around. The sun was rising here, wherever here was.

I glanced into the water to see Alex further out than he should have been. "Alex, get your furry ass back here!" With no effort, he turned and headed back to the shore.

The waves crashed around us, and Alex was back in a few minutes, grinning like a fool. "Seals are fun."

I stared into the water, saw dark spots humping up and down in the water.

And then the unthinkable—a set of jaws burst out of the water around one of the seals, clamping down on it, then dragging it under the water. Alex's mouth dropped open.

"Sharks in water."

"Holy shit, Alex! That could have been you."

Doran stepped beside us, affecting a strong Aussie accent. "Can I interest you in a shrimp on the barbie?"

Australia, we were in the land down under. Shit, first time for everything, I suppose. Well, since we were here, I Tracked the Blood.

Expecting nothing.

Shocked as hell when I got a resounding thread to follow.

"They're here," I said, striding off in the direction of the Blood.

"Wait, are you serious?" Doran grabbed my arm.

I stared at him. "Well, what the fuck did you think we were going to do?"

"Wait for Faris?" He quirked an eyebrow at me, his piercing catching the glinting sun. "You know, since we just had to run like hell from Berget and Jack as it is?"

"We'll be ready for them next time." Shit, even I didn't believe me.

"Fuck, Rylee. We need help. If not Faris, then can you connect with Blaz?"

I shook my head. "No, he's too far."

Doran held me loosely. "We should get you out of the sun."

"I'm not frail."

He frowned at me, the piercing in his lower lip dipping downward. "You sure as hell aren't ready to go flitting across the continent right now, are you?"

A wash of fatigue and I had to concede he was right. "A few hours. Maybe Faris will catch up to us tonight."

"Are you ill, Rylee?" Doran's concern was heavy in his voice.

"No, I think I've finally just hit the wall."

Then again, maybe we were on our own again. I tried to figure out how Faris would find us and I knew there was a reason he should be able to, something to do with Alex, but the thoughts slipped through my mind over and over, and then I realized I wasn't awake any longer. I was out cold and dreaming.

Deerborne Park again. Hell, my life always seemed to circle back to this place. Berget and I were on the teeter-totter this time. Up and down, her hair floated around her face for a moment before she went down, like she was in water.

"Rylee, you have to be careful. The madness is growing stronger without any blood to feed my body."

I pushed off the ground. "Figured that out already."

She shook her head. "I do not know if you can save me. I am fading." As if her words were the ignition, she flickered, like in an old movie where the reel jumps from scene to scene.

I wanted to grab her and make her stay, but again, she shook her head. "If I must go, then I will. But when you try to stop the madness, realize it might be too late. I don't think I will be able to reach you again."

The teeter-totter creaked as we bounced up and down, the old wooden seat jarring when it met the ground . "Are you saying goodbye?" I whispered.

"I'm saying thank you, for never giving up on me. For being my sister to the bitter end." She smiled, a tear slipped down her cheek, and then she was gone and I blinked in the bright sunlight.

Doran peered down at me. "Hey, none of that. No passing out on me." He reached out and brushed a tear off my cheek, his voice softening. "And none of that, either."

I swallowed the lump in my throat, but didn't try to sit up. Nausea rolled through me, and I was afraid if I moved I'd puke.

Never mind.

I twisted to one side and spewed whatever minis-cule amount of food I had in my stomach onto the floor. Wait, floor?

I looked around us. We were in an open roofed room, but there were walls and a floor and I was com-pletely confused. "Where are we?"

Doran smiled and helped me move away from the bile. "Shamans are all over the world, you just have to know where to look."

On cue, a wiry old Maori man stepped into the room. He was dressed in loose khakis, but no shirt and his feet were bare. Tattoos covered his torso and several strings of beads and bones hung from his neck. Yet I didn't feel animosity flowing from him. He reminded me of Louisa, despite the fact they were different genders, and worlds apart. There was that same calm knowledge deep in his eyes.

He crouched beside me, his fingers hovering over my forehead. "My name is Al." He touched me gently. "You're feeling rough, eh, little Tracker? You have the look of your mother, that you do, but it is the fire that comes from your daddy that drives you."

My jaw dropped and I stared him, his words bouncing inside my head. "You don't mean my adoptive parents, do you?"

Making a duck face, he shook his head. "Nope. But we don't have time for stories, do we? Not today."

He held up a piece of pottery, a barely molded cup, steam curling out of it. Fuck, the last thing I wanted was something hot, but Shamans were not to be ignored.

I took the shallow cup and put it to my lips. The liquid started out hot, but as it trailed down my throat it turned to ice. I gasped and choked, Doran pounded on my back.

"What is this?"

"A drink of my people. It will keep you cooler as you cross the desert. You won't need water or drink for several days. But after, you need to take time off. Time to let your body heal. Understand?"

I nodded and the Shaman handed a drink to Doran and one to Alex. They swallowed and gave the same kind of response I did.

There was no way I could resist asking. "My parents, are they alive?"

He shook his head. "No. They died protecting you. It's a long story, Rylee. One I have only a small part in. I have their story in your mother's journal. When you are done, come and get it."

I nodded, grateful beyond words. If I was going to lose Berget, maybe I could at least have the memory of parents who did love me. I wanted to ask the questions burning in my gut, but Al was right, there wasn't time.

Revived beyond belief, I stood. "How long was I out?"

Doran's eyes slid away from mine. "Almost a day."

Holy shit. "Faris?"

"Yes. He was here all night. He can find us through Alex, since he took his blood. For some reason, he can't find you anymore. He'll catch up with us as night falls. But we have to hurry. We have less than a full day to get to the Blood."

"Berget is in the same boat."

His face was grim. "Which will make her desperate and even more dangerous."

I thought about what Berget said to me. "I don't think it will matter. We will try to get the opal on her, but . . ." I shook my head. Perhaps I was too naïve for this life, to keep believing the outcome would be anything but death and pain. Yet, with everything that had happened, I needed to believe there was hope, there was a possibility we could see this through and bring Berget back. Otherwise, what was the point, if I stopped believing?

"Something you want to share?" Doran asked, his eyes watching me closely.

"Nope. We're going to kick ass, leave the names behind, and do this right. We're bringing her back, and then we'll figure out what the hell we're doing about the vampires' leader." I checked my sheaths and thought about asking Al for a pair of shorts. The cocktail dress was really not doing it for me. Though, at least I'd get a tan.

A half-smile slipped across Doran's lips. "Well, I've been wondering where you've been."

"What are you talking about?"

He shrugged and turned away, saying nothing more.

Al loaned us his truck. Mind you, it was a Willy, an old army beast that looked like it had been through the desert more than once. The paint peeled in multiple places leaving gaping holes to the bare steel, but when Al started it up, the engine turned over no problem.

"Here's a map, not that you should need it, but I've marked where you can find others who will help you if you have need of it."

Grateful for his foresight, I took the map and had a look at it. Half a dozen places were marked with red dots. Al put his finger at the top center. "You're starting here, we're on the Cape York Peninsula." He moved to the back of the Jeep. "Extra water and fuel in the back." Al tapped two canisters marked diesel, then a third marked drinking water. "This one is in case you get stuck out there when my drink wears off."

Alex yipped and leapt into the back, his front paws on top of the cab. "Car riiiiiiiiiiide!"

I slid into the driver's seat without asking Doran if he wanted to drive. "Thank you, Al. I'll be back for that journal."

The old shaman winked at me. "Of that, Rylee, I have no doubt."

We drove out of his place and I locked onto the threads of the Blood. They were a fucking long ways away. Like I barely felt them. Only enough to know what direction.

"How far do you think?" Doran rested his arm on the door of the Jeep, the wind whipping in around him.

I focused on the threads, their signature weak inside my head. "Could be on the other side of the continent, or could be they are just faint. Fucked if I know; I don't have a sense of distance here like at home. They've been closed off for how long?"

Doran grunted. "I don't know for sure. Several thousand years, at least. There are secrets held by these vampires, the Blood are a mystery, even us Daywalkers don't know. It is part of how they keep us in line."

I laughed at him. "That, and the fact they can kick your fangy butts into next week."

"Smart ass."

"Better than a dumb ass." I grinned at him, feeling light, and better. Belief—who the hell knew that a little faith, a little hope, could give me so much?

We drove south until the Willy was nearly out of gas, stopped, fueled up, and continued on. We were well into the interior, and the landscape was nothing short of mind boggling. Blazing blue sky, empty as far as I could see, and the ground wasn't any better. Scrub grasses and the occasional lone tree.

"Pretty barren." I found myself driving more to the west now, heading toward what I knew was the center of Australia.

The desert. Even with Al's drink coursing through my veins, I was soaked, the backs of my knees dripped sweat onto the floorboards and my back stuck to the seat. A glance at Doran showed me he was soaked too, his shirt clinging to his chest and abs, clearly showing he had at least one piercing I'd not known about.

I squinted against the bright, hot sunlight pouring in around us. If Al's drink ran out on us, we were so screwed.

Killing someone with premeditation was not really his forte, and while he knew Ingers had to die, planning it was not easy. So he avoided it.

He stood with Milly and Pamela, watching Eve and Frank take off to bring the Harpies to their side. Good thing Rylee had a harness made for the Harpy, or he wasn't sure they would have gotten Frank onto her back.

But to be fair, Liam could hardly keep his mind on the task at hand. Morning had come and gone, and Rylee hadn't come back. Ingers would have to wait.

"If the task was so easy, why isn't she back yet?" Pamela moved to his side and he glanced down at her.

"Where did she go, Pamela?"

She let out a sigh and seemed to struggle for a moment before spilling the beans. "She went to see Doran. That's it."

Liam frowned at this revelation, and not because he didn't like the Daywalker. Pamela was right; Rylee should have been fine. Faris wasn't due to show up for at least another five days.

His heart clenched, and a heavy premonition settled over his whole body. "Faris came early for her."

Milly spun to face him, her feet slipping in the snow. Out of instinct, he reached out and grabbed her, stopped her from hitting the ground.

She pulled out of his hands, her eyes more than a little disbelieving. "How do you know that?"

He wiped his hand on his pants and headed toward the house. "Doran would have been a pain in the ass, but there was no reason for her not to come back. The only thing that makes sense is Faris. He's a liar, we know that."

Which meant Liam had to hold to his word, and let Rylee do her job. And he had to do his. In the doorway of the farmhouse, he paused, struggling with his wolf and the desire to run after his mate, to keep her safe until his very last breath. A hand settled on his shoulder.

"Liam, she's strong enough to survive this." Milly's scent and voice wrapped around him and his reaction was as instinctive as the one to catch her from falling.

His hand snapped out and wrapped around her tiny throat, the growl in his chest rumbling outward. "Do not touch me, witch."

He dropped her before he could do any real harm, but it took more than an effort to do.

On his way to the house, he saw her slump to the ground, her hands going to her throat, but she said nothing.

Smart witch.

He strode through the house and into Rylee's room, slamming the door behind him. Her scent filled his nose and the anger in him soothed away slowly with each breath.

One way to make sure she stayed safe was to get these guns off the market. To make sure no one could take her out from a distance. That much he could do.

A timid knock on the door turned him around. Pamela, he smelled her.

"Liam, are you okay?"

He sat on the edge of the bed and put his hands in his lap. "Come in, Pam."

She opened the door, her movements uncertain and her eyes full of fear. "Is your wolf going to attack me?"

"No. You aren't Milly."

Pamela let out a quick breath and then got right down to it. "I think we should just hit the FBI office, and take all the information they have. Then we go after the coven."

He couldn't help the way his eyebrows shot upward. "You've thought this all through?"

She stepped in the room and began to pace. "Well, that seems like the best place to start; humans are easier to take out than a whole coven of witches. And you and Rylee pointed out they already have some technology to block us. They use it on their planes."

Her ability to break it down to such simple terms both impressed and worried him. She spoke about killing as if it were easy.

"Pamela. You aren't going to kill anyone. That is a last resort, do you understand?"

She frowned at him. "I can handle it."

There was no way he was going to beat around the bush. "No, you can't." Her jaw dropped open and he knew he'd offended her. "You are too young."

"I've killed before."

"Zombies don't count. Killing a person for no reason other than you need what they have, isn't acceptable. Ever." He stood and walked to her, and put both hands on her shoulders. "Ever. You kill to protect those you love, and those who cannot protect themselves."

"Yet, that is what we're going to do." Defiance radiated through her and into him, and when she would pull away, he tightened his grip.

"No. That's what *I'm* going to do. This will be on my shoulders, not yours. Whatever death comes, I will deal out. Understood?"

She again tried to pull away but he held her tight. Sure, she could have used her magic, forcing him to let go. But this wasn't about magic. This was about who was in charge.

Slowly, with great reluctance, she nodded. "Fine."

"Good." He pulled her in tight for a quick hug, surprising them both. Despite her abilities, she was still a child. Her arms circled him for a brief second before she stepped back.

"So do you have a plan, then?"

"Your plan is good, Pamela." He watched with amusement as his praise made her eyes light up. "I think it would be smart to hit the FBI first. I don't think they'll be expecting it."

They headed to the kitchen where Milly was nursing a hot drink. Her eyes flicked up to him then back to her cup. "Would you rather I stay here?"

Her question surprised the shit out of him. "You're offering to stay behind?"

"I don't want to get strangled again for trying to give someone comfort." Her words were sharp, but they didn't work, not on him.

"You're lucky I didn't snap your neck. See how far we've come?" He strode past her and aimed toward to cellar. The last stash of Rylee's weapons was there and he needed something from it if they were going to do this.

In the cellar, the light bulb flickered above his head, swaying left and right.

Only a few weapons left, but he knew which one he wanted. Rylee's back up crossbow was smaller than her main one, and wouldn't take as much strength to pull back the draw.

He grabbed it along with a handful of bolts and then climbed back up the stairs. Once more in the kitchen, he put the crossbow and bolts on the table in front of Milly.

"If you're coming with us, you'd better be useful."

She swallowed hard and nodded. "Just like throwing a spell."

With a snort, he walked away. "How the hell would I know? Just make sure you don't shoot Pamela."

The FBI offices were dark. Weird for this time of day, and it made the back of his neck crawl. Or maybe that was the fact Milly crouched behind him with a loaded crossbow.

Yeah, that seemed a likely culprit.

"Pamela, can you blow the transformer?"

She nodded and lifted her hand, a delicate tendril of magic curling out and around the box at the top of the power pole. A muted pop, a flash of light, and the rest of the buildings on the street went dark.

In the light of day, it was not easy to sneak in. So they went in bold as could be. He took the lead, the guns he'd snatched from the warehouse snug in their holsters, a comfort he'd missed.

Milly held the crossbow easily. Apparently, Giselle and Rylee had given the witch rudimentary lessons in weapons.

Pamela was only a half step behind them both. Though she'd argued the whole way over, even Milly agreed. The kid went in behind them. End of story.

With the power gone, the front door had locked. Now Liam did motion for Pamela.

"Keep it soft, Pam."

She put a hand to the door and the lock let out a groan, the door swinging inward. Damn, her lessons with Milly were paying off in dividends. The entrance was dark and they slipped in, closing the door behind them.

He held up his hand, fingers spread, voice pitched low. "Five minutes. You two take the front desk; I'll take Ingers's office. Ears and eyes peeled."

The two witches nodded and headed around the side of the front desk. Liam jogged through the building to the back where Ingers's office was. Her door was ajar and the slightest flicker of movement froze his feet. He dropped to a crouch and inched forward, hands curling around the butts of his two guns.

The figure seemed to be searching through Ingers's office, flipping papers and pushing things around. Liam lifted his nose and took in a deep breath.

Fucking Trolls, they were like rats; they seemed to be everywhere. Staying in the crouch, he slid forward and pushed the door open a fraction more.

In the dim light, his eyes picked up details he wasn't sure he wanted to. The Troll was hurt, and it was the first female Troll he'd seen. She was crying softly, her hands searching through the paper on Ingers's desk. "You bitch, you fucking bitch. I'll kill you."

She wasn't as heavily built as the male trolls, her body more human in proportions, her skin tone softer and . . . delicate even. It was hard to put her in the same category as the males he'd seen. He frowned and knew he had to do something; he couldn't crouch there forever.

Standing, he held up his hands. "I'd like to kill her myself, if I could find her."

The Troll scrambled backward, luminous grey eyes widening, her hands fisting up. "Get away, get away!"

He knew panic when he saw it. "You want to kill Ingers?"

She trembled, but didn't back down. "Is that the baby killer's name?"

He let out a slow breath as understanding dawned. "She's been testing her weapons on your children?"

A sob caught in her throat as she bobbed her head. "Half-breeds are not worth any less. Yet, our families turned us over to her." Her eyes lifted to his and he let out another slow breath. There, under the scent of Troll, was the other half of her.

Human.

Shit, this was unexpected. He couldn't help but pity her and her plight. He moved deeper into the office. No matter how bad he felt for this . . . woman, he had to find out the meeting time. And where Ingers might be hiding.

"My name is Tara."

"Liam." He didn't lift his eyes from the desk and she moved out of his way. She didn't ask what he was.

"Can I help?"

He pointed beside her at the tall grey metal cabinet. "Check the files, quickly. Won't be long before the fighting starts."

Tara did as he asked and dove into the cabinet. He searched Ingers's desk, ripping open the locked drawers with ease.

There it was, a green file folder labeled "Army." He grabbed it and spread it on the desk, his blood running cold.

Ingers had more than the coven working for her.

There in black and white was the date and place of the meeting, set up for the winter equinox. "Fuck." His brain couldn't form what he was seeing, what was coming for them.

Tara spun. "What is it? Did you find her?"

"Yes and no. We have to get the fuck out of here. Now."

They ran out of the office as the first round of bullets shattered through the building. "Everyone down!" he roared, ignoring his own advice and continuing to run forward.

Tara hit the deck only a few feet from the front entrance, right next to Pamela and Milly.

Liam knew he was the only one who couldn't really be hurt. Through the front doors he ran, guns out, though his wolf fought with him to be unleashed, a snarl of bloodlust curling through him.

Three cars, three agents.

Running full tilt toward them, he took the three of them in quick succession with shots to the head before they knew what hit them. They dropped, surprise etched on their faces for eternity. They had no idea what they were up against, but they weren't the ones he worried about. No, the humans were the least of his worries, if the file was right.

"Pamela," he called, and the young witch came bolting along behind him, Milly and Tara following. He moved to the first black sedan, an idea forming. One of the dead agents was a woman. He frisked her and found her cell phone.

With a flip of his wrist he tossed it to Milly. "See if Ingers is in there. Call her and tell her it's taken care of."

Milly lowered the crossbow and flicked the phone open.

He looked around, saw people peeking out of the building windows.

"Time to move, ladies."

He hoped he was right about the sedans. Sliding into the driver's seat of the one closest to him, he turned the key. The engine rolled over without a single hiccup.

"Finally."

The three "ladies" (he wasn't sure a Troll could be a lady) slid into the car, eyeing one another, making introductions warily.

As he pulled away from the building, the phone in Milly's hand rang. She flicked it open. "Yes. Yes, Agent, we've cleared the building. Excellent, we'll meet you there." She hung up, a wide grin on her face.

"Got her."

Even though it was Milly, Liam grinned back. "Time to wipe out the bad guys."

Tara's face was grim. "I want first shot at her, she killed my babies."

Milly and Pamela turned to stare at the half-Troll, both with tears in their eyes. Liam nodded. "As soon as I have my questions answered, she's all yours."

"Thank you. I couldn't do this on my own." She burrowed deep into the seat, her baby pink skin standing out against the black leather seats. Pamela, being Pamela, slung an arm around her.

"Hey, you're with us now. And we always get the bad guys."

Liam wasn't so sure that was true, but he sure as hell wasn't going to correct her.

Let her believe they would win the day. For a little while longer, let her believe it would always work in their favor and they would all survive.

15

We sat on the outskirts of Alice Springs and the thrum of the Blood hovered inside my head. The closer we got to them, the more my nerves jangled like live wires.

"It's like they know we're coming." I rubbed my hands over my arms, a chill chasing along my skin in the 120-plus degree weather. "Fuck, I might as well be standing in an ants' nest."

"I'm sure we could arrange that," Doran said, pouring the last of the fuel into the gas tank. "Here, drink some of this." He handed me the water jug.

"Al said we didn't have to."

"Doesn't mean we shouldn't."

He had a point. I took the jug and held it to my lips, drinking until my belly was full, then handed it to Alex. The werewolf slobbered and slopped at the opening, getting more water poured down his front than into his mouth.

"Thank the gods I can't catch his virus," Doran muttered, shaking his head.

I snorted and climbed into the passenger side. "Not like you would end up a submissive."

Doran started the Willy. "Maybe not now, but in the beginning, perhaps I would have been like Alex."

A quick glance his way showed he wasn't kidding. "You were submissive?"

He didn't answer. "I need to stop in Alice. Pick up a few things. Just in case."

Hmm. Interesting. The idea of Doran being submissive, excepting the fact he'd been bonded to the former Empress and then Berget, was odd.

Not that it mattered right now. I stared out the window and Tracked the Blood, then tossed out a thought for Jack and Berget.

I sat straight up in my seat.

"They're in Alice."

Doran glanced at me. "Who is?"

The sky was still bright over head, how the fuck had they gotten here ahead of us? Tonight was the equinox, but I'd hoped they'd mess up. "Jack and Berget are holed up in Alice."

He put the pedal to the floor. "We can take them both while they sleep, Rylee. The gods *are* looking out for us."

My heart stuttered. Killing Jack, well, maybe he deserved it. And the beasts residing in Berget, they deserved a final death too. But my sister, what was left of her, didn't deserve anything of the sort. No, I had to believe the opal would work, that it would be enough, buy us some time.

"Rylee, where?"

I gave directions numbly and within a few minutes we were parked outside a squat building, only one level. Which meant they were in the basement, well away from the sun.

I stared at the sign. "Donny's Fishing Hole." The sign on the door said the place was closed, but I didn't pay much heed.

Checking my weapons, I slid out of the Willy, my boots hitting the sidewalk. Up and down the street, everything seemed quiet. As in no humans. Alex jumped out of the back of the old truck and bounded to me. I crouched to look him in the eye.

"Alex, there are going to be vampires in here, so we have to be very careful. One of them looks like Jack, but he isn't our friend anymore, do you understand?"

The werewolf frowned, his lower lip sticking out. "Bad Jack?"

Teeth gritted tightly, I nodded, unable to say anything past the sudden lump in my throat.

The door was locked, but a slide of my blade through the latches and we were in. Inside smelled musty with an overlay of fish, but the thick coating of dust was the tip off.

No one had been in here for a long time. Two sets of footprints left a path on the floor. One large, one petite. I loosened my swords and started forward. Behind the counter was a small selection of flashlights. I grabbed one and flicked it on, the battery sputtering only once. Not bad.

Doran put a hand on my shoulder. "We kill Jack first. That won't wake her. But if we do anything to her, he'll be up before we can say 'fuck it, we're dead.'"

"Got it."

I tried my best to not think about Jack as we located the trapdoor, but it was hard. Though I hadn't known him long, and he'd lied to me several times, he'd also helped me swallow some hard truths. And I'd wanted so badly to believe he was going to be the mentor I needed.

Finding the trapdoor was easy enough following their footprints. Doran pulled the door open and peered into the darkness. "Leave this open. Just in case."

Doran went first, and I followed. We were about halfway down when he cleared his throat. "Rylee, I have to tell you something in case this is the last time we speak."

Shit, I hated it when people got maudlin, but if he wanted to talk, I wouldn't stop him. "Okay, what?"

He took a deep breath and let it out slowly. "Those panties you're wearing make me want to bite your ass."

I glared over my shoulder at him, but there was nothing I could do. The Daywalker had a perfect view right up the short skirt. At least I was wearing panties.

"Ass."

"Tease."

I swung a boot at him, and with a quiet laugh he dropped to the floor. Following his lead, I did the same, a puff of dirt swirling up around us. Alex landed next to me in a crouch, sniffing the ground in soft whuffles. Doran had broken my train of thought around Jack, and I suspected he knew it.

Clever boy.

I handed him the flashlight and let him lead so I had both hands on my swords. Down here, the musty scent was far stronger, and Alex sneezed twice. At first, I worried he would alert them to us, but the further in we walked, the more I realized the place was damn well cavernous.

"How far?" Doran asked.

"Twenty feet," I said, keeping my voice low.

Doran glanced back at me. "They're dead to the world, you don't have to be quiet. The only thing that will wake them is when we take Jack's head."

I swallowed hard. "Will it be that simple?"

Doran stopped and turned to me. "Never killed a vampire?"

"No, Faris was the first I'd met, and he never gave me the chance." True and not true. One time I'd been able to kill him was when he flooded me with his power, not because of anything I was on my own.

"Take the head, then pierce the heart. Your swords are edged with silver, are they not?"

"Yes."

"Then that'll do it."

We rounded a small curve in the underground complex and there they were, asleep on two separate beds. Mind you, Berget was in the princess bed, a canopy swooping between the bedposts, bright white sheets curling around her small body.

Jack was on a basic bed, more like an army cot than anything. On the side wall, there was a simple white wooden door.

"Fuck, you want to bet that goes to the castle?" I strode over and yanked it open, looking straight into the hallway where we'd seen Jack and Berget originally.

"I bet she's cheating," Doran said, rapping his knuckles along the edge of the door. "Using the memories of her parents to further herself."

They hadn't been searching for the right door like us; they'd known where they were going, or at least, which continent.

Moving away from the doorway, I looked at Jack. Alex had his head on the Tracker's chest, tears streaming down his furry face.

"Bad Jack. Alex sad." He scrubbed his paw over his face and Jack stirred.

"Alex," I hissed. "Get over here."

"Rylee, quick," Doran said.

But even that was too late. Jack was on his feet without me even blinking.

"Hello, Rylee. Be glad the Empress sleeps, or I would have to kill your friends where they stand." His voice was strong and deep, nothing like the shaking tremor I'd last heard in him.

"How could you, Jack?" I held my swords up, pointing them at his neck and heart. "How could you let her use you?"

His blue eyes, those three tones of blue, swirled. "She didn't give me a choice, and she took my memories of her visits. Until I stood before her, a vampire fully fledged, I had no idea what had happened."

"Doran?" I didn't know who to trust, though I wanted so badly to believe Jack. But that would mean one more person to try and rescue.

"I don't know," the Daywalker said. "I don't think he's lying."

Alex, though, was the one who sealed it for me. "Smells honest, like Jack."

"Jack, if we take you away from her . . ."

Doran was beside me, shaking his head. "Sunlight. We'd be better off to kill her now, get it done with."

This time Jack shook his head. "Rylee, there is only one thing to be done. You won't be able to kill her. I tell you this because I believe there is only one thing that *would* be able to kill her, to finally end her life. She must walk into the sun by her own choice."

"Well, that ain't going to fucking well happen, is it?" I growled, but I wondered if that was just what she'd told him? To make him believe she was unsinkable. It wouldn't surprise me, but then again, she was carrying the blood and powers of two very old, very strong vampires. "And why aren't you cussing up a storm?"

His lips twitched. "The Empress doesn't like bad language, so I'm forbidden from using it."

I couldn't help laughing; it was the most ridiculous thing I'd ever heard. "Seriously?"

He shrugged. "I have no say in my life. Ask Doran, he was her pet too."

"I was far enough away that she let me say whatever I wanted until she remembered I belonged to her and found a use for me." Doran folded his arms over his chest. "Shit, what are we going to do, then?"

Jack smoothed his hands over his head. "She has commanded me to find the Blood. But she has not told me to take the most accurate route. I can slow her down, let you get there, and get Faris on the throne.

If what I understand is true, once the new Emperor has the blood of the old ones in him, she won't stand a chance."

I turned, lips tight, and looked at Doran. "Good plan if Faris hadn't fucked it up."

Jack sucked in a sharp breath. "He's not with you?"

Doran filled him in. "He couldn't hold out. He doesn't have the control to finish the task."

Jack's whole face tightened, as if in pain. "She's waking."

I didn't say goodbye, didn't think of anything but getting to the ladder. Doran shoved me ahead of him, and I shoved Alex, praying Jack could hold her off long enough for us to reach the ladder and the relative safety.

No such luck. Doran's hand on my shoulder disappeared, when we were just steps from the ladder. "Alex, up," I screamed as I turned around and faced the gloom, my flashlight showing Jack holding Doran against his chest.

There was no choice now. I rushed them, and Jack held still, his eyes meeting mine one last time. In slow motion, I leapt into the air, my blades arcing forward.

But Jack jerked away and Doran dropped to the floor before I could contact anything. Doran caught me midair and all but threw me partway up the ladder. "CLIMB!"

Berget's laughter floated from the depths. "Run away, sister. I will see you soon enough. Tell Faris I said hello."

I scrambled through the trapdoor and flopped onto the dusty shop floor beside Alex, who stared into the hole. Doran climbed out and slammed the door shut behind him.

"We shouldn't have survived," he said, holding a hand out to me.

"Yeah, I kinda thought that myself."

Though we didn't run out of the store, it was close. Spooked, my body knew how just *how* close it had come to getting snacked on, even if my brain was trying to tell me everything was fine. Alex, like always, was already moving onto the next adventure.

"Car ride?"

I pointed at the truck and he leapt in, dancing in one spot, or maybe bucking would be a more accurate term. "Seat too hot?"

"Nope, just dancing."

Shaking my head, I let the smile slip across my lips. We had to take the bright spots when we could, even just a werewolf doing his version of the chicken dance.

Again, I let Doran drive. "Do we have time for your pit stop?"

"We have to." His face was closed off, zero emotions to read.

Maybe he'd been more spooked than I thought. So I left him to his own thoughts, and me to mine.

Mine, of course, were dark and less than pleasant. Jack hadn't made the choice to become a vampire, yet I wasn't sure there would be a way to save him. Or if we could even get past him to get to Berget. Shit on a stick. I couldn't reach Liam, but I tried to Track him anyway. Of course, nothing but a big empty hole with all the oceans between us. A low sigh escaped me and I scrubbed a hand over my face.

"I know you said there would be no rest for me, when you Read me. But really, did it mean I would feel like I was wrung out, completely done in, exhausted with every breath I took?" I glanced at Doran, watched as a smile slid over his lips. Ah, so I could still get him to respond.

"Dramatic much?"

"I was trying out my 'Milly.' Did you feel any sympathy at all?"

He snorted. "Sorry, none. She's much better at laying the guilt and begging for sympathy. You just sound irritated."

A few minutes later, we were at his pit stop, which turned out to be a hokey-looking crystal shop on the far edge of town.

"You're kidding, right?" I couldn't help the way my eyes widened. This was supposed to be what, some sort of Shaman's place?

"Sometimes the best defense to the world is showing them who you really are and letting others believe you're fucking crazy." He jumped out, jogged inside, and within two minutes was back in the truck, no bag in hand, nothing I saw brought back with him.

I lifted an eyebrow. "Care to share, fang boy?"

"Not really."

There he went, gone again, deep into himself. I slumped in my seat. Fine by me and I would try to sleep a little. I dozed as he drove, wishing I'd been joking about the fatigue dragging at my limbs.

When we hit the edge of the true desert, Doran slowed the Willy and then stopped. "Do you see that?"

I sat up and squinted as something moved along the horizon.

Something big and sinuous, scales catching the bright, hot sun and reflecting it across the desert.

"Blaz!" I shouted—hell fucking yeah, we had back up! But how had he gotten here so fast?

And why wasn't he answering me?

I stared at the shape humping toward us, the size and velocity of it far bigger than any 'native' fauna I knew. A niggling memory, the smell of snake musk and the fear of my first real battle swam in my head. I'd faced a giant snake before, but how could I have forgotten until now? Of course, if my spotty memory served me at all, the last time I'd faced a snake this size, I'd almost died. Not a good omen.

"Oh, shit."

Doran let out a low whistle. "You can say that again."

From the back of the truck Alex thumped the cab, his words screamed out in a high-pitched cry. "Ohh-hhhhhhhh, shiiiiiiiiiiiit."

From the mouths of babes and werewolves. We were in trouble.

Surprise, surprise.

16

As they drove, Tara filled them in on the details of the firing squad. When Trolls raped humans, which happened more often than anyone liked to believe, the product were children like Tara. Children who were more human in mind-set, more Troll in body. A rough combination even on a good day.

The half-breeds had started their own secret colony, using what little magic they had to blend in with the human world.

"The pure bloods, they've never paid us any heed, but then they started coming around. Acting like they were worried about us. My own sire, he showed up to check on me." She took a slow breath and then went on. "It was all a ruse. They were working with Ingers to bring in targets. They rounded us up, said if we helped them, they would help protect us. From others. Most supernaturals kill us on site."

Liam met her eyes in the mirror. "Seems rather hypocritical."

Tara dropped her eyes. "Survival of the fittest. We are weak like humans, yet look like a supernatural. Only a very few have any sort of magic, usually those gotten by a Lighteater."

Pamela spoke up. "How many of you are there?"

"A few hundred."

Milly sucked in a sharp breath. "How could so many go unseen for so long?"

Tara met Liam's eyes again. "People see what they want to see, not what is truly there. You understand, don't you?"

He of all people did.

They were almost at their destination. A warehouse situated in the industrial part of town. About what he expected of a supposed 'secret' hideout.

"I'll subdue Ingers. Milly, Tara, take out anything that moves. Pamela, you make sure no one slips out."

They drove to the warehouse's main door and it slid open to let them in. Milly let out a gasp.

"Bad, this is very, very bad, Liam. You have to trust me on this."

People moved in and surrounded the vehicle. Liam threw the gear into reverse and hit the gas. But the sedan didn't move.

Words spilled out of Milly. "Liam, I can get us out of this, but you have to go along with me. Do you understand? You have to trust me."

Fuck it all, the last thing he wanted was to trust her. "Black Coven?"

"Yes."

No choice, no fucking choice.

"Pamela, follow her lead. Tara, the same." The women nodded and then the doors were yanked open.

Milly stepped out, her demeanor immediately that of one who was used to being in charge.

"Sven, fancy seeing you here, Liam, come, my pet."

Ah, shit. His wolf curled up and he fought not to shift. Aching all over, he slid out of the car and stood, moving to her side.

Biting his tongue, he managed to keep it together. Milly waved her hand. "This is Pamela, my young protégé, and her companion, Tara."

"Milly." An average-looking man strode to her and held out his hands. "I knew you would see the light after we destroyed Terese's coven. Where were you? We could have used your help."

The tension in the air rose and Liam moved closer to Milly, looming over Sven. The man went very still, looking up into Liam's eyes. All Liam saw was darkness around the man, like his very self was made of death and chaos.

Black Coven or not, the man was evil.

Milly waved her hand at Sven, very nearly smacking him in the face. The fury rolled off her, and Liam had no doubt if she had her abilities, she'd go on a rampage.

"I was out of the country, Sven. I told you before I left."

"True, but one likes to be sure the story told and the story now given are one and the same."

She stiffened. "Do not push me, Sven."

"Or what?" His voice was low and the challenge obvious. Not good, this was not good when she couldn't even—

"I won't even bother, I'll let my apprentice wrap you up," Milly said, beckoning Pamela forward.

Pamela tipped her head toward Milly. "Of course, you have but to ask."

Sven threw his head back, laughing like it was the best joke of the day. "Please."

"As you wish," Pamela said, a wicked grin slipping across her face. She barely moved her hand and Sven went flying, spinning in the air and then sticking face first to the far wall.

The room quieted and Milly put a hand on Pamela's shoulder. "Leave him there, love. He needs to remember who is the strongest here, and it surely is not him."

Liam did a quick count. Including Sven, there were ten witches. In that moment, the smell overpowered him, dropping him to his knees.

Pamela reached out and put her hands on his shoulders, whispering softly to him. "Liam, hang on. You can do this, you are strong."

He focused on her voice, and tried to hang onto thoughts of Rylee. Being out of control was not a luxury he could afford.

"Nice pet, Milly. Looks like you'll need to collar him to show him some true manners."

The words seared through the last shreds of his control and he let out a roar, shifting at lighting speed. The witch who'd spoken was in his jaws, her neck snapped before anyone took a breath.

Kill them all.

Chaos erupted around them. Milly was using the crossbow, Tara picked up his guns, and of course, Pamela was laying waste, her power ripping through the warehouse like a forest fire.

But it was not enough; these were not inexperienced witches or Druids who didn't like to fight.

Liam leapt toward another witch, a male. The spell that hit him rippled across his fur, pain flickering along his nerve endings. But the pain was gone almost as fast as it started and another neck was in his mouth, blood searing his tongue.

"Come on then, Guardian, let's see what you have." He turned to see a young man, eyes bright with the fever of battle, sword in hand.

This young pup seeks your life and knows how to end it.

Yes, Liam saw that. He circled the younger man, waiting for his opening. With the battle raging around them, there was not much time. What he didn't expect was to be pinned down.

Another witch sidled up to the first, her magic swirling around his four legs, binding him tight. She curled a hand around the sword handle.

"Take his front right. We will piece him out and see if that slows these interlopers."

He was unceremoniously flipped onto his side, his right leg held up as if in sacrifice. He let out a howl, long and rising in power. Pamela would hear him; she would come to his aid.

But it was not Pamela who answered his call.

It was Milly.

A crossbow bolt took the man in chest and he crumpled to the floor, his eyes rolling up in his head. "Let him go, Veronica," Milly challenged.

Veronica laughed. "Why don't you make me? Ah, yes, so it seems the great one has been brought low. How lovely."

Liam could just see Milly, see her crumple to the floor, her face twisting in pain. Veronica stalked past him to stand over her.

"I always hated you, did you know that? Did you know how long I have dreamed of this moment?"

Milly struggled to breathe, her words shocking him. "Let them go. Take me, and then let them go. You don't need them."

Veronica shrugged. "It is not up to me, *pet*."

Milly's eyes widened and a slow smile slid over her lips. Her eyes flicked to Liam's but he couldn't read her well. If he didn't know better he'd have said she was happy. But that didn't fit.

Slowly, she sat up, a fierce light in her green eyes making her seem, almost protective. Again, that seemed off to him, yet there was no other word to describe Milly in that moment. She was trying to protect him and Pamela at the cost of her own skin. "No, you're right, Veronica," Milly said, "it isn't up to you. It's up to me."

She flung her hand at Veronica who sailed backward, into the wall with a solid crack, her body sliding down and crumpling onto the concrete. Freed, Liam scrambled to his feet.

Pamela was backed into a corner, squared off against four witches, sweat pouring off her face. He didn't think, just sprinted toward them, leaping at the one on the left side, taking down the Black Coven member without a single whimper.

Milly dispatched two, and before Pamela could take the life of the last, Liam crushed the black witch's neck with a single bite.

The teenager glared at him. "I had it, Liam."

He snorted and shook his head. Milly stood beside him, breathing hard. "That was close. Where's Tara?"

A groan whispered, "here."

They found her under the body of one of the Black Coven members. She shot him, but not lethally and it looked like he retaliated. Milly crouched beside her, and laid a hand to her head. "Easy, it'll be okay."

Tara stiffened, let out a low moan, her body twitching like crazy. Slowly, her twitching eased, and then she blinked at them, her eyes free of pain. "You healed me. I didn't know such a thing was possible. Thank you." Tears glimmered in her eyes and he had no doubt she thought of her children.

Milly stood and brushed her hands on her skirt. "Liam and Pamela, are you okay?"

He bobbed his head. Fuck, he owed his life to her. How the hell could he go on hating her when she'd been ready to sacrifice not only herself, but her child? Maybe he wouldn't hate her as he had, but that didn't mean he was suddenly on the Milly train.

Pamela reached out and touched Milly's hand. "You have your magic back. So you know we're all family now. That's what Giselle said."

"I suppose I do." Milly looked at Liam as she spoke, then toward the interior of the building. "Do you think Ingers is still here?"

Only one way to find out. With a toss of his head, they headed out on a hunt together. The weirdest pack around, but one he knew without a doubt he could trust with his life.

Gods be damned, even Milly.

"Doran." I shifted in my seat. "I don't think we can outrun this."

"Are you sure about that?"

My head snapped around and I was shocked to see a grin on his face. He winked. "I never knew just how much trouble you managed to find, Rylee. Let me say this now, if I never meet another Tracker, it will be too fucking soon."

A giant snake was in front of us, with most likely our death on its mind, and I burst out laughing.

"Doran, I don't think you will ever have the pleasure of meeting another Tracker. Besides Jack, that is."

The snake stopped moving about four hundred yards in front of us. Still, too close for any sort of comfort.

"Let me guess." Doran squeezed the steering wheel and pushed himself back in his seat. "No plan."

"No plan, I don't have a fucking clue."

Really, the only upside I saw was the snake hadn't moved any closer, just seemed to be watching. Doran's eyes didn't leave the creature. "I'd bet there is a territory she's in, that she protects, that's how it was with Seps. I'd also lay a bet she is one of the 'challenges' the supplicants have to face."

Seps. Someone else had said that name and suddenly it rang in my ears, an entire memory cascading over me. Scales and the old mine shaft, Milly and Giselle. My head throbbed with the suddenness of the images assaulting me. Was this part of what Milly erased from my mind all those years ago? Fuck me.

I cleared my throat. "Seps wasn't bad, she could be reasoned with to a degree, if I remember right."

"Yes, did you meet her?"

Leaning forward, I put my head on the dash. "I was there when she died. I think. Giselle killed her."

He sucked in a sharp breath. "Well, that explains her sudden disappearance. I'd wondered."

"Listen, that doesn't matter now. Obviously, there is more than one giant fucking snake. Who are we dealing with here?" I lifted my head and stared at the coiled body.

Doran frowned. "I know Seps had sisters. Could be one of them."

The snake's scales glinted red and orange, a flash of gold. Beautiful and deadly, like so much in our world.

I Tracked the Blood, and the fuckers were, of course, directly on the other side of her. "Seps wasn't a Guardian, not like Eagle or Bear. So this one should be able to be killed if we have to."

Doran laughed. "You want to try and kill that on our own? Even you can't be that ballsy."

"I have my days," I muttered. "Let's see if we can get around her. We'll go north, staying close to the edge of her territory. If she follows, we have our answer."

Doran nodded and backed the truck and headed north. The massive snake uncoiled and slithered parallel to us. I ground my teeth in frustration. Tonight was the night of the equinox; we had to be at ground zero to stop Berget or it wouldn't matter if Orion was alive or not, if the demons wanted to take over.

There was no way the power in Berget would allow any of us to live, not once she didn't need us.

"Enough of this, head straight for her, slow down when you're about fifty feet away." I shimmied out the window, my ass on the edge of the window ledge.

"You sure?"

"Nope."

"Excellent, I was worried you suddenly had a plan."

Laughing, I worked my way out the window and clamored to the top of the cab. I had to believe we could do this.

Alex let out a barking laugh and thumped the roof, claws scratching the paint.

"Ryleeeeeeee!"

I grinned down at him. "Ready to rumble with a big snake?"

He gave me 'thumbs up' with one claw. "You bet-cha."

I slid down to the hood of the truck and stood up, legs braced for any bounces, swords drawn at my sides. We drew close and Doran slowed the truck to a stop. The giant serpent raised herself into a cobra-like position, without the flare of a hood. It didn't take a fucking genius to realize with the length of her body, she could probably strike me from where she was.

Liam's voice seemed to whisper in my ear. *Keep it simple.*

"We need to pass."

She swayed where she was, tongue flicking out and tasting the air. "Tracker. You come for the Blood, but you bring no supplicant for the throne. You may not pass. Not until the equinox has come and gone."

Keep it simple. Right.

Doran leaned out of the truck and hollered, "She has a supplicant."

I frowned at him, totally confused. "What the hell are you talking about? Faris isn't in the running anymore." Assuming he would show up as he said he would. And that he would actually be able to find us via Alex's blood.

The snake seemed as confused as me. "You are not a proper vampire, Daywalker. No matter the size of your fangs."

He looked up at me and shrugged. "I tried."

Enough of this talking shit.

"We *are* going to pass you. Either you are going to let us, or I'm going to make myself a brilliant new jacket and boots."

"I don't think that was a good idea," Doran said, his voice floating up to me.

The snake hissed at me, once before answering. "You may hold the fate of the world in your hands, Tracker. But I will not be threatened."

"Whoopty fucking do da." I flicked one sword tip up and pointed it at her.

Her tail lashed out, slamming onto the ground with a force that rippled out like a bag of dynamite. And yes, I know what that feels like from experience.

I went to one knee, grateful the material of the dress was stretchy enough to accommodate rather than split down the middle. There were days that even small mercies had to be acknowledged. This was one of them.

The tremor passed and I stood. "That's all you've got, you big—"

"Rylee." Doran pointed. "Look over there."

Squinting, I tried to see what it was he pointed out, somewhere to the left of the truck. "What?"

"The ground is moving."

I blinked several times, and then it clicked. "Oh fuck." Snakes, hordes and hordes of snakes headed our way, and in Australia, I was betting they were all venomous. I might be Immune to their bites, but Alex and Doran weren't, and there were enough of the slithering masses to kill them both with leftover venom.

I banged on the roof as I slid off and into the truck bed. "Go, get us out of here." Son of a fucking ass monkey. We had to get past her, time was ticking and sunset was only a few hours away at best.

Doran and Alex would be killed by the sheer amount of venom.

Berget had to be stopped.

I was the only one who could get away with being bit.

Doran had the truck turned around in a split second and took off. And I did the only thing I could.

I jumped from the back of the truck and hit the ground rolling, sprinting toward the big-ass snake.

What I didn't expect was Alex to jump with me. I slowed for half a heart beat. "Ah, fuck! Alex, run!"

He bolted ahead of me, and the snakes on the ground shifted their paths, as if to intercept us. I didn't dare put my swords away. A large, black snake about four inches around launched at me. A back swing took its head, but it was so close the bloody stump sprayed my legs.

"Faster, you have to go faster, Alex!"

"Yuppy doody!" He cranked on the speed, claws digging into the hard ground for traction, easily leaving me in the dust. Which was what I wanted. Only thing was, it meant he was almost at the big girl.

Another snake struck at me and I cut it in half. The first bite hit me on the back of my thigh, just above my knee. Then another, and another, the bite marks literally coming one after another all up and down my legs. I cut the snakes off as I ran. Felt the poison flow though my blood, but just as quickly, swallowed up in my Immunity.

"Fucking dumb-ass snakes. I'm a fucking bitch of an Immune!" Not like everyone else in the supernatural world didn't know it already. And maybe the big girl would call them off seeing there was very little they could do.

Or maybe they'd just change tactics.

I was struck again, this time in my lower back, right over the scar of a Daywalker's bite.

Pain, searing and dark ripped up my spine, but it wasn't the poison. Nope, just the feel of a wicked sharp set of fangs clamping down on me.

Alex skidded to a stop. "Alex, help!"

"NO! Get away, Alex!" I didn't see him, but he didn't come to my aide. So maybe he'd listened.

The small snakes hissed and writhed around me, but they stopped striking. I ripped the one off my back, threw it on the ground, and sliced its head off. Blood ran down my legs, and flies and bugs swarmed around me.

That, however, was not my largest problem.

A shadow shifted over me, blocking out the sun.

"Tracker, you are of the Blood of the Lost?"

I blinked up into the calculating eyes of a snake easily four feet across with fangs big enough to kill me simply based on size, never mind venom.

"I am."

"Then for a moment we will speak. If I like what you say, I will let you and the wolf pass."

Well, shit, this was unexpected.

She lowered her head, her tongue flicking out and tickling along the side of my face. "You would face danger without your friends, to save them?"

"Yes." A twinge of pain trickled through my guts. Fuck, maybe my Immunity didn't want to let me get through this one unscathed.

"And do you truly understand the prophecies, what they ask of you?"

I put a sword tip into the ground and leaned on the handle. "To face the demon, save the world, all that shit."

Her tail flicked forward, snapping me in the bare skin of my thigh. "Insolent."

"I've been told that a time or two."

Her tongue flicked out several times. I rubbed my thigh. To me, this was looking like a standoff that would result in a fight.

"My name is Tespa. And you, young Tracker, have no inkling of what comes for you in the future."

I snorted. "You going to try and Read me?"

"I don't need to. I understand the prophecies. And for that reason alone, I will let you pass. You will need all the help you can get." She shifted her body, all her coils in one smooth rolling motion to the side.

"Why, you had to know I was the one the prophecies spoke of when I showed up. Why would you do this?"

If snakes could smile, this one did. "You are not the only one who must challenge me. There is another who must prove their worth. You have shown to me that you do what your heart demands, not what others demand. And now, one more must face the same challenge."

"Then I wish that person better luck than me." Another twinge ran along my belly and up through my lower back. If I didn't hate snakes before, I fucking well did now. I fought back a moan that started low in my throat, every bite on my legs burning and aching as I moved.

One step, and then another and another. Neither she nor her snakes got in our way.

Alex waved at me from about thirty feet away, his tongue lolling out, a big paw waving at me. "Alex listens."

As I walked, the burning faded and the pain in my lower back eased. "Good job, buddy. You ready to run?"

He yipped at me, high-pitched and excited. Sliding my two swords into their sheaths, I caught up to him and ran a hand over his head. Looking back, I saw Tespa watching us, her collection of snakes coiling about her huge body.

Tracking the Blood, I broke into a jog and headed toward them. The first vampires ever made.

The battleground where I'd face Berget and Jack. My heart squeezed as I realized in my hurry, I'd left behind the opal, the one thing that might give Berget a chance.

I was a fucking idiot, and she would pay the price for my haste, for my reckless behavior. The arid desert dried my tears before they slid down my face. There was nothing for it now; I'd made the choice, I would have to live with it.

And so would Berget.

The only thing I hoped was something would intervene, that maybe, just maybe the gods would favor me once.

If I was lucky, I'd be able to save at least Jack.

If I wasn't, I'd be lucky to get me and Alex out alive without any new puncture marks, our blood still singing through our own veins and not someone else's.

What a freaking awesome day.

17

The sun kissed the horizon goodnight as we stepped into the long shadow of Ayers Rock. Hanging onto the threads of the Blood filled me with a sense of foreboding now that we were so close. Somewhere within the rock, those fanged fuckers were silently held. The energy of their lives gave off a low vibration, one that made my bones ache as if with a deep cold.

I put my hands on my hips and took a long deep breath. "It can never damn well be easy, can it?"

Alex mimicked me, wobbling to his back legs, not something he often did. "Nope."

Ayers Rock was big. As in *block out the sun* big. Even if night hadn't been falling, we'd be standing in shadow.

Nothing but to see where the hell the Blood was hidden.

Searching the rock was something akin to searching holy ground, or at least, that's what it felt like to me. The age of the place weighed on me, the pulse of the past seeping into my pores. Moving close enough to touch the rock, I put my hand on black lines. I traced a design of a large snake surrounded by many, many squiggly marks. Tespa and her minions.

Perhaps here the people saw more clearly than at home, maybe the supernatural wasn't so hidden from them. Of course, no one in their right mind would believe a tale of a giant snake. Not in our day and age.

Alex sniffed at the rock. "Vampires."

I wanted to let out a groan. Surely Jack and Berget weren't here already, were they? Or was Alex just picking up on the Blood? I tested that theory, but Jack and Berget still felt distant, though they were closer than before. I refocused on the Blood.

Locking onto the threads, I jogged along the length of the rock, trying to find a way into where we needed to go. "Alex, can you smell vampires still? Old ones?"

He put his nose to the ground, sniffing in and out, puffs of red dust blowing up around his face. "Yup. Oldy old."

Perfect. Using his nose and my Tracking, we worked around the rock until the stars were our only light source. Dust stuck to my bare skin, the sheen of sweat acting like sticky glue of the worst kind. And the bugs, fuck me, were everywhere, sticking to me alongside the sweat and dirt, their flimsy wings tickling the shit out of me. I swiped a hand down one arm, came away with a mixture of muddy bugs.

"Fucking awesome."

Alex snickered, then snapped at a large bug, catching it and then spitting it out, gagging. "Shitty bugs." He took a step then froze, one ear flicking back. "Truck."

I spun to stare into the darkened landscape. "You sure?" I couldn't see or hear anything, no headlights, no rumble of an engine.

Alex nodded. "Truck." Then he yelped and scrabbled away from the rock. I dropped to one knee, yanking out my swords, pointing them at the figure who'd snuck up on us.

Faris leaned against Ayers Rock, still all in black. "I told you I could find you through the wolf's blood, why again are you surprised?"

I blew out a breath, hesitating for a moment. "You're actually going to help?"

"Are you actually going to kill the Child Empress?"

Ah, here we go. I nodded as I slid one of my swords into my back sheath, while I reminded myself I was not lying. I just wasn't going about Faris's plan his way. "Of course. Consider the Child Empress dead and gone from your life. IF we can slow her down first, which requires Doran. Can you get him?"

Faris stepped toward me and I saw the difference in him. The slightest glow of his blue eyes, the pink in his cheeks, the way he moved like water. He'd obviously fed, and fed well. "He's on his way. Though I do not think you will be pleased with the shape he is in. No, not pleased at all."

Despite the lingering heat of the day, ice seemed to travel down my spine. "No games, I said no fucking games. What do you mean?"

Faris seemed to fight with himself before spitting it out. "The snake, she gave him a fair choice. Either take her venom and pass, or stay behind."

"How the fuck do you know that?" I glared at him, wondering if he'd somehow set up Doran. It wouldn't surprise me. Nothing Faris did at this point would.

A tight smile slipped across his lips. "I watched from a distance, saw what happened, and then jumped the Veil to where I sensed Alex. I have no need to face the overly large reptile."

Fear tightened my throat but I forced the words out. "Doran, he took the venom, didn't he?"

The vampire gave me a grim smile. "He did."

"Then I'll give him blood. It worked with the spider guardian."

"This has been too long, the venom will be through his whole system by now; ah, here he is."

Finally, the sound of a truck reached my ears, the soft flicker of headlights. The truck stopped about twenty feet away, the headlights on us. "Faris, help me." I ran to the truck. Doran was the only one who knew how to lay in the opal, the spell that would bind it to her. Even if he wasn't my friend, I couldn't let him die, not today.

Surprising the hell out of me, the vampire did as I asked and ran ahead of me, pulling Doran out of the truck. In the headlights, everything was illuminated, and not kindly.

Doran was limp in the vampire's arms, his body convulsing, blood trickling from his ears. His white shirt was stained red over his heart. Tespa had stabbed him in the heart with her fang?

"He's still breathing, but not for long. There is nothing we can do for him." Faris laid Doran on the ground in front of the truck and I knelt beside the Daywalker.

"Doran, listen to me. You know there is a way to save you, don't you? That's why you let her do this, isn't it?"

Please let me be right about this.

"Let him have peace in his final moments, Tracker," Faris snarled, his hand clamping on my shoulder. "Give him that much, at least."

I didn't have to say anything; Alex did it for me, as he shoved the vampire backward with a big paw. "Fuck off, Faris."

Doran let out a low moan. "The bag. Do it."

There could be no more hesitation. He'd known what the choice was; he'd known there would be no turning back. "Alex, get the bag out of the truck!"

"What are you doing?" Faris drew close as Alex dropped the bag in front of me. I yanked it open and poured out the contents, my brain scrambling with the recipe. Please, gods, let me get it right. I mixed the ingredients, used the mortar and pestle. "Doran, the moon dust."

He tapped his front pocket and I slid my hand in, feeling a thin paper bag. Faris let out a long, low hiss. Of course he would know, or at least recognize this recipe. He'd been planning on using it on a Daywalker himself. Which was how I'd gotten my hands on it.

"You planned this all along, you were going to turn him and let him take the throne instead of me."

"Give the vampire a prize," I snapped, ignoring him, pouring the dust into the pestle, the air snapping with sudden ozone. Above us, clouds rolled in, blocking the stars. Shit, this was going to get ugly.

"Yes, I have the recipe that will turn a Daywalker into a vampire." I stared at Doran, pale and unmoving on the ground. "Who better to lead the vampires than one who is powerful both in mind and magic—and has no desire to lead?"

Faris's jaw dropped and then he slowly closed his mouth. "Mother of the gods, it might work. Technically, he has not drunk any blood the entire time he is a vampire. Yours does not count as it is what will *make* him a vampire. That should be good enough to meet the requirements. Stunningly simple and . . . brilliant."

Shocked he would compliment me, I ducked my head and focused on the ingredients going into the shallow bowl.

"He could drain you completely." Faris dropped to a knee beside me, a look of concern etched around his eyes, softening them. Concern, for me.

I didn't take my eyes from him. "I trust him with my life."

"But I don't. I won't let him live to lose you. None of us will survive if you die this night, Tracker. You understand that, don't you?"

Unfortunately, I did. All too clearly, I knew what was in the balance. But if I was willing to let my friends and loved ones die without fighting for them, what the hell was I fighting for in the first place?

"Believe, Faris." I pulled my sword free and laid the blade gently against my forearm, over the scar where I'd given Doran my blood the first time we'd met. What seemed like eons ago.

My skin split and I held my arm over the pestle. There were no words, no incantations, just the potion, and the timing.

His heart had to stop beating, his life gone, but only for a split second. Any sooner this would fail, any later, same fucking result. I slowed my breathing and put two fingers to Doran's throat, felt the slowing throb of his heart. In my other hand, I held the small pestle poised over his lips. Faris moved around me, ripped away a thin strip of his shirt and then wrapped my dripping arm with it.

"It will not be your arm he pulls from, but your neck."

"I know." And I did. I Tracked Berget and Jack, felt them closing in on us, a few miles at best. But they still had to get past Tespa.

Time, I had to believe we had enough time.

Under my two fingers, Doran's heart beat once. Twice. Nothing.

I didn't hesitate. With a single swift motion, I poured the concoction down his throat. "Come on, Doran. Don't give up. Not yet."

Alex sat across from me, his lower lip stuck out. "Doran's gone."

I swallowed hard. Had it been too soon? Fuck me, how were we going to know? I looked at Faris in time to see his eyes widen, just as a set of fangs drove hard into my neck, bowling me over.

Dragging me down into memories that were anything but my own.

"Milly, are you *sure* those weren't all the coven members?" He strode beside the witch as they searched the warehouse for Ingers.

"Positive. They've been actively recruiting for years, stealing children, and even taking adults fully trained." Her skirts rustled as she did her best to keep up to him.

"How the hell could they take adults?"

Pamela moved up beside them. "I didn't think there were that many bad people in the world. How could they all be black witches to start with?"

Milly lifted a hand, stopping them, her head cocked to one side. "Do you feel that, Pamela?"

The young witch went still, but Liam could tell what they were tapping into. Someone was throwing around a lot of magic, a lot of power, and they were close. The hairs along his arms stood at attention. That was more power than even Milly and Pamela had combined. This was not good.

"Yes," Pamela whispered, her eyes widening, "I feel it. That is a great deal of magic."

"That," Milly said, "is the rest of the coven. They no doubt know we are coming. There are too many for us to take. We must leave." She turned to seemingly do just that.

Tara moved in front of Milly, stopping her. "I will not leave. They killed my children, as if they were ants to be crushed under their heels. I will make them pay for this."

"Be my guest." Milly made a sweeping gesture. "But you will not get three feet into their presence before they do the very same to you. Though, they have ways of controlling people, perhaps they will use you as a spy and a puppet against the rest of your people. Would that be preferable to death?"

Tara's face lost color, and her breathing quickened. "So we run away?"

"We plan." Liam put a hand on her shoulder, doing his best to be gentle. "Too many witches, you saw what happened with those we dealt with. It was far too close for comfort." The feel of a blade against his leg was still rather fresh in his mind. He didn't discount there were times and places to be smart and back away. This was one.

Pamela sagged with relief. "I didn't really want to fight them."

"We should hurry," Milly said, her gaze flicking around the room. "They will notice soon enough we aren't drawing closer and they will come for us."

Liam nodded and the four of them started to jog. A dark premonition slid over his skin and he felt Giselle's words as if they hovered over him.

"Pamela, no matter what happens, you get the hell out of here. Understand? Take Tara and go to Giselle's, wait for Rylee."

Her blue eyes darted to his. "Liam—"

"Don't argue, just do it," he growled, the wolf in him wanting nothing more than to protect this pup. To keep one of his own safe.

The premonition grew as they approached the exit. He couldn't stand it any longer. "Stop." The three women stilled and he shook his head, hearing the sound of feet scuffling in the snow outside. They were trapped. "Milly, get them out of here. Jump them, now."

Her green eyes widened for a split second and then she nodded, taking both Pamela's and Tara's hands.

The Veil opened and on the other side he saw the inside of Giselle's living room. They stepped through as the front wall of the building exploded in shrapnel. He let the change take him, let the wolf have his head for the first time. In that moment, he needed the instincts of a survivor, not the instincts of an agent used to commanding others.

Spinning on his haunches, he galloped deeper into the warehouse, the air around him charged with electricity and magic.

This was going to get ugly, and there was no way to avoid it.

His only regret was not being able to see Rylee one last time. To tell her—

The ground in front of him erupted, concrete flying in every direction, shards driving into him. A chunk the size of his head smashed into his front right leg, snapping the bone. With a snarl, he went down, felt the weight of magic curling around him.

Pinning him to the floor.

Trapping him.

He closed his eyes and waited, knowing there was nothing he could do.

Not this time.

18

I don't know what I expected from Doran's memories, maybe some enslavement, some pain. In a way, those would have been normal for a supernatural.

What I got was a past so riddled with overwhelming despair and horror it drove my own fears out of my head.

His whole life flickered in front of me.

Being snatched from his family's arms when he was barely out of his teens, trapped by his maker for a hundred years in a life of slavery and debauchery that made my blood run cold. His escape, scrounging and scavenging to survive, the realization of being a Shaman, the things he Read in others, the unimaginable sorrow of knowing those he loved were dying, or would soon be dead.

Loss, so much loss.

And yet through it all, he'd hung onto a belief that he was meant for better, and all he'd suffered had a reason behind it. That he wasn't done yet. There would be a love great enough to save him.

Son of a bitch, under all that had happened to him, under all the loss and horror he'd suffered, he'd never really been broken, because he never allowed himself to give up. His heart would never let him grow dark in disbelief and cynicism. How long had he hidden this side of him from others, from all those around him? Apparently long enough that no one knew who he really was, and the strength of his heart and soul.

In that moment, and that heartbeat, I knew I'd made the right decision; Doran would lead the vampires better than Berget or Faris.

From a distance, I heard shouting, and the howl of a wolf. Hands gripped me and I knew I was getting close to having too much blood taken.

I lifted a hand and touched the side of Doran's face. "I believe in you."

Just like that, his mouth left my neck and I opened my eyes, the spell broken. He cradled me with one arm; the other held Faris around the neck. Slowly, he released Faris, and the vampire slumped to his knees.

Faris rubbed his throat. "Rylee, you crazy Tracker. He's stronger than me. How did you know?"

I smiled at Doran, knowing I could trust him. "I didn't."

Doran's lips twitched and the differences in him were there. Subtle and yet profound. He'd always been good looking, but now he was downright gorgeous, the angles and planes of his face, the deep green color of his eyes drew me in . . . I looked away. No need to get bespelled this close to the finish line.

"I thought you trusted me," he said, helping me to my feet.

I held onto his arm, my strength slowly returning. "I do. But you don't know your own strength yet."

Faris grunted. "Though you two might like to continue this lovely conversation, we have a Child Empress to kill."

Tracking Berget, she was a hell of a lot closer than she'd been when we'd found Doran. Tracking the Blood next, I breathed a sigh of relief. Berget's threads and the Blood weren't overlapping. It seemed perhaps Jack was having the same difficulty I was.

Finding the Blood wasn't the issue. We both pin-pointed them. But getting to the Blood was a whole different ball of wax.

"Come on, this isn't finished yet." I let go of Doran, and the world swayed. I grabbed for Alex, who put himself under my hand.

"Alex gots Rylee." He blinked up at me and I gripped the ruff in his neck tighter.

The Blood was close, so damn close.

The two vampires flanked me, exchanging glances over my head that I chose to ignore. I knew I was wobbly, my feet catching on every rock and dip in the ground, my breathing shallow. This was the price to giving my blood for Doran's transformation.

The curve in the rock was subtle and as we rounded it, a series of caves were revealed. Shit on toast, it was going to be like a fucking labyrinth.

"Alex, what do you smell?"

"Rylee, the Blood wouldn't have been walking around here." Faris so kindly pointed out.

"I fucking well know that," I snapped, my weakness making me more irritable than usual. That didn't mean I was going to apologize, or explain. Alex had a nose like no other.

He lifted his head and pointed with a single claw. "Alex smells Jack, and Al."

Bingo. "Wait, Al? You smell Al, too?" What was the Shaman we'd met on the far coast doing here?

Alex nodded and gave me a grin. "Al and friends."

Shit, we did not need cannon fodder at this little shindig. But it looked like we didn't have a say in the matter if they were already here.

Doran moved closer to me, and Faris stepped away, spinning in a slow circle. "I cannot sense them."

I snorted. "Always trust the wolf's nose, dumb ass."

Alex and I led, and at each cavern I felt the pull of the Blood. Either they were in every cavern, which wasn't possible, or they were so deep in the rock, every cavern felt like the right one. My gut instinct was the latter and less easy of the two.

In my mind, that made the solution simple. Look for the cavern that felt furthest from the Blood and head in. I could only hope I was right. If I was wrong, we were in for a long night.

The feel of Berget's thread getting closer forced my feet to move faster.

But not fast enough.

We stood in the front of the last cavern, the one that did indeed feel the furthest from the Blood, when they hit us. And I mean hit.

Jack slammed into Faris, and Berget tackled me to the ground, her fangs extended. I'd love to say things slowed down, that I was able to get my swords free, but that is so far from the truth, it's scary.

She was on me, her teeth inches from the bite marks Doran left when she froze. "Who has been feeding from you, Tracker?"

And then she was flung off. "That would be me." Doran stood over me, power all but rumbling off him.

She snarled and leapt at him. "Daywalker, you are no match for me!"

Ah, she couldn't tell yet. I pushed to my feet, wobbled, and Alex caught me. I used him for balance as I did my best to follow what was going on. Jack was giving Faris a serious run for his money, the two of them exchanging blow for blow, sharp as lightning that suddenly broke above us. As if that wasn't enough, the skies opened and the rain fell; the densest downpour I'd ever experienced in my life.

I pulled out a sword, knew I could only handle one at a time. This was what I got for not thinking things through, though it wouldn't have changed my mind when it came to saving Doran. With the blood loss, I was weaker than I should have been going into a fight.

Faris threw Jack to the ground and held him, immobilizing him. "Rylee, he is no longer your friend."

"Just hold him. We end her, and he's free."

The look Faris gave me said it all. I was a fool in his eyes, but he would do as I asked. Small mercies.

The rain hammered around us and I sloshed forward to where Doran and Berget grappled. I couldn't let her kill him, anymore than I could let him kill her. She was on top, one hand over his heart, the other wrapped around his throat.

But I knew what would draw her attention. "Berget, I found the Blood. I know exactly where they are."

Her head snapped toward me and it was all the distraction Doran needed. He flipped her over and pinned her hands. All that power from her adoptive parents, where had it gone?

"She's weak," Doran said. "No blood for a lot of days. This is our only chance."

Faris grunted. "Kill her quickly."

Doran made eye contact with me. "The opal is under my shirt."

"Opal, what the fuck are you talking about? Kill her."

We ignored Faris, and I knew he wouldn't let Jack go, which meant he was conveniently out of the way with his hands rather full.

I reached his side and slid a hand into Doran's shirt, the warmth of the opal drawing my fingers to it. "Anything I need to say?"

"No. But Faris is right, make it quick." The strain in his face and voice were obvious.

Much as it might seem that putting the opal under the skin of her chest would be best, I doubted there was enough skin for the size of the opal. "This won't hurt a bit," I said as I slid my sword across her belly, in the general vicinity of her appendix, through skin and muscle.

She bucked and writhed, her blood making her slippery. Worse, the skin began to knit as she screamed obscenities in several languages at us.

I dropped to my knees and grabbed the edge of the wound, holding it open as I slid the opal into the opening. I let go and the wound sealed in a matter of seconds.

Doran let go and grabbed me, yanking us away from her. But she didn't move, just laid there, the rain pelting her face, the bare twitch of her muscles the only thing giving away that she lived yet.

"Come on," I whispered, my heart beating wildly. I had to believe, had to. She would pull through this.

Her body stilled, and a whoosh of air slipped out of her. I grabbed Doran's arm. "Doran, what's happening?"

"I don't know. It will either work or it won't."

"Kill her!" Faris screamed again, his voice bouncing off the rock.

Berget trembled and then her back bowed, a scream ripping out of her. Heels and head were all that touched the ground as she continued to scream, her arms straight out to the side.

I dug my fingers into Doran's arm.

Please, please let her come back. Let me have her for a little while.

Her screamed faded, like the sound of an engine slowing, sputtering, and then dying. With the loss of sound, her body slumped with a splash into the puddle below her.

Alex pressed against me, lifting his nose to the air. "Smells different."

"You are breaking your oath, Tracker," Faris screamed. I'd had more than enough of his shit. Fury and grief merged and I screamed back.

"No. I'm not. You said to kill the Child Empress."

His eyes blazed with fury. "Then kill her."

Berget sat up, a hand going to her side, her clear blue eyes wide as they met mine. Her hands fluttered in front of her face, then dropped to her side.

Fuck, was she going to rip out the opal?

Blinking several times, she put a hand to her throat. "She did kill the Child Empress. Rylee, I knew you'd come for me." Tears streaked her face alongside the rain and she stumbled to her feet, ran to me.

Was this really happening, had it worked? I caught her in my arms and we dropped to my knees. She sobbed into my shoulder, her arms tight around my middle. "I knew it. I knew you would save me."

I didn't try to stop the tears, just held onto her, Berget. Finally, after everything we'd been through. After all the years. I smoothed her hair and held her. My belief validated.

Love won this round.

A hand struck out, driving a wedge between Berget and me.

"What the fuck?" I snapped as I rolled to my feet. Faris stood between us, crouched and ready to leap.

"It is a ruse, Tracker. I have seen this so-called soft side of Berget before. She lulls you in, so you will not kill her this day, only to end your life when you least expect it."

Berget sat on the ground, looking up at him. "Faris, I mean none of you any harm. And I will prove it." She swept her hair back offering up her pale neck. "Take my blood, see the truth of what has happened."

Faris let out a low growl and before I could say yes or no, he'd slammed her against the rock, his fangs buried deep in her neck. Her eyes found mine over his shoulder, and I saw the edges of a smile.

"It's okay, Rylee. He needs to believe and this is the only way."

I ran toward them. "Let her go, Faris." I lifted my sword, ready to force him to drop her when he did so on his own, stumbling back. He swiped a hand across his lips and shook his head.

He looked stunned. "I have underestimated you, Rylee. You and Berget both; you kept your oath." He shook his head again. "Though I barely believe it, there is no denying the madness is contained." He continued to shake his head, finally reaching out to touch Berget on the cheek, and then jerking his hand back as if burned. "Truly, I did not think it was possible."

Berget smiled up at him. "Faris, you would have been a fine leader, far better than me, trapped as I was."

Ah, there was my little sister, always believing the best of people. And in this instance, it smoothed things over. Eased tension, though not all of it.

Doran and Jack eyed each other, but Jack spoke first. "Well then, old man, are you taking the throne then?"

We all looked to Doran, the only one who could take the throne, and I had a sudden thought, a whisper of a prophecy I'd read while in London. Though I asked, I already knew the answer, felt it in my gut.

"Doran, the prophecies said I would bring the teeth together. Do you understand what that means?"

A smile flitted across his face and he shook his head slowly. "The teeth are the two branches of blood drinkers. The vampires and the Daywalkers. If I take the throne, they will finally be united and the prophecy fulfilled. And you are the instrument of it all."

There was silence except for the pounding rain, and then Faris lifted a hand to the sky. "If we are going to do this, then we need to leave now."

Berget stood and helped me stand. "Faris is right, we should hurry, the equinox will pass soon and then there will be trouble."

We headed toward the cave and within seconds were plunged into darkness. "What kind of trouble are we talking about this time?" I put a hand to the wall and let my Tracking guide me.

"If there is no leader by the close of the equinox," Faris said, "the vampire nation, which includes the Daywalkers, will go mad and unleash on the world in an epic meltdown."

I grimaced and kept walking. "Sounds like fun."

Doran laughed and the sound flexed around us, echoing in the cave. "Fun, yeah, not so much. I saw it happen once; I do not recommend that happening again. It not only decimated the human population, it decimated our own. That is why there are so few of us now."

There seemed to be a light growing ahead of us, though I couldn't be sure. "Anyone else seeing this?"

"Rylee, you are fucking kidding, right?" Jack grunted. "You've got the bloody worst fucking eyes of the bunch of us, and you want to know if we see glowing shit ahead?"

That was the Jack I knew. "Yeah, well, you aren't always that observant."

Laughter tripped through the group, but it ceased in a sudden biting halt as we stepped out of the long tunnel and into a cave.

Thirteen Shamans (and yes, I was sure they were Shamans because one of them was Al) sat in a circle around a fire. On the walls petroglyphs depicted what some might say was the past. Humans with oversized fangs, winged serpents, lines shooting out of people's hands. Made sense to me, and I wondered what the humans made of it.

Doran stepped forward. "I am here, to claim the throne."

Just that? That was it? No way, that was too fucking easy.

Damn me for being right.

Pain was far too weak a word; pain was a fly bite compared to a body being skinned alive. He couldn't stop the screams, the howls erupting out of him. The magic they used, it burned like fire, like a thousand knives jabbing into his organs, the brutal pain of bones snapping and splintering, and then played with. At some point, they'd forced him to shift back to human form. Or had he done that on his own? He couldn't be sure what exactly happened. Everything was a blur beyond sending Pamela and the others away.

At some point, the assault stopped, and a voice whispered in his ear, male, but high-pitched like a young boy's voice. "You are a stubborn one. I will give you a single chance to join us, wolf. And if you do not, we will kill you. It is apparent you are far too capable of slipping bonds. How you got the collar off, I would truly like to know, though, will you tell me that much?"

Liam focused on his breathing. There was no going back. The equinox would be here soon enough and there would be no stopping Ingers or the Black

Coven. Maybe he could fool them though, stop this long enough to—

"And believe me, if you lie to me, wolf, I will know."

He drew in a deep, burning lungful of air. "Go fuck yourself, witch."

"Ah, I thought that might be your answer; then let us end it, end it right now, yes?"

A voice rang out. "I think not, Jaron."

The smell of roses and magic wrapped around him, and he knew Milly had come back. But he also knew she couldn't jump them both out of there. Not with his inability to cross the Veil unless it was a physical crossing. Like a doorway in the castle.

"Milly, go." He barely managed the words over the fighting.

"Liam, I can't. I can't leave you." She was battling too many, he knew it, knew he couldn't help her. Not the condition he was in. Couldn't even open his eyes past the swelling.

But she would lose. And no point in them both dying. He forced himself to his knees, swayed and slumped forward, his face smashing into the unforgiving concrete.

Power surged and then Milly lay on the ground beside him. She pressed a hand over him, and the healing flooded him was almost as bad as the pain the coven inflicted on him.

"Run, Liam. Run," she whispered and he heard the pain in her voice. She was hurt. He opened his eyes, saw blood running down the side of her face as she passed out. No way he could leave her behind.

They were so screwed.

19

The Shamans turned to us as a unit, their eyes widening as they saw me and Alex.

"You're shitting me. You've never seen a werewolf before?"

Al rushed to me. "You must leave, now. This is a place only for vampires and the Shamans who oversee the ceremony. We are protected from the old ones' hunger. You are not."

He shoved me backward, but Alex was behind me and I flipped over his back, hitting the ground hard. My right arm hit a serrated rock and my skin split.

"Fuck, I'm going." I rolled to my side, arm dripping bright red droplets to the ground.

Al let out a groan. "Too late, too late."

A rumble in the ground and the rock bent and flexed around us, like a giant hand. Spikes of rock shot up through the ground, and down from the ceiling, blocking the doorway.

I pulled my swords free. "Al, tell me this is for show."

The old shaman closed his eyes as he sank back into the circle and raised his hands above his head. "We cannot protect you, Rylee. I am sorry."

Berget moved to stand in front of me. "I won't let them hurt you."

Faris gave a slow nod. "Neither will I."

Alex gave a shiver and a low rumble, deeper than anything I'd ever heard from him rolled through the cavern. "No hurts Rylee."

A soft laugh escaped Doran. "Nor will I allow them to harm you."

Jack snorted. "Do you even have to fucking well ask?"

A solidarity I never expected filled the room. Four vampires, who all at one point had been my enemy, now stood between me and a sure death. I gave a slow nod, accepting this for what it was. I could not survive on my own; there was no way, even if I wasn't dealing with a massive blood loss.

That didn't mean I was lowering my blades, not for a second.

The far wall cracked, a jagged line ripping through the hard rock, through the symbols etched thousands of years ago.

Dust rolled ahead of the crack, filling the room, dimming the light. The fire sputtered and spit, flickered, and then grew in intensity as the particles settled. Blinking to clear the grit from my eyes, I stared hard at the four figures emerging from their stone coffins.

Skeletally thin, their clothing—what was left of it—barely hung in tatters from their frames. Their eye sockets were deep and black, no apparent eyes to poke out if they got too close. They stepped forward, fanning out to face us along the wall.

They spoke as a unit. "Fresh blood has come to waken our sleep, no longer to be feasted upon by those who wish power seek us out, but to seek out our rightful place in this world."

I braced myself, but it wasn't me they came for.

The four of them launched at the circle of Shamans. Despite what Al said, he was wrong. They were no more protected than I was.

I didn't stop to think if I was being smart; there was no way I could let the Shamans die. My fanged tag team jumped in, pulling Shamans out of the way and pretty much throwing them behind our "line" of defense.

"Al!" I ran to him as an old one snaked an arm out. Fast, but not the freaky scary fast of vampires I was used to. We had a chance. "They're still weak, kill them!"

Easier said then done. And of course, me and my big fat mouth got their attention. I drove my sword through the heart region of the one holding Al and twisted hard. Bones broke and shattered under the force. The old one dropped Al—who scuttled backward—but it didn't die. The other old ones drained Shaman after Shaman, faster than I could have imagined; we couldn't save them all.

I pulled Al and another Shaman with me, back to the blocked entranceway. Half the Shamans had been drained in a matter of seconds.

Faris, Doran, Berget, and Jack didn't stop them once they got the shamans away. "What the fuck, are you four just taking in the performance?"

"Doran needs their blood, all four of them, if he is to be our leader. We can't kill them, we have to subdue them," Faris said.

Oh fan-fucking-tastic. How do you subdue vampires who were full of blood lust, and enraged they'd been imprisoned for who the fuck knows how long? Yeah, I didn't know either.

Four vampires on our side, four very old and very angry vampires on the other. Like some sadistic version of red rover, red rover, let's call the weak one over and eat her.

I didn't take my eyes from the old ones who in turn were eyeing up the younger vampires in front of them. "Al, tell me you can put them back to sleep."

He leaned heavily on the wall. "Yes, there is a way, but they must be drained of all their blood once more." He let out a moan and under his breath I heard him whisper. "I cannot believe our spells did not protect us."

More than likely, they had the spell wrong. Shit, I could only guess how long it had been since the last time the ancients had been brought forth. Thousands of years, maybe.

With everything I had, I fought the groan that tried to escape me. Nothing, nothing could be easy or go the way we planned.

"One at a time, boys and girls, let's keep this orderly." I swung my swords in loose circles beside me, my confidence wavering under the steely-eyed gaze of the old ones. They weren't really looking at anyone else.

Just me.

Awesome, just what I wanted for Christmas, whole new sets of bite marks.

Alex moved in front of me, teeth snapping, and suddenly he looked the part, no longer the cowering wolf that hid behind me. For the first time, he looked like the scary, vicious werewolf he could be.

We were in a deadly standoff, tension rising as the old ones seemed to debate how best to take us out. It was pretty apparent we were on their dessert list.

Not really how I saw my life ending.

A breath in, a breath out, and the old ones attacked. Faris, Doran, Berget, and Jack each took one on.

Faris, Doran, and Berget held their own, using their physical abilities, along with vampiric powers to keep the old ones from breaking through to the rest of us.

Jack, on the other hand, was not doing so well. Being the youngest of the vampires made him the weakest. He was pushed back, step by step, until closer to me and the Shamans. I wanted to help, but they moved so fast, I only saw what they were doing a split second after it happened. I couldn't keep up with them. So I balanced on my toes, fatigue and nausea rolling through me, waiting for what I knew was coming.

Jack couldn't fend this one off. The blows from the old one came harder and faster, like a lion feeling his prey weaken. The old one's power rippled forward, smashing Jack in the chest, dropping him to his knees.

When it picked up Jack to feed on him, I hesitated, my heart faltering with what had to be done. If the old one took Jack's blood, it was even more power for those we fought.

Jack's eyes met mine, the swirl of the three blues filled with sadness. "My blood will give him too much. Do it."

With every ounce of strength and regret I possessed, I drove my sword, through Jack's neck, clipping into the old one behind him. Jack's body convulsed, his eyes frosting over as his head rolled. The old one dropped the husk of a body that had moments before been Jack to the floor. A snarl rippled over his blood-stained teeth as he spoke to me, his English heavily accented but still clear.

"The young ones, they can't take a blow like that and survive. But you knew that, didn't you?"

I held my sword up. "You old timers can't take a blow like that and survive either, asshole."

As the old one advanced, I backed away. Sure, I'd stopped him from feeding on Jack, but there were still a number of potential victims. I couldn't kill them all.

"Al, you and the Shamans stay behind us!"

Alex moved to my side and let out a snarl that under any other circumstance would have startled the shit out of me. But there was no room for shock, not here.

The old one, grey hair hanging to his shoulders, pitch black eyes with the barest hint of white in them, and a set of fangs that would put Tespa to shame, attacked. The eyes were different than when they'd first emerged. The fresh blood was bringing them back to life. Not good, not good at all.

His mistake was discounting Alex. The old one swept a hand to knock Alex back, but the werewolf had tangled with vampires a few times now. He ducked under the hand and tackled the vamp to the floor, snapping both of the its knees. I jumped forward and drove my sword through the old one's heart and into the stone floor.

I lay my second blade against his neck. "Let's keep this nice and simple. You don't move, I won't take your ugly head, got it?"

His black eyes glared up at me. "Heathen bitch."

"That's a new one. I'll add it to my collection." I grinned until something tried to sweep me backward. I say try, because it was an old one using power against me. Power that slid around me, melting like ice in a volcano.

I lifted my eyes to the old one, a woman, and grinned at her too. I even gave her a wink. She was in the middle of a fight with Berget, but seemed to be attempting to take us both. Not smart on her part. "Try again, dipshit."

Yes, egging on a very old, very angry vampire didn't tend to be good for one's health. She leapt at me, launching through the air over Berget's head.

Thank the gods I had kick-ass vampires on my side of the fence. Doran snatched her midair and burrowed his fangs into her neck, draining her so fast I saw her skin shrivel and shrink, tightening over her cheekbones until as skeletal as she'd been before. Maybe even more so.

He dropped her body and she hit the ground with a rattling thump, the sound of a bag of bones clacked together. Behind Doran lay another lump of bones that twitched periodically.

Faris pinned his opponent face down to the ground. "Take him, Daywalker."

Doran came toward me, calling over his shoulder, "Hold him, Faris."

No animosity hinted in their voices, more of a camaraderie I didn't expect. But then again, they fought for the same reason now, finally working together.

Doran drained the old one I held, then Faris's captive. Four lumps of bones under rumpled cloth scattered the floor.

Just like that, it was over, the battle done. I moved to Jack's body, felt the momentary high at surviving another near death situation dissipate.

Another friend gone. I bent a put a hand to his face, my heart whispering goodbye to. I glanced at Berget and she smiled, though it was tired; maybe not all of this was a loss. A year, Doran said the opal would last a year. I refused to think about what would come after that. There would be a way to keep her here, to keep her from the madness.

Doran and Faris dragged the remains of the old ones back to the hole they'd come out of, bantering back and forth. Like old friends.

Al and the remaining Shamans stepped forward like nothing had happened and Faris stepped back, leaving Doran to face the Shamans on his own.

"You chose well, Tracker. Doran will make a good leader," Faris said softly as the Shamans conducted what I assumed was the final ceremony.

"How could Berget not have known this was where the Blood resided? She held the memories of the last Emperor and Empress. Why didn't they tell her where to go?"

Berget slipped beside Faris. "Because there is a different task every time. This is the first time in thousands of years, perhaps the first time ever, that the task involved the Blood. From what I understand"— she frowned and I could almost see her accessing memories that were not her own—"something of this magnitude only happens in times of desperation. Doran will be, is stronger, than any other vampire this world has known. He holds not only the strength of a vampire and Shamanic abilities within him, but now carries the strength of all the old ones. And he has not lost his soul. I do not know why, but it resides in him yet."

I couldn't help the shiver that ran down my spine. Faris and Berget stared at me, perhaps guessing my thoughts. If either of them had taken the blood of the old ones, there would be no stopping them.

Fuck me sideways—that had been closer than I dared think about.

It all happens for a reason, Rylee. You know that, Giselle's voice whispered through my brain. Yes, it all happened for a reason, but sometimes seeing the reasons laid out were more than my measly brain could handle.

Alex grinned up at me. "Alex kicks ass."

I reached a hand and touched the top of his head. "You sure did."

He continued to grin, a horrible twisting of lips and teeth that was as goofy as ever. But behind that grin, I felt a change in him. Submissive to me, maybe I always would be. The submissive werewolf he was, though, with everyone else, that part was gone.

Going home would be interesting.

Home. The very word made me ache for it.

I could only hope I had a warm welcome and Liam wouldn't be pissed as hell with me for being gone so long, and leaving so much sooner than I'd thought, and without even saying goodbye.

I let out sigh and leaned against the wall, the stone cool against my skin.

Yeah, Liam would be pissed. Maybe he'd even try to punish me for it.

A grin slipped over my lips.

Yeah, one could hope.

20

Alex and I were kicked out for the final parts of the ceremony, which was fine by me. All I could think was that we'd done it, that I'd kept my oaths to Faris, and still managed to fulfill a prophecy. And I was still alive.

Lying in the back of the truck, I stared at the wide open sky. Dawn approached, which meant the vampires were either getting their asses in gear, or staying another full day.

I almost didn't care.

Almost.

Alex lay stretched out on his back beside me, his eyes at half mast, his tongue hanging out the side of his mouth. "Vampires coming."

"About fucking time," I grumbled. With all the battering and blood loss, I was sore and grumpy. Even thoughts of Liam's arms around me weren't helping.

We both sat up and the three vampires stood at the side of the truck. I shook my head at them. "Stop sneaking around. Make some noise would you?"

"Alex hears them." He grinned at me and almost—*almost*—winked.

Doran held out his hand, his eyes serious. "Come on, you have to go home. We"—he motioned to himself, Berget and Faris—"have business to attend to."

The soft shuffle of feet drew my eyes and attention. Al and the remaining Shamans limped out of the cave and gathered around the opening. Hands raised to the sky, they started a chant, their feet drumming into the hard, red earth, splashing in the puddles that had accumulated, in time with their voices.

Ayers Rock answered them. A low-pitched hum emanated from the giant rock.

I backed away. "Seriously?"

"They are closing the entrance. No need to have a human wander in and cut themselves," Faris said, for once without a trace of condescension.

It took seconds for the rock to blend and meld, the entrance gone as if it had never been. Sweet baby Zeus—that was *some* magic trick. The Shamans backed away, one by one, melting into the darkness around the rock. Except for Al, who came toward us, a book in his hand, a wry smile on his face. "I didn't know why I needed to take this with me, but it seems fortuitous for you."

I knew what it was. I hopped out of the truck and met him part way. "This is the journal?"

He smiled, though I saw it was strained. How could I think we hadn't lost much? Six people died. Shit, I really was getting callous.

"Yes, this is your mother's journal. Rylee, you have done your family proud tonight. You fought where you could, but allowed those around you to fight as well. That is the mark of a leader, one who knows when to let the troops take the brunt of a battle."

I swallowed hard and lowered my eyes. "That doesn't bring your friends back."

"No. But we all knew the possibilities when we took on this calling to watch over the old ones." He rested a hand on my shoulder, giving me a squeeze, but said nothing else. Just turned and walked away.

The journal was a thin, spiral-bound book with a black cover. Nothing fancy. I didn't dare open it, not yet. I needed a time of quiet to finally meet my parents.

"You ready to go?" Faris asked.

I glanced at him, took in his disheveled appearance, the fatigue in his eyes. Berget wasn't really looking that much better.

"You sure you can manage dropping us off?" I lifted an eyebrow at him, baffled by the trajectory of our— what would you call it—relationship? Friendship? Neither really applied, yet what did you call a person who'd alternately saved and threatened your life?

Fucked if I knew.

Faris swung his hand and twisted the Veil. On the other side was the front porch at Giselle's house, sunlight dimmed by heavy snow clouds. I didn't question him. It was time to go home.

"Let's go, Alex."

The werewolf bound ahead of me, through the Veil, and barreled into the house with a howl of excitement.

"You will find me when you've done your business?" The question was meant for Berget, but all three nodded.

Good enough.

I stepped through the Veil, into the early afternoon of the day before. Weird, very weird.

Here, the equinox hadn't occurred yet. But I'd already lived through it. I shook my head and walked into the house to hear . . . crying?

"Pamela?" I pulled my swords, gripping the handles tight. "Alex?"

"Are you Rylee?"

I spun to face a woman I'd never met and looked suspiciously like a Troll.

I didn't answer, just whipped my swords forward, stopping them at the base of her neck. "Who the fuck are you?"

Her pale pink skin paled even more. "My name is Tara. Liam saved my life."

"Where is he?"

"I don't know. Milly brought us here and then left to help him."

Help, why the hell would he need help from Milly? I Tracked both Liam and Milly. They were together and they were both afraid, even if it came through differently in them. Liam's was a fury born of fear, and Milly's was a terror born of fear for her child. Only one of them was hurt.

Liam.

I lowered the tips of the swords. "Where's Pamela?"

"I don't know, I went to lie down for a moment and when I opened my eyes she was gone."

"FUCK!" I was, to say the least, not happy about this. I Tracked Pamela. She wasn't far, just down the street. "Tara, stay here."

She nodded, and I bolted for the door, forgetting it was like barely 15 degrees outside, if I was lucky, and I'd just come from 130. I sucked in a sharp breath, my lungs seizing up. "Alex, go get Pamela. Hurry!" I opened the door and he galloped out, nose buried in the snow. I slammed the door and ran upstairs. The extra clothes I had stashed away were in my hands in no time, and I could finally get out of this fucking dress. Easier to be mad at the clothing than worry about my friends. It took me less than a minute to change into jeans, layered tops, boots, and another heavy winter coat. Not my leather one; that had been lost somewhere along the way. Damn, I hated to break in new leather, but looked like I might have to. Again, easier to think about a new coat than worry about those I loved.

The front door slammed and then feet pounded up the stairs. Pamela flung open the door, her face a mess of emotions. "Rylee, the Black Coven has Liam and Milly and there are too many. I couldn't stop them."

I grabbed her arms and held her still. "How many witches? Were there other supernaturals?"

"No, I don't think so."

"Okay. I'm getting Blaz, and he and I will deal with this, got it?"

"What about me?"

Al's words about being a leader wrapped around me, and as much as I wanted to leave her behind, she could help.

"I want to come too." Tara stood in the doorway.

Before I could ask, Pamela was nodding. "You can trust her, Rylee. They killed her children."

My jaw twitched. Baby killers; just fucking perfect. And they would be the same ones who helped kill Dox and the others.

The mother Cyclops came to mind, her fury at the loss of her children, and I let out a slow breath. This wasn't perfect, but baby killers were baby killers, and maybe this would go a short way to evening the scales of justice for her, as well as Tara.

"Then we go together, come what may."

Come what fucking may.

21

Blaz was more than happy to get us.

The farm is quiet, but I did not come here for quiet. Now, hunting witches, that's more like it.

Three of us were bundled up tight, but Alex needed no bundling. He was quite happy with his thick fur and tongue hanging out in the wind as we flew. I Tracked Liam and Milly, felt the injuries doled out to Liam. Broken bones, one at time, the witches let him heal and then broke the same ones again and again.

Fury rippled through me, very much like facing the Trolls at the Landing Pad. I was weak from blood loss, despite the food and juice I'd guzzled before Blaz reached us. But that wouldn't matter. I felt it surging in my blood, a demand for the death of those who'd truly done wrong. Those who would stomp out the light in the world around them.

The Blood of the Lost sings strong in you, Tracker. Have you yet begun to understand yourself?

I shook my head, kept my words to myself.

Perhaps when this is done, you and I will seek out the favor I've asked of you, and you will see what you truly are.

"Why can't you just tell me, lizard?"

He laughed, the sound rolling back through the clouds to us. *What fun would that be, bitchy woman?*

"Is there a plan?" Tara leaned forward, her hands gripping Blaz as best she could.

Pamela shook her head. "There's never a plan with Rylee. You just go in and kick ass. Right?" She looked at me, like I had all the answers.

"Yup. That's how we do things here. Kick ass, leave the names written in blood."

Blaz circled a warehouse that could have easily housed ten Blazes. Liam's threads drew us to the back side.

"Pamela, blow out the roof and walls. Blaz, can you take what they throw at you?" He answered for all of us to hear.

You know I can. And I do believe the little witch can do more than windows and roof. Why don't you shake them up while you're at it?

Pamela grinned, but it was not a kind grin. "Good idea, Blaz. I think I will do just that to those damn bloody bastards."

The dragon's wings beat hard as he hovered midair and Pamela lifted her hands, a spell rolling off her tongue and fingers. Her power drove into the building, literally blowing the roof off, then the walls, scattering the structure like matchsticks. But when she fisted her hands, and the earth began to shake, I knew she was pissed. And I was really glad she was on our side.

The Black Coven fired back, but Blaz dodged and ducked, taking hits here and there. But like me, he was an Immune. So saying he took hits was a misnomer.

But the Black Coven didn't know that. Pamela rained down fire on their heads. They scattered, enough for Blaz to drop to the ground.

Now, time for a meal.

We slid from his back as he began to *chase* the fleeing witches like a giant dog. Alex tore after him, alternately howling and snarling.

"Alex, no!"

I'll watch out for him, get your other wolf.

I grabbed Pamela and Tara and we ran toward the building, toward where I felt Liam hurt and bleeding, broken in too many places.

There were downed I-beams and I leapt over one, pulling my sword as I landed in a crouch on the far side.

Liam was sprawled out on the floor, completely unconscious. Milly was pressed against him, her eyes wide, a collar on her neck studded with rubies. Fury in me built to a crescendo; I needed something, or someone, to unleash it on.

Three of the Black Coven members remained. Two men and a woman. Perfect.

Pamela didn't wait; she stepped forward and snapped her hands up, the ground erupting in front of them, sending them flying backward.

"Tara, help Milly," I said softly before running into the fray. The spray of dirt and dust still floated and provided the screen I needed. The woman was closest to me and I drove my sword up, through her jaw, and out the top of her head. She bobbed and arched against the blade. I yanked it out and she dropped to the ground, twitching.

I turned slowly to face the two men, but only one was standing. His eyes closed tightly as he whispered a spell. Only it wasn't a spell.

In his hand was an orb covered in spikes, an orb I knew too well. A demon stone. I had to kill him before he completed what I knew he was doing. I felt the darkness rising, felt Orion drawing near.

"Kill him!" I ran for him, but wasn't going to make it. A black streak of death wrapped around his neck, feet from where I stood. The spell strangled him, cutting off his words. His eyes bugged out, but I didn't wait for the spell to finish the job. I swung hard with my sword, taking his head to the ground.

Disrupted, the spell slid away. I turned, expecting to see Milly.

But it was Pamela who faced me, who'd called up one of the deadliest spells I'd seen.

I gave her a nod, though my heart ached for her lost innocence, gone sooner than my own. "Good job."

Milly got to her feet, and Tara held the ruby-studded collar in her hands. Milly took it from her and showed it to me. "They can collar witches now, like I collared Liam. They had me in thrall, I would have done anything they asked."

I frowned as I strode toward Liam. He was already healed, though still completely out of it. "Why didn't you fight for them, then?" I sent the words over my shoulder to Milly as I dropped to my knees and put my hands on his back. To be sure. His breath rose and fell in slow beats. Good enough for me.

She gave a half-smile. "Because like me, they were stupid and told me not to use my magic. I had to obey them, even when they screamed for help."

Pamela laughed, and even Tara smiled, though it seemed forced. "We still have to stop Ingers, before the equinox."

"Do I want to know?" I stood and Blaz trundled around the corner, his mouth blood stained. Alex pranced at his side, tail flagging high.

"Alex kills bad witches." He snapped his teeth, and fuck me if he didn't have blood on his lips too. "Watches boss. Learns."

Again, an ache shot through me. He would always be Alex, but to see him lose some of that gentleness that was a core side of him was a physical pain.

Milly put a hand on my arm. "Liam will be unconscious for awhile, he's been healed twice in a very short time from major injuries. He can't be here for the rest of this."

"Tell me about Ingers. Who is she, why are we going after her, and why the time limit? Blaz, take Liam back to Giselle's then come back to us."

Bossy. But he did as I asked, scooping up Liam in his front claws.

Milly and Pamela filled me in on Ingers, the guns, and the potential Army connection.

"What does she look like?"

"Tall, mocha skin, pretty, dark hair and eyes—"

An image of the woman in the sedan on the highway came back to me. "I've seen her."

Pamela's eyes widened. Apparently we'd all had a

run in with the same chick. Awesome. I locked onto the image and name in my head, Tracking Ingers with ease.

She was about a half mile away; hopefully far enough she hadn't heard the commotion and wouldn't know we were coming. "Come on, let's end this, I have things to do."

That stalled Milly. "What do you have to do?"

"I'm taking a fucking vacation."

Alex moved ahead of us, nose to the ground, and he snickered. "Yuppy doody, taking a vacay."

The other three kept up with my slow jog, I couldn't do much more than that. "Rylee, are you hurt?" Milly caught up to me, putting up a hand to slow me.

"Just. Yes, I don't know. I had to donate a lot of blood."

"I can't heal that, I'm sorry."

I didn't answer. No point and talking would take more air than I wanted to use.

The fatigue rushed through me out of the blue, and I wobbled mid-stride, stumbling to my knees.

"Rylee!" Pamela grabbed at me and I remained down, breathing hard, my heart pounding in overtime. My gorge rose and I knew I was done. I was at the end of my stamina.

"Just give me a second."

A second turned into a minute, which turned into five. I couldn't pull it together, and I was trying. Alex circled us and I found myself lying in the snow. "How long before the meeting?"

Milly crouched beside me. "A few hours."

I Tracked Ingers. She was so close, yet she might as well have been on the other side of the continent. "She's human, but has guns that work; is she cocky?"

I was stalling and the look in Milly's eyes told me she knew.

"Rylee, we can finish this."

"You can't find her." I pushed to my feet and called Alex. Using him, I started forward again. No one argued. We were far slower, but at least I was moving. And fuck, just moving at all at that point was a bonus.

We reached the building as the sun began its dip below the horizon and shadows stretched around us. Like fucking déjà vu.

"Let's hope there are no vampires this time." Shit, was that my outside voice?

"What?" Tara squeaked.

"Never mind, just reliving an equinox past." No need to mention it had only been the night before.

"Well, I'd think you'd like at least one or two vampires to show up." I turned my head, unable to spin around. Doran stood behind me, grinning. Berget and Faris stood behind him, and although Faris was not grinning, he gave me a nod.

Berget moved to my side with the speed her kind were known for. Pamela took a step lifting her hands as her eyes narrowed.

"Stop." I laid a hand on Pamela's shoulder. "Things have changed. This is my sister, my real sister, Berget. No longer a puppet of the Emperor and Empress."

The two girls were close to the same age, but I saw Berget had more control. She'd learned it at the knees of two monsters.

"Pamela, another time we can discuss this, but I believe we have things to accomplish tonight." I watched as Pamela's face shifted from wariness to reluctant agreement.

She let out a slow breath and then nodded. "Yes. That's true."

"Rylee," Doran said. "Let me give you a hand with this." He winked and a flood of strength rippled through me, washing the fatigue away in less than a heartbeat.

"You invoked the bite?"

He gave me an oversized grin, more than flashing his fangs. Tara squeaked and stepped farther back. "My soul is intact, and it was you who kept it grounded. I owe you my life and my soul. Seems like I should at least invoke the bite when you needed it."

With Doran's bite invoked, I temporarily had a burst of strength, speed, and stamina that would rival any vampire. This was what I needed to get through the next few hours.

Feeling like myself for the first time in what seemed like forever, I snorted and turned away from him. "Well then, let's deal with Ingers."

What came next was almost boring compared to everything that had happened so far. Ingers was waiting in a small office, oblivious to what had been going on. No witches were waiting with her, which surprised me.

A small cage held two tiny, what I learned were half-breed, children.

Ingers never even got a shot off. Tara saw her, saw the children, and went mental. Literally tore the agent in half. Messy, but effective. It made me think a few Trolls, or even half-Trolls on our side wouldn't be a bad thing.

We let the children out and they clung to Tara. Orphans who needed a mother, and a mother who needed wounds to heal.

All we had to do was wait for the Army contact who was supposed to show up for his "meeting."

Again. Boring. The vampires fed well that night, and we staged the scene to look like a lover's tryst gone very wrong. Mind you, we had to put Ingers back together again, which Milly was able to do.

Tara took the children home. Doran, Faris, and Berget left, and just me, Pamela, Milly, and Alex remained.

And a hell of a long walk home.

You didn't think I'd forget you, did you?

My knees sagged with relief. Even with the burst of energy from Doran, I was done. "You took long enough; what'd you do, tuck Liam in bed?"

The dragon roared with laughter.

No, but perhaps next time I will do just that.

Blaz dropped out of the sky in front of us, his claws digging into the earth for balance. The four of us climbed onto his back and he took off. Finally, finally we were done.

About fucking time.

22

"What are you going to wish for?" I poked at Pamela who stared into the candles like she'd never seen them before.

"I don't know," she said softly, her eyes round with childlike wonder that surprised me. Though she could be a truly tough little witch, it was easy to forget her early life was far from kind. Simple things like a birthday party with friends, presents, and a cake meant a great deal to her.

I glanced at the clock above the stove. "Almost midnight, you'd better decide and then blow them out or it's not your birthday anymore."

We'd held the party late so Doran and Berget were able to attend. Faris decided not to come, which was just as well. I might have accepted what he'd done and how he'd got my oaths, but I was pretty damn sure Liam hadn't.

When everything had been said and done with Ingers and the weapons, Liam showed me the two files he'd pulled from Ingers's office. In them were details that made me shudder, and we burned them.

Ingers had been tracing the movements of several supernaturals, Faris included. Her goal had been to set up the supernaturals not only to kill one another, but come "out" of the closet.

She'd even been working with Denning—Will's boss and head honcho at SOCA in London.

The weapons they'd been making were the first step in starting the "cull," as they'd tagged it. But now with Ingers and her Army contact dead, that left only Denning to carry on.

And I would deal with him soon enough. For now, Will watched him, and kept tabs on everything the piece of shit did.

It would have to be enough; I needed a fucking break.

The birthday party was in full swing when Doran pulled me into the kitchen. "You said you have a young necromancer in your pack now. Be careful, Rylee. Necromancers innately hate vampires and it goes both ways. If Faris had come, and your Frank had been here, there would have been bloodshed. I have the control to hold back, and amazingly so does Berget. But not Faris. He has always hated necromancers."

"Are you shitting me?" I whispered.

Doran shook his head. "Just be wary. The hatred goes both ways—Frank would take a shot at us too, even if he didn't understand why."

And of course, the whole pulling me into the kitchen to "chat" had Liam's feathers ruffled. Despite the fact he knew Doran didn't have a chance with me, Liam couldn't relax around him.

Speaking of . . . Liam curled his arm around my waist and tightened his grip on me. Since I'd been back, he'd been particularly possessive. I couldn't blame him; it would not have been easy on his wolf to let me wander off on my own.

"Ease up," I grunted, pushing at his arm. "I need to breathe."

He relaxed, but then Doran grinned and gave him a wink from across the room. I shook my head. They would work it out. More so than ever, this was a game to the Daywalker. No, vampire. That would take some getting used to.

Pamela finally leaned forward and blew out the candles. "Do I tell you what I wished for?"

We all shouted no at the same time, Berget included. Even Milly.

Pamela smiled and sliced into the cake, handing out pieces. Of course, Alex was first, his drool making a shallow lake on the warped floor. We were still at Giselle's, but only for twenty-four hours. Eve was on her way back with Frank, and I felt her anxiety at hurrying home. Not too long at all and she'd be at the farm.

A day off seemed like a luxury at that point. And I would take it.

Everyone brought gifts for Pamela and I eased myself back, watching the pure delight on her face as she carefully opened each gift. A book of spells from Milly, a mortar and pestle made of clear quartz from Doran, a pair of diamond earrings from Berget.

"I can't, these are too much." Pamela looked more than a little horrified at the fine gift. Berget stepped close and put her hand over Pamela's.

"You took care of Rylee when I couldn't. That is worth all the diamonds in the world, Pamela."

Pamela, being who she was, was not tentative in the least. She wrapped her arms around Berget, hugging her tight.

The party went on for a few hours, and Pamela didn't mention that neither Liam nor I had given her anything. Doran and Berget slipped into the basement when the sun began to crawl through the sky, and Alex and Milly had gone to their separate beds.

Liam was sprawled on the couch. "Think we should give her the present now?"

Pamela's eyes widened. "I don't expect anything from you, I truly don't."

I gave her a wink. "Well, too bad, you're getting something anyway, kid." I held out a long, narrow package. By the look in her eye, she knew what it held.

There was no care in her as she ripped the paper off and opened the box. A sword lay in the bottom, already edged in silver, spelled by Milly to cut deep.

"You can't always protect yourself with magic; you've seen what happened to Milly," I said, lifting the sword out. "This was Giselle's sword, and the one I learned with before I graduated to the two I have now."

I held it out to her and she took the handle carefully. "Thank you, this is all too much." Her eyes filled with tears and I gave her a hug.

"Never. It will never be enough if it keeps you safe."

Liam cleared his throat. "On that note, I have something for you too."

From his pocket, he pulled a small black bundle that fit in the palm of his hand. I frowned; I had no idea what it was.

He unfolded it and put it on her wrist. "It's made from my and Alex's fur, woven using a spell Milly knew to keep it strong. It will make other wolves fear you, even if they don't know why. They will avoid you at all costs."

Well, that was wild. Not the bracelet, but that he'd worked with Milly. Maybe they had gotten past things. Maybe I'd needed to be out of their way for a bit.

Pamela thanked us again, and again, and finally, I sent her to bed.

Liam flopped back onto the broken down couch, and I sat beside him, my hand curling around his thigh.

"Rylee, I'm still pissed at you for sending me away with Blaz."

"Hmm. I'll take a spanking for it if I must."

He cleared his throat. "Woman, you are a devil, you know that?"

I chuckled. "Yeah, I've heard that a time or two."

We fell silent, the sunrise peeking through the windows.

"Liam?"

"Hmm?"

"It's the calm before the storm, isn't it?"

He turned my face to his, kissing me lightly. "Yeah, I think it is."

So much to do, so much was coming, and yet for the first time, I felt hope. The crushing despair that had nearly consumed me after Dox's death had lifted. I knew there would be more losses—that was the way of things. There was never a world so perfect that everyone survived a war.

But since this really was the calm before the storm, and it wouldn't last forever, I took advantage of it.

"Liam?"

"Yes?"

"About that spanking . . ."

COMING JUNE 2017 FROM TALOS PRESS

VEILED THREAT

A Rylee Adamson Novel
Book 7

"My name is Rylee and I am a Tracker."

When children go missing, and the Humans have no leads, I'm the one they call. I am their last hope in bringing home the lost ones. I salvage what they cannot.

Demons are putting rips in the Veil in order to cross over and steal my friends and allies away.

But, going after them isn't even close to simple. The deepest level of the Veil is not a place you can just open a doorway too, after all, and of course, that's where they've been taken.

As fate would have it, it looks like I might get some help from a trained demon slayer and his fire-breathing ride.

The only problem? Said demon slayer claims to have family ties to me. And I've never trusted my family. Nor am I about to start now.

$7.99 mass market paperback
978-1-945863-01-1

AN EXCERPT FROM *VEILED THREAT*

While the castle always felt deserted, something was different. A definite chill . . . like a graveyard vandalized and the graves dug open. I had no illusions about this being a place of peace; we'd shed enough blood on these stones to dispel any of those kinds of thoughts. Still, it seemed wrong to brake it down and turn it into nothing more than an ordinary castle.

It took an hour before we found an unbroken doorway besides the one leading to the North Dakota badlands we'd come through on the first level. On the third level, near one of the few windows looking onto the courtyard, was the only door untouched.

A part of me expected something black and charred, a literal entrance to Hell or the deeper parts of the Veil I kept hearing about.

This door though was steel, thick and polished to a shine catching light from the window. A heavy, old-school padlock clamped down on a bar that rode across the middle of the doorway. I knew this door; I'd been here with Alex. Fuck, I did not want this to be happening.

I put a hand on the cool steel. "Does it surprise you this doorway is left standing?"

"No, not really," Liam said, bringing his hand next to mine on the door. He barely touched it and was thrown back, an arc of lightening slamming him into the far wall.

With a groan he sat up, rubbing his head. "Let me guess, the door is spelled?"

I chuckled, knowing it would take a hell of a lot more than a simple bolt of lightning to take him out, and ran my hand over the door, my Immunity to magic protecting me. "I suppose; I didn't touch it last time."

Stepping back I shook my head. "Let's go, there's nothing we can do about this now."

Liam brushed himself off as he stood. "What about Sas and the ogres?"

I slid my swords into their sheaths. "Blaz, or maybe Eve can take us. That'll be faster than driving. We still need them, but not so badly we'd take the long route."

The clank of steel against steel, soft and quickly silenced, rose through the window. Moving to the side of it, pressing my body against the cool stones, I peered out. Liam did the same on the other side.

In the courtyard below, row upon row of red caps covered the ground. Big hulking bastards covered in muscle and armor. They had their pikes in one hand shield in the other. They looked like the Hulk pumped up on steroids. Yeah, they were that big and ugly. Shit, we'd faced them before in the castle and I'd nearly died, and Pamela was with us, blasting her way through them. Where the hell had they come from? Maybe another doorway was still open.

They stood tall and proud, blood trickling down their faces from the gruesome organic hats on the top of their heads. The thing with red caps was they loved their "hats," but only if they were made of the guts of enemies they'd slain. One stood in front of others, a half-head taller and what looked like viscera on his shoulders that dripped with blood. He paced in front of the other red caps, finally coming to a stop. "There are intruders here, ones who have destroyed the doorways."

A deep rumble rolled through the red caps and even at this distance I saw their large hands tighten on their weapons and lips lift into snarls. Shit, this was not good. Particularly since I was pretty sure we were the only intruders in the castle, and I doubted red caps would wait for us to explain we hadn't blasted the doorways apart.

"We should go, now, while they're busy." Liam stepped away from the window and motioned for me to follow him.

"Wait, just wait." A part of me wondered whose side they were on, because if we could get them on our side, they would be an amazing fighting force against Orion. Lots of them, and blood thirsty as they came.

Below us, the leader let out a loud snarl. "We will hunt them down and use their bellies to brighten our caps and their skin to shit in." His troops roared their agreement.

Never mind, time to go.

On the second floor, nearing the stairway down to the main level, the first red cap loped around the corner behind us.

He let out a roar, his head thrown back as he lifted a six-foot long pike over his head. That was the opening we needed, but Liam beat me to him.

Liam lunged, his blade snapping forward and driving through the red cap's neck. His head rolled, held by the spinal column.

"Not even a clean cut? I'm disappointed." I headed down the stairs as the body thumped to the ground behind us.

"The blade is too short, which makes it somewhat useless. Besides, don't I even get a 'thank you'?"

No doubt he still wished he had guns. For the safety of the supernatural world, we destroyed the spelled munitions while in Europe. So Liam was back to blades or teeth and claws. I was happier with them gone. The guns made me so damn nervous I could barely sleep at night, dreaming of Orion finding them. In the wrong hands that technology would have literally been the death of our world.

Liam trotted down behind me as the sound of footsteps on stone echoed around us, probably called in by their buddy's last roar of defiance. I jogged faster, skipping steps where I could. We were nearing the first floor, but our doorway was on the other side of the castle.

Not that I was dawdling, but I was doing my best to keep quiet. Red caps en masse were not something I wanted to deal with if I could help it.

And the stairwell was dark and shadowed. Of all the things in my arsenal, night vision was not one of them. Last thing we needed was me falling and breaking a leg or an arm and alerting the red caps to where we were. Liam wouldn't break if he fell; I on the other hand was all too capable of snapping a bone.

"I'll thank you later. Besides, you keep telling me your job is to protect me. See how I let you do your job?" A smile twisted across my lips and Liam laughed under his breath. Being hunted by red caps doesn't seem much like a laughing matter. Yet, in my life, it was a fairly minor deal on the scale of scary shit I'd seen and gone through. At best, a five out of ten.

Water dripped down the walls of the castle, hitting the pitch-covered torches, flames hissing and flickering with each droplet of moisture. But we were almost to the doorway, so who the hell cared if the lights went out? Or so I thought, until Liam grabbed my arm, his voice low. "We aren't alone."

Every muscle in me tensed as my eyes searched the hall ahead of us. With the light dancing, every shadow seemed alive, every dark spot could hold someone waiting to take us out when we least expected it. I'd been ambushed more than once in dark places like this. Being supernatural you'd think I'd learn to avoid them, but honestly it seemed my life was nothing but dark places and battles.

There will be no rest for you, Rylee. You know that. Yeah, I did. The echo of Giselle's voice in my head was not needed to remind me of that particular fact.

Behind us, at the far end of the hallway, came a loud sniff, as if a creature were scenting the air. Red caps didn't scent the air; they were more human like than animal, even if they did bathe in the blood of their enemies and wear intestine scarves.

Liam let out a low growl. "Some sort of hound, we have to move."

So be it.

I strode toward our exit point, the only door besides the steel one unbroken. The shadows beside the door shifted and a man stepped between us and our exit.

Unfortunately for him, I had very little patience for this kind of shit. "Move or I'll move you in pieces."

He let out a soft laugh that tickled along the back of my senses. The hounds behind us let out a unified howl that filled the air, doing far more than tickling my senses.

The man didn't move. His face was shrouded by shadows, his arms loose at his sides. Almost like he wasn't sure what to do with himself or what he was doing next. I didn't like it. His eyes darted from us, to the doorway, and then back to us. Uncertainty was a good way to get killed in our world.

"Rylee. I never thought to see you again, child." His voice was thick with an accent I thought might be Russian.

"Good for you, you know my name. Now move your ass out of our way."

Hesitating slightly, he opted for a sweeping bow, then stepped away from the door. "After you."

Heavy feet and armor along with the scrabble of claws behind us propelled me forward. I didn't trust this shadow man, but I didn't have a choice. We couldn't face all those red caps, not without serious casualties. At least once on the other side of the doorway we'd be safe. One of the few perks with using doorways—very little would come through after you.

I yanked the door open and paused to stare at the man. "I suppose you're wanting to come with us?"

He nodded and I pointed to the dark on the other side. "You first."

He obliged and Liam let out a growl. "Go, I'm right behind you."

I didn't argue, took a torch from the wall and stepped through the doorway. Liam followed, shutting the barrier hard behind him. We crossed the Veil, a tingle of awareness crawling over my skin, and then we were through to the other side, back home in North Dakota.

The air in the cave was cool and still.

"Where'd he go?" I swept the torch high, but saw no one beyond the cusp.

Liam pointed and I followed the scuffled footsteps to see the man leaning against one of the walls.

"Who are you?"

He lifted his eyes to mine. His face was familiar, but I couldn't place him, couldn't remember where I'd seen him. There were flecks of green and gold in his eyes, and he watched me carefully. He ignored my question, staring intently at my face. "You have the coloring of your mother mostly, but those eyes . . . they might as well be my brother's staring back at me. At least in color, if not design." He smiled and I just looked at him, unable to move, his words tumbling inside my head. The implication stunned me to the core. No, he wasn't saying what I thought he was. He couldn't be.

Before I said anything the doorway behind us flew open and the leader of the red caps stepped through.

Funny enough, he didn't look all that happy.

Fan-fucking-tastic.

ABOUT THE AUTHOR

Shannon Mayer is the *USA Today* bestselling author of the Rylee Adamson novels, the Elemental series, and numerous paranormal romance, urban fantasy, mystery, and suspense novels. She lives in the south-western tip of Canada with her husband, son, and numerous other animals.